PINELANDS

PINELANDS

A NOVEL BY

ROBERT BATEMAN

PLEXUS PUBLISHING, INC.
MEDFORD, NEW JERSEY

Fiction
Bat

Published by:
Plexus Publishing, Inc.
143 Old Marlton Pike
Medford, New Jersey 08055

Manufactured in the United States of America

ISBN 0-937548-27-8 (Hardbound)
ISBN 0-937548-28-6 (Softbound)

Cover Photo: Thomas H. Hogan, IV
Cover design: Jennifer Johansen
Book design and composition: Shirley Corsey
Publisher: Thomas H. Hogan

FOR DONNA HAINES

PINELANDS

ONE

1909

Zauber was behind her. Elizabeth braced her arms on the back of the damask-covered chair. Her brown hair slid from her shoulders and draped her face. She felt the warm press of his body, but she couldn't keep her mind on him and looked at the rug, tracing its ornate pattern, following each twist and swirl with growing displeasure. The colors, at first glance, appeared bright and filled with vitality, but as the minutes passed they grew dark and lifeless. The design became ineffective and she floated above it, waiting for him to finish. He whispered something, then repeated the phrase, which dissolved against the nape of her neck. His breathing quickened. He spoke again, but she remained mute and didn't make an attempt, beyond her compromising position, to please him.

They had been spending time together in and around Atlantic City for just over two years. Three years before their affair began, Zauber had been declared dead; his bones along with faded identification had been found just south of the Texas border in a Mexican cave. In 1907, he wrote to tell Elizabeth that he was still alive. He had fallen away from his calling, away from mysticism and healing, and into madness. Zauber had spent over a year wandering in the Mexican desert, fleeing what he thought was death. Ironically, he discovered that death had arranged a meeting with him and that his flight was an illusion. He drank heavily then and was certain that his alcoholism had obliterated any trace of his psychic powers. His cryptic letter to Elizabeth hinted that his earlier stay at Worthing Mills in 1889 (most of which was spent weaving in and out of a coma) and his aborted performance

1

there had something to do with his present dilemma. He implied that Elizabeth was partially responsible for his failure and near death. She had, in his words, "interfered with his sensibility." Their earlier acquaintance, which was little more than that to Elizabeth, had led Zauber to a state he feared more than the loss of his powers or even his death. He was in love. After Mexico, Zauber drifted toward Atlantic City. Three years passed, and by the first weeks of 1907 he had regained his sense of self and purpose. He began to think that his diminished powers might return. His love for Elizabeth, which grew more apparent with each passing month, finally drove him back to the city where they had met.

Zauber knew about her husband's accidental death in 1904. He had read about their cart-pulling moose, Bully, and how Elizabeth's husband was gored to death by the automobile-frightened animal after a political victory ride. Her husband's broad, bearded face had stared back at Zauber one damp morning from the creased page of a nameless city newspaper. The obituary listed Samuel Worthing's accomplishments: his early success as a New England industrialist and entrepreneur, his unbridled resolve to save the paper mill town he renamed Worthing Mills, his great concern for social justice and the welfare of his employees. Saintly was the first word that appeared in Zauber's mind, but he knew about the darker side of Samuel Worthing's life: the abandoned first wife and son, his bigamy, his addiction to coca wine, and the rumored political chicanery. Although Zauber held no animosity toward the man, he found himself sneering at the glowing account of Worthing's life and triumphs.

When Zauber asked to see Elizabeth, she readily accepted his invitation. The time spent at Worthing Mills, twenty years before, hadn't afforded Elizabeth an opportunity to satisfy her curiosity about Zauber. On the day of his arrival in 1889, before he was able to take part in Elizabeth's newly founded lyceum series or demonstrate to Elizabeth and others his powers as a spiritualist, he lapsed into a coma. She cared for Zauber while he struggled to regain consciousness and insisted, once it was discovered he had no known relatives in the country, that he stay in the house rather than become a county charity case. He appeared preoccupied as he convalesced in the garden, sipping the Irish tea made by the Worthing's housekeeper, Mrs. O'Malley. When he recovered, the man spent little time in Worthing Mills. He stalked the town's streets, taking time to learn the names of the town's inhabitants and the function of each building of the paper mill complex. Then he grew aloof and disinterested, ignoring those he had befriended and avoiding the streets which surrounded Worthing's home. Within a week, he was gone.

Now Elizabeth and Zauber were lovers. Their relationship had been tempered by disagreements and reconciliations. A child had been born in secrecy without Zauber's knowledge. The infant was entrusted to Mrs. O'Malley's niece and her husband. Elizabeth was afraid that her pregnancy would influence the outcome of the dower suit brought against her by Beatrice Worthing. Although Elizabeth had lived as Worthing's wife for fifteen years, Beatrice had never consented to a divorce and legally was still his wife. Above anything Beatrice wanted her wayward husband to pay for his decision to leave her. This was her chance to hurt him, even though Worthing was dead. Revenge was foremost in her mind. It was true that Beatrice had laughed about her restive husband's interest in Elizabeth. But as the weeks turned to months and then years, her laughter turned to incredulity. She never thought his restlessness would lead him to the arms of another woman, at least not permanently. Beatrice imagined that her consent, or lack of it, would somehow influence her husband. But she was wrong.

Once Worthing was dead and his estate passed into Elizabeth's hands, Beatrice's lawyers appeared. They were determined to prove that he was married to Beatrice and that they had produced a son—something Worthing had steadfastly denied for the last ten years of his life. An attempt was made to establish that he was not of sound mind to make and publish a will. A court-appointed trustee oversaw all company transactions. Until now Elizabeth had managed to hold them at bay, but she was fearful of the court's ultimate ruling. Before Worthing's death, large sums of money were removed from his accounts and placed in her maiden name. Samuel Worthing foresaw trouble and knew that Beatrice wouldn't graciously accept the terms of his final will and testament. He even predicted that someone would be appointed by the courts to oversee all the transactions at Worthing Mills Incorporated and that Elizabeth might eventually lose control and ownership of the company.

Elizabeth was a pragmatic woman and knew her husband was right. Her goal was to keep Worthing Mills intact, regardless of ownership. She hoped that Beatrice wouldn't liquidate the company's holdings if she succeeded in taking control of the town. Unfortunately, Beatrice wasn't interested in a monetary settlement. Elizabeth's lawyers had tried to buy Beatrice's silence, but Beatrice's motivation went beyond money. Elizabeth suspected that she wanted to destroy Samuel Worthing's greatest success—Worthing Mills.

As Elizabeth worried about Beatrice's vindictive attack, Zauber had renewed his interest in raising money to found a school. He was contacting people who had contributed to this cause before his failure, thinking that they would give him additional financial backing. He had succeeded in putting together a small building fund, a fund that matched what he had lost at the time of his self-proclaimed spiritual crisis. Many were stunned to hear that he was still alive. Elizabeth wasn't enthusiastic about his dream. Establishing a school based on love and its ability to end all human suffering sounded like a line from a Victorian stage comedy. It had been attempted before with dubious results. His idealism and sincerity had remained intact over the years, but the country had changed. New Mysticism was dead. The West had been tamed. Fortunes were being made. Opportunities were everywhere. His revelations, as he once called them, weren't miraculous or awe inspiring. His powers, which in their heyday she respected, now lacked force and seemed hackneyed.

And along with the trying repetition of his philosophy and prognostication was this—their lovemaking. It had started like an adventure. Clandestine arrangements would be made in advance. Anticipation would build as the time came near. Finally, they would meet. At times, she found it difficult to think of anything but Zauber. But after a few months, it was routine. Now, when she faced him in a darkened room, she longed for her dead husband. Then, to her surprise, she was pregnant at forty-three. Her husband had desperately wanted another child, but their attempts had ended with disappointment. Years passed; doctors were consulted; scientific cures were exploited; home remedies were tried. But nothing worked. Until Zauber reappeared, having a child was a fantasy that had eluded Elizabeth. With Beatrice and her lawyers on the doorstep, it still seemed to be so. Elizabeth's child was not her own.

Zauber finished and fell onto the bed. When she glanced over her shoulder, he looked like an angry outcast—his long hair and beard more disheveled than usual. His breathing was strained. His chest and face were flushed. He had remained slender over the years and looked much younger than he was, a fact that amazed her because the past hadn't been easy for him. She could see a weariness in his grey eyes. They weren't the same hypnotic eyes which years before drew people to the front of the hall where he was speaking. Gone too were the seizures and the scramble of unintelligible words that had poured from his mouth. In place of this was a quiet severity that could be mistaken for shyness. He had become critical and unforgiving of anyone who disagreed with his plans. His once odd but gentle eccentricity had transformed itself. Sympathy and its attendant virtues had vanished. He was obsessed, not only with his school, but with having Elizabeth by his side.

At first, she was complimented by his interest and thought that he might be confusing financial needs with emotional ones. She was a wealthy woman and would continue to be so, even if Worthing Mills was lost to her. He professed great love for her and said that he had loved her on their first meeting. As Zauber accumulated money from other sources, she started to see that he was truly in love with her and not her bank accounts. He wanted her to relinquish control of

5

Worthing Mills and marry him. Initially, she was amused, but he insisted that Worthing Mills was the only thing standing between them, that the devotion he required couldn't coexist with anything else. Elizabeth realized after this that she must escape. He could be emotionally overwhelming at times, but she wouldn't allow him to totally rule over her. With Worthing Mills, she was an important and respected woman. Without it, she would become merely a wife under his hand. Their relationship was marked for failure. His school was bound to create a scandal. But it wasn't controversy that Elizabeth feared. Within a few years the school would probably collapse, and they would be left with only each other.

She sat next to him, her lack of passion evident.

"Do you have to leave this morning?" he asked.

"Yes."

"Couldn't you forget about the dinner?"

"We've already discussed this." Elizabeth's voice was distant.

"This club...you say there will be wealthy people there?"

She pulled the sheet around herself and said, "Yes."

"And that man, what's his name?"

"Ruspoli."

"Italian nobility?"

"Yes."

"Do you think he'd be interested in our school?"

"No, I don't think so." Elizabeth considered his endless barrage of questions, knowing they must stop.

"Or any of the others?"

"No."

"None of them?" He paused, considering her motivation. "Why go?" he finally said.

"We've discussed this before. I go because it's good for business. There's always information floating around, things that I wouldn't be privy to if I didn't go." She was annoyed with his persistence.

"But you just went."

"The costume party was different."

"How?"

"That was a costume party. Everyone was in disguise, and

I never mentioned business, not for the entire evening."

He was disgruntled and left the bed. He stood at the window, looking out over the city, the Boardwalk, and the blue-grey Atlantic. He could see the double-wheeled Roundabout. Zauber remembered riding on the earlier wooden Roundabout, which was built by William Somers, and destroyed in 1892 when a gasoline lamp exploded. The new structure's double wheels ran in opposite directions. Customers strained to catch a glimpse of friends as they passed on the parallel circle; below them the Boardwalk, bounded by hotels, piers, amusements, novelty shops, restaurants, and food stands, stretched for miles. The Somers' wheel and its contrary motion, with each wheel spinning endlessly, negating the opposing force, mirrored Zauber's emotional state. He had needs, desires, and plans but frequently found himself in a quandary. Nothing was synchronized. Each inner movement was stymied by a counterforce. This lack of control and his inability to right the situation with Elizabeth baffled him.

"I'll be back next week," she said, suspecting she wouldn't.

"And you still think I shouldn't come to Worthing Mills?"

"Not until the suit is over."

He started to pace in front of the window, looking at the carpet with the same intensity she had experienced minutes before.

"We don't have a choice. You'll get used to it," Elizabeth added.

He didn't answer.

"You will!" she assured. "Truly."

Zauber shook his head and said, "I don't like it now, and I never have. A woman like you going to that place alone. It can't be good—not for you, not for us."

She crossed the room and tried to stand in his path.

"I never go unescorted. You know that."

"Don't remind me."

"So?"

"That doesn't make it easier," he said, shaking his head again.

"Well, what else can I do?"

He stopped and rested his spare hands on her shoulders. "Tell me that you won't go."

Her face tensed.

"Tell me." He squeezed her shoulders.

She remained silent.

"Tell me," he repeated firmly.

His eyes blazed for an instant, reminding her of the past. At that moment, Elizabeth decided that she wouldn't return. She hated his badgering. When his eyes flashed, she found them easy to ignore because now they were cold.

"You're hurting me."

"That's your answer?" he asked.

"Yes."

"I can't make you change your mind?"

"No."

He tightened his grip and said, "Who is it this time?"

She shifted her weight away from him. Suddenly, her nakedness made her feel vulnerable.

"The same," Elizabeth said.

"That's wonderful." He released her and turned back to the window. "A regular escort."

"He's only a friend. Listen to me! I've been faithful to you. He's not my lover." She heard her words but knew that they didn't matter. He wouldn't be swayed.

"Oh." His voice was filled with the sound of abandonment.

"Karl." She reached for him, but he stepped around her.

"I guess you'd better leave then so that you'll have plenty of time to get ready for him—whatever his name is."

She looked at his back and wondered how she came to be there with him. She resisted any impulse to allow her past feelings for him to infuse the moment with sentiment. Although she still cared for him, it was obvious that their relationship was crumbling before her.

"I'll see you next week." She waited for a response, but he remained resolute. After a minute passed, she gathered her clothes from a chair and went into the bathroom, her bare legs slicing the still air of the room.

When Elizabeth emerged, he was gone. She knew that he

would go to the beach where he would pace the long strand, intermittently broken by piers and people, for hours. He would be oblivious to the people watching him. Their hushed comments would be blocked by the rhythm of the ocean and would never find his ears. His anger would subside; then he would return to brood in silence for the remainder of the day.

Elizabeth left the hotel, driving away in her car. An odd sense of relief overcame her. The city streets were busy. Merchants anticipated the arrival of summer and the tourist season. Beach surreys and buggies, along with a few automobiles, clogged several intersections. The long brick city hall, with its single clock tower, loomed over Tennessee and Atlantic Avenues. She maneuvered through a crowd of early vacationers who gathered along the curb in front of a hotel. Several men were startled to see Elizabeth behind the wheel. One man pointed, making a comment to the woman on his arm. The woman laughed, then waved, but it was too late for Elizabeth to notice because she had left them behind.

The congestion of the city quickly gave way to the stillness of the forest and its dominant scrub pines. It was warm, even for a spring day, so she left the top down and allowed the wind to whip around her head. Within twenty minutes, the city and Zauber were only muted images in her preoccupied mind. May pinks bloomed in random clumps along the road. The hardwoods were thick with swelling buds and new leaves. Nothing around her would suggest that Atlantic City was only a few miles to the east.

She had traveled the road many times. She thought about Samuel Worthing and how quickly their time together had passed. She still remembered the first day he had appeared at the Pennsylvania hotel where she was the assistant manager. His search for a new business endeavor had led him to the hotel which was several miles south of Harrisburg. After a few days, his interest suddenly turned to Elizabeth, a woman who was young enough to be his daughter. Their romance developed and deepened in the fragrant spring of the Pennsylvania countryside. Before long she was at his side in Worthing Mills. Years passed. Elizabeth never regretted her decision to be-

9

come his wife, even though Worthing had never obtained a legal divorce from Beatrice.

Now, at forty-five, time seemed very valuable to Elizabeth. The days were short. Running the company with a trustee in tow was demanding and time consuming, but trying to keep Zauber away and her child a secret while working with the lawyers who helped stave off the attack on the property, proved to be exhausting. She could let her manager do more, but she enjoyed the work. Elizabeth knew that without the company to fill her days she would be unhappy and might still find her way to Zauber's side, if not for love then maybe for companionship. So she accepted the pressures and inconveniences of her life at Worthing Mills and hoped that her energy, luck, and patience would survive.

She drove confidently along the road, moving to the side whenever there wasn't enough room for an approaching vehicle or wagon. She made several turns and within an hour she was on the road to Worthing Mills. Many people in town felt that she shouldn't be riding on miles of narrow, mostly deserted, sand roads by herself, but she scoffed at them. The roads around the town weren't normally traveled by outsiders. She controlled over two hundred salaries in the area. She was convinced that if her car broke down someone would recognize her and offer help.

Many residents of the state thought of the local people as uneducated and hostile. Stories of alcoholism, domestic violence, and dire poverty appeared in Philadelphia and New York newspapers. Tales of inbreeding, deformity, and brothers and sisters not being able to distinguish parents from aunts, uncles, and cousins, abounded. Rumors of robbery, rape, and murder filled the minds of outsiders. Social activists called for drastic measures. State agents were sent into the forest to investigate. The nickname Piney appeared in print and it stuck. The natives adopted the name and sometimes relished the imagined horror springing up around them. As distasteful as they might seem, these exaggerated reports helped keep the region relatively crime free, at least more so than the rest of the state. The Pineys knew this and hoped that their fortunes wouldn't change.

Within five miles of the town, a downed tree limb stopped her. Elizabeth could see that it was too heavy for her to move by hand. She carried a length of rope for emergencies and tied one end to the front bumper of the car. Reaching for the other end, she moved toward the limb. She had become adept at clearing the rough roads and bent over, trying to find the best place for the rope. A killdeer scurried out of the roadside brush, dragging its wings in the dust. The engine chattered and tapped behind her, masking any sound from the surrounding trees. Then she fell, her head swinging violently forward as her legs dissolved beneath her. She didn't move until she was lifted from the road by a passing collier, who was returning to town with a load of pit-made charcoal.

T W O

1937

The two canoes floated just beyond the mouth of a flooded spong that drained into the river. They took turns diving from their canoes—first Billy Wescoat, then his brother, Sammy. With each dive, the canoe rocked wildly in the cedar water. And each dive brought a new record for staying beneath the surface. Andy Johnson went next, beating the other boys by twenty-five seconds. They splashed and laughed as the water trickled down their backs and the sun burned their shoulders. The cedar boughs rustled for a second; then the shrill pitch of katydids swelled around them.

Will Johnson was next and was frightened. He didn't like diving from the canoe and found it nearly impossible to pull himself over the gunwhale and back to his seat. The other boys taunted him. He was the youngest, but this didn't bother him until someone older emphasized it. He stood, shaking the canoe slightly. He looked warily at his brother.

"Go on Will," Andy whispered. "You'll be all right."

Will glanced at the boys in the other canoe. Both of them were laughing.

"Willy. Willy. Your mama's calling you."

The Wescoats laughed and jabbed each other in the ribs, causing their canoe to bounce in the water.

"Watch out for that snapper down there."

"Yeah, it's the big black one—the one that ate my uncle's fyke."

"Don't listen to them, Will. There ain't no stinkpot in there. You know that," Andy said.

"Go on, Johnson. You ain't no woodjin. You'd be in the

12

water already. Jump!"

The other boy repeated his brother's last word. "Jump! Jump! Jump!"

Both of them joined together. "Jump! Jump! Jump!" they cried, beating a hollow rhythm on the side of their canoe.

Will looked up into the milk-blue sky, catching the dark cedar tops in his peripheral vision. He thought about praying but didn't. The surface of the languid river was alive with striders. Their rapid, jerking motions made him uneasy. A neon dragonfly hovered above the water. He closed his eyes, took one long breath, and sprang from the canoe.

The other boys hooted as he struck the water with a back-stinging whack. Then he disappeared. He hadn't planned on breaking the record or even participating in the contest, but now he decided to remain under for as long as possible. He was surprised to see that the river was shallow and clearer than usual, but then he remembered the rainwater flowing from the spong. If he stood, the top of his head would only be a few feet from the surface. The bottom was sandy and didn't bother him like the soft muddy bottoms filled with rotting debris or eelgrass.

They waited for him to resurface. As the seconds passed, his brother became worried. Andy looked at the others and they sensed his fear. He leaned over and searched the molasseslike water.

"Will. Will!" Andy could see parts of the bottom as the sun filtered down through the liquid. They waited for something to happen.

"Shit. Where is he?" one of them said.

"Will!" Andy yelled as he prepared to dive.

Nothing.

Suddenly, Will broke the surface on the opposite side of the canoe. His face was contorted; his mouth produced a wrenching scream.

Andy reached for him, ignoring the unstable canoe.

"There's a head down there," Will shouted between the ripples that reached his open mouth.

Andy tried to swing him over the gunwhale, but the canoe

tipped, throwing him into the water next to his brother. He grabbed Will's arm.

"What are you talking about?"

"A head...a head," the younger boy said, kicking his legs frantically as if he wanted to prevent something from touching them.

The Wescoats jumped from their canoe, unafraid, and swam to Will and Andy.

"Where is it, Will? We'll get it."

"Down there." He pointed.

One boy vanished, then the other, both breaking the water with strong kicks. Within seconds, the surface of the river became polished, as if nothing had occurred.

"Are you sure Will?"

"Andy," he brushed the hair from his forehead, "I saw it."

A moment passed. Then the Wescoats resurfaced.

"You're full of it, Johnson. There ain't nothing there."

"It was probably a snapper. You're lucky it didn't take one of your toes off."

"Yeah, or your dick."

They laughed, each splashing Will, who shielded his eyes with a hand.

"It wasn't a snapper. I saw it."

"Show us then."

"Yeah. I'll bet you a dollar that you're full of it," Billy said.

"You're sure?" Andy questioned.

"Yeah. But I'm not going back down there."

"Okay." Andy looked at the others. "He's not going in."

"Bullshitter!"

"I'll go down and find it," Andy offered, "but let's right this thing first."

Two of them got under the canoe and pushed it up and over. Its keel slapped the river.

"Get in Will. You watch the canoes and don't let them get into the current and drift downstream."

The three boys made two more dives, and when they returned to the surface one of them said emphatically, "There is something down there."

Will looked at them smugly. He had won but didn't want to see his discovery again. His mind filled with fears developed from Saturday afternoons at the movie theatre in the county seat. Horrible creatures prowled the bottoms of rivers and creeks, and he had no desire to encounter one today.

They went under once more and two of them struggled to bring it up. Will thought that it seemed heavy for a head.

"It's a head all right, but it's made of stone."

"Damn thing must weigh seventy-five pounds," Andy said.

They moved to the side of the canoe where Will sat. Andy got in, and along with his brother, he hoisted it aboard. Will stared at the face that had gazed up at him from the sand bottom.

"Jesus Andy, she's pretty."

"What are you talking about?"

"The head."

"It's marble or something. It's not alive."

Will looked indignantly at his brother and responded, "I know that."

The Wescoats flopped into their canoe, each cursing the other for not doing what was right. Once inside they leaned back and caught their breath.

"I could go for a smoke."

"So could I."

Billy shook his head as he peered into the pack. "There's only one left and it's wet."

"Balls. We could get some johnnysmokers."

"Have to go almost back to town for that."

Sammy exhaled loudly then said, "Where do you think it's from?"

"Maybe it's part of a pirate treasure. You know, someone like Captain Kidd who used to sail up from the bay and hide his loot," Billy speculated.

"Do you think there's gold down there?"

"You guys," Andy interrupted, shaking his head. "How could a ship get this far up the river?"

"They could have used a rowboat or something."

"What about a lost civilization?"

15

"Yeah, like Atlantis."

"That wasn't around here," Andy reasoned.

"I think it belonged to a king, and it was his queen and she died and..."

Andy hit his brother with his wet ballcap. "Goofy."

"Maybe we can get money for it."

"Who knows...it could be worth a thousand bucks and we could sell it."

"I doubt it. But Will was the one to find it, so I think he should be the one to decide what to do with it." Andy waited for an answer. "Well?"

Will stared at the face and wondered what the woman was like if she ever lived. She reminded him of his mother.

"Well?"

"I want to take it home and show Mom."

"That's it?" shouted a voice from the other canoe. "Oh brother!"

"She'll know if it's worth anything. If I decide to sell it, I'll give you guys some of the money."

"Dumb kid."

"Could be worth a thousand dollars or even two thousand. We could buy the whole town and live in the mansion like old lady Jenkins," Billy added.

"And ride around in a big car," his brother said.

When they finally paddled to town, each thought about the discovery and what it might bring him. Will glanced at the head more than once to reassure himself that it still rested on the floor of the canoe behind him. Satisfaction overwhelmed him. For once, he thought, they had to admit he was right. Finally, he wasn't just Andy's kid brother.

The Johnson brothers carried the head between them in a twisted towel. They walked past two derelict houses—their shutters drawn, front gates hanging open, and yards overgrown with weeds. They rounded the corner and approached their house. The burned shell of the paper mill's main building gaped through the trees behind it.

"What do you think Mom will say?"

"We'll find out in a minute. She'll want to know where we

found it."

The boys shouted as they entered the house. No one answered. A plate of cookies and a note rested on the kitchen table. When the brothers noticed the food, they temporarily forgot about the head and their mother. Andy found the milk in the icebox, and their afternoon was suddenly complete. Their mother's note went unread until most of the cookies were gone.

"She'll be back in twenty minutes," Andy commented.

"Where did she go?"

"Checking on Mrs. Sooy."

"How old do you think she is Andy?"

"Over ninety."

"God."

"She was around when old man Worthing was alive. Her husband managed the place." Andy reached for another cookie.

"When the paper mill was working?"

"Mom was around then, too."

"Naw."

"Yes, she was."

"Get out."

"She was!"

Andy continued to taunt Will about their mother's age until she came through the back door. His younger brother seemed so stupid to Andy. His mother had told him that Will was an exact copy of him when he was the same age. But he didn't believe it. How could he?

"What kind of day have you two had?" she asked, removing the empty plate and glasses from the table.

"We found something and brought it home."

"Not another snake?" She reached for a green and white dishcloth.

"No, Mom. This is different," Andy said.

"Yeah, Mom. This is really something. Why don't you close your eyes, and we'll show you?"

"I don't have a lot of time for games. Your father will be wanting his supper when he comes home, and I haven't started it yet."

"This will only take a minute."

"Sit at the table and close your eyes." Will quickly grabbed her hand and pulled her toward a chair. "You'd better put your hands over your eyes, too."

"Okay, okay." She smiled. "But it better not be a snake."

"It's not."

"Or a turtle."

"No."

"Or a frog or toad."

"Come on, Mom!"

She sat and placed her hands over her eyes, fully expecting to see one of the things she had mentioned.

"Or anything that crawls," she exclaimed.

The boys lifted the head from the corner and managed to sit it on the table with a thump.

"What is it?"

"Don't look yet."

"No peeking."

They stood it on end. The break at the neck was flat so it was square and upright when they shoved it in front of her.

"Okay. Open your eyes."

She removed her hands and looked at the face which serenely returned her gaze. She gasped.

"Where did you find it?"

"In the creek up above town."

"I can't believe it." She reached out to touch it, but her hand balked.

"Isn't it something, Mom? I found it when I was trying to break the record. They didn't believe me, but I told them it was down there," Will said excitedly.

"You were scared to death. You thought it was real," Andy added.

"It is," she said.

"No, it isn't Mom. It's some kind of rock."

"No, I mean it's Elizabeth Worthing. The woman who lived in the mansion.

"Old man Worthing's daughter?"

"No, his wife, Andy. His daughter died when she was very young."

"Was she an Indian or something?"

"No, honey. The water has turned the stone a little brown."

"What was it doing in the river?"

"That's a long story."

"But why..."

"Some people wanted her statue destroyed. I guess you found the spot where they threw it."

"I don't remember any statue around here," Will said.

"It was a long time ago."

"She sure was pretty."

"She was."

"The Wescoats say it might be worth a thousand dollars."

She didn't hear him. She recalled the time when it all happened: when Elizabeth was murdered, when the statue was destroyed, when Samuel Worthing's son vanished.

"Mom," Will said, tugging at her sleeve.

"What?"

"Do you think it's worth anything?"

"Not much. Not many people care."

"About what?"

"Oh, the Worthings and what they did here and what happened to them."

"You mean when the paper mill was open?"

"Yes."

"I think she looks like you, Mom." Will smiled.

"She reminds me of Miss Harris," Andy interjected.

"Can we put her in our room?"

"Now? It must be heavy. Why don't you wait for your father?"

"We can lift it. We carried it from the canoe twisted up in that towel," Andy said.

Agnes Johnson stood and watched them pull it from the table and into the hallway. As her hands mechanically prepared their evening meal, her mind was transfixed on the image of Elizabeth Worthing's face and the days before her own marriage. The town had flourished when the Worthings were alive. During her last year in high school and after graduation, she had worked for the county newspaper. With amplified interest and frustration, she observed the unexplainable as it unfolded before her. Misfortune and tragedy overshadowed the town's everyday existence for years. Now she lived with her husband and two children in the quiet, half-deserted place that had caused her so much consternation. And the past, one which she had conveniently relegated to old boxes and partially remembered facts, had unexpectedly returned.

T H R E E

1990

*T*he heavy gate was ajar, set
*hard against the root of a blackjack that had grown up and
around an adjoining section of rusting ironwork. He looked
down through the scrub into the cellar hole of the vanished
bleaching house at Maggie, who snapped at the intermittent,
fluttering white flags. The sun made everything luminous except for the crumbling sandstone walls of the paper mill which
rose behind the hole and remained bathed in the black shade
of the encroaching trees. As he approached the fence, the
crushed green glass which was spread on several graves
sparkled in weed-filled pools. Sand rose around the soles of his
boots, leaving a faint trail behind him.*

Crack!

Will broke the rack and the balls scattered across the dirty
felt. He moved his stocky frame around the table.

"I suppose Tommy isn't coming," he said to the bartender.
"Been an hour, hasn't it?"

"I guess he's still out at the bog." Dunphy wiped the
formica counter. "Everything is late this year. He says nothing
grows right nowadays."

Will missed his first shot, and his opponent leaned over
the table, the ragged edge of his red beard touching its top.

"Six ball, corner pocket."

*Maggie leaped from the cellar hole with a piece of white
ribbon in her mouth. She barked as if she had lost track of
him. The plastic dropped from her mouth; then she bounded
toward the fence at the far end of the road.*

*"All right, girl," he said as she reached his side. "I'll only
be a minute. I just want to do something." He rubbed the dog's*

21

neck and she jumped at him, resting her sandy paws on his khaki shirt. "I know. I know. You're ready to eat. And then I have to see Tommy." He gazed at the sky. "Maybe you'd like to stay in town. Sun's out. Not many more days of peace left around here."

"Probably should leave and come back around three or so," the bartender suggested.

Will sipped his beer, glancing at the 33 on the backside of the label.

"Hear you're moving," the other man said, pointing to a ball and pocket with his cue.

"Yep."

"You the last one back there?"

"The last."

The man sank the ball and pointed to another.

"My parents were the last family to stay. I still live in their house."

"You're kidding?"

He passed through the gate. Cedars grew between the stones. A locust tree arched over one corner of the enclosure. The grass, brown and ragged, was knee-high. He walked toward them, noticing a dead yellow leaf as it floated over the ironwork and down to the marble. A pine lizard sat rigid on the light-drenched stone.

"There's nothing I can do. Absolutely nothing," he said. "The lower court's ruling stands. I swear to Christ it's all money. If I had enough to fight...but that doesn't matter now." He glanced at Maggie as she pulled a lathe free from the grey sand. "They're ready to start clearing." He crouched next to them, and a sharp pain shot down his legs. He scanned the stones until his eyes found the largest monument, which was surrounded by an additional iron fence. "Worthing would have an idea or two. Maybe if I could be there beside you, it wouldn't matter. This place has become a damn crazy house.

"Not many people live like that today."

"True, true. But I'm not most people." Will rested his bottle on the counter.

"Why are you leaving?" His opponent sank another ball.

"Not because I want to."

"I thought that land was protected or some bullshit like that."

"You've got that right."

"What do you mean?" The other man chalked his stick absentmindedly as he circled the table.

"Around here you never know. My place and the whole town—what's left of it—was supposed to be preserved. Some big shots from the power company came along and said they needed the ground. They went to the state, oiled a couple of palms with the green stuff, and bingo—the state said no problem. It isn't the first time they've done it. Back in '61, another utility got a chunk of state forest and a piece of the Appalachian Trail as well." He finished his beer and signaled Dunphy for another. "Hell, even you could wave a few million around and the state would give you anything you want."

Rather than responding, the other man concentrated on his newly discovered shot. He flexed the fingers of his left hand on the green felt.

He walked back to his house and could hear the tea-stained river rushing over the sluice into the race and then down to the hollow guts of the stone paper mill where the turbines once turned. Down the slope, behind his home, he could hear its whisperings at night as the water traversed the switchbacks and the sound made its way from the rockless sand river bottom through the labyrinth of laurel and huckleberry and black gum to his bedroom. It always caressed him, transporting his spirit back to a more satisfying time. In the dark night, it was stealthy and had healing power.

"Condemned is what they said. They're a funny bunch up there. They have control of all these historic sites and a pile of money to preserve and restore them. But what do they do?"

The other man shrugged and finished the game by sinking the eight ball. He began to whistle the melody of a George Jones song.

"Let them rot—the majority of them at least. Especially the ones in this part of the state. Remember the old Fleming Cotton Mill over in Atsion?"

"Another game?" his opponent asked, ignoring Will's complaints because they were beginning to sound like a tirade. He looked at Dunphy who shrugged in agreement.

Will finally nodded and said, "Damn, I should write a book." He stopped and reached for his beer. "And give me a chance to shoot this time."

The other man racked the balls, and Will motioned for him to break.

"Shit!" he muttered when nothing fell.

"Well, it's about time." Will slipped from his barstool and looked at the clock behind the counter. Its numbers and hands rotated counterclockwise. The clock was framed by two mounted deer asses. "I'm not playing anymore after this one. If Tommy isn't here by the end of it, I'll catch him later. I have things to do." He squatted behind the cue ball. "That duck there in the side." He gently stroked the ball into the plastic-lined pocket and pointed to the next ball and pocket with his cue stick. The ball fell into the hole. He looked at the younger man. "Not bad for an old fart."

The other man leaned against the aqua-blue cinderblock wall and folded his arms. He tapped the end of his cue on the concrete floor.

"Two ball, corner pocket," Will said, but the ball careened out of the hole and slammed into another ball.

"That's it," his opponent remarked as he studied the table.

"You're full of yourself today." Will gazed at Dunphy who wasn't watching the game.

"Nothing unusual," the man said, resting his arm on the table. "I'm running out of competition around here." He tilted his head back for a moment. His beard wasn't trimmed and it covered his neck. He burrowed his fingertips into the matted profusion and scratched.

Fire still smouldered in the cans behind his house. He had started to burn the accumulation of several lifetimes. Things that had sentimental value would be given to friends or distant family members. Will imagined they would be silent when presented with something that appeared to them to be worthless. He had anticipated that the court's final decision would force him to leave the town where he was raised. Anything that couldn't be used or given away went into the burning ashcans where the black smoke rose from the rims into the sky and disappeared. He liked the idea that this haze would be blown over and back into the Pines. After feeding Maggie, he stood on the porch and watched the plumes begin their journey.

"Another five or six loads and we'll be finished," he said to the dog as she darted from the porch toward the cans. "Don't worry, I won't burn your things." She sprinted around the yard and returned to the porch. "It'll be fine girl."

Months before the animal has sensed the upheaval about to take place. He hadn't touched any of the house's contents yet, but she was aware that a major change was near. She stayed in a different room each evening—something she never did—until she finally reached his bedroom, the place where she had always slept.

"Eight ball, side pocket," the younger man said as he bumped the ball solidly into the hole. He rested his cue against the table and looked at Will who shook his head. "Are you sure you don't want to play another?"

"No thanks." Will opened his wallet and placed two dollars on the covered slate. "You're too much for me today. If I didn't have so much on my mind, I would have kicked your ass though." He laughed. "Try not to drink it."

"You never said where you're going," his opponent said as he collected the money from the table.

"Garden State Gun Club until deer season is over. And then I'm heading south."

"Really. My sister lives in Georgia."

"How old is she?"

"Twenty-seven."

Will smiled. "Maybe I'll stop by and see her if I get down that way." He returned his pool stick to the wall rack. "Dunphy, hit me with an eight-pack of those little green bottles." He placed a hand on the bar and watched the man remove the beer from one of the two white refrigerators that sat against the rear wall and flanked a raised platform. "Tommy going to start up with those dancing girls again?"

"Not sure."

"Good for business, isn't it?"

"On Wednesday and Thursday nights, the place is jammed. But the rest of the week, it's dead. He thinks that having them dance might hurt business more than it helps."

"Why?"

"There's a different type of customer around now. A lot of houses up the road a couple or three miles. Those folks don't want to come in here and look at a bunch of Pineys get rowdy."

"What's the world coming to?"

"Haven't you heard, Will? We're what's known as a metropolitan state. Tommy might dump some cash into this joint and make it nice, more classy...suburban. Tips would sure as hell be better."

"Christ."

"Don't be surprised if the dancers go the same way as Worthing Mills."

"I'll be out of here by then. Vamoosed." Will gazed around the bar. "This place has started to give me diarrhea anyway." He lifted his beer from the counter and left his money. "There's a good tip in that." He winked as he pulled his tan jacket from a barstool and slipped it on. "Don't forget to tell Tommy that I'll be back this afternoon."

Will left the square block building with its flat roof and got into his truck. Sunlight glistened across the windshield and hood. It was past noon when he drove out of the gravel parking lot. The vertical sign that flashed 'Tommy's' was on, but its sporadic blink was invisible in the daylight. Dust kicked up behind him as he rolled over the shoulder and onto the tar. He turned on the radio, but interference disturbed the only station he cared for.

"Damn it," he cursed, opening a beer. He took a long swig, catching his bloodshot eyes and uncombed grey hair in the rearview mirror as he braced the bottle between his sore legs.

FOUR

1937

Martin Kelly left Wescoat's at four o'clock. One wall of the paper mill, orange with the light, stood lifelessly above the town. He drove slowly, finding it difficult to believe that this town was the same one where he had spent most of his life. The streets were free of traffic. His truck, it seemed to him, was the only thing moving in the entire town. Vacant houses were left to decay along with much of the abandoned paper mill facility. Nature, temporarily abated by progress, now ate away at the periphery of the enterprise, shrinking it year after year. Unless nothing short of a miracle occurred, Worthing Mills faced obliteration. And Kelly knew that a miracle wasn't likely. The entire operation had been reduced to a small machine shop, which occupied one of the old papermachine buildings; cranberry bogs and blueberry fields, which played an increasingly prominent role in the company's unstable finances and added to the demand for hundreds of seasonal, agricultural employees; and a sawmill, which barely made enough money to support its work force.

When compared to the town of forty years before, the present Worthing Mills was a parody of itself, an imitation which mocked its former prosperity and glory. The population was only a quarter of what it once had been. Nearly eighteen years before, after a not too vigilant attempt by Beatrice Worthing to run the company from another state, the business was on the verge of bankruptcy. Anthony Jenkins bought the property for a fraction of its value and proceeded to make it worth a fraction of what he paid for it by extremely poor business decisions and a lack of imagination. Within a few years he died, and his wife was left with a morass of debts and obligations, as well as a family who wanted nothing to do with the isolated, problematic company. Her lawyers devised a plan to postpone the creditors: valuable timberland was sold; the paper mill was permanently closed (her husband had closed it once, but reopened it in the early 1920's); the agricultural holdings were enlarged; and the permanent work force was cut drastically.

In a few short years, the town fell from being a leading employer in the area to a minor one. With this plan came a nonchalance toward the maintenance of the overall physical plant. Worthing's vision, which he had succeeded in making a reality, was gone. The idea of a beautifully synchronized company town was lost. Beatrice Worthing, as well as the Jenkins family, had neither the creativity nor the desire to sustain his dream. What Samuel and Elizabeth Worthing, along with their workers, had made was exquisite. The others, with the aid of nature and fire, had destroyed it.

Kelly passed the machine shop and counted eight cars in its yard. Dismay overcame him when he thought about the paper mill that once ran twenty-four hours a day. People had filled the streets; wagons carrying rags and rope and salt hay arrived constantly; paper products, lumber, and shingles were shipped to the train station with regularity or loaded onto ships for sale in faraway markets outside the United States. All of the normal activities of a thriving mill town had ceased. He was one of the only people who had witnessed the arrival of the Worthings. Oddly enough, he had contributed to their ultimate departure. Now the town was filled with ghosts.

His sister and her husband were gone also. They had died, leaving him without family in the state. Their children had left to live in different parts of the country. He hadn't seen any of them for close to ten years and remembered them with fondness, but he made no attempt to reach out to those still living. His dwindling memories of Sunday afternoon meals and the conversations that stretched into the evening had helped him remain with them. Occasionally, he thought he saw his sister waiting for him at his cabin when he returned after a day's work, but she was gone by the time he reached the drive. As the years passed, it became more difficult for him to recreate those pleasant times in his mind, and he suspected that a day would arrive when the memories would be lost.

He still worked as a gardener and handyman for the owner of the town, although the nature and demands of his job had become less important and strenuous. Mrs. Jenkins wasn't a yearlong resident of Worthing Mills and only spent an infrequent weekend and a two-month holiday in the mansion. She had no delusions about preservation. If the structure was no longer useful, it was allowed to fall. She refused to spend money. If there was no foreseeable return on an investment, she wouldn't agree to it. Primarily, Kelly's duties revolved around the mansion, but he did provide special services, free of charge, to a few unfortunate town residents who had faced some kind of calamity.

When he turned onto the road leading to the town dump, the empty hulk was behind him. The lake twisted its way beyond the trees to the right. Water still tumbled through the sluice, but its roar wasn't what it had been. The lake had filled with silt and was being choked by chain fern, yellow pond lilies, and other aquatic plants. The remains of a dead stand of cedar, their grey, bleached trunks standing akimbo, clogged one section of shore. As its role in the town's well-being was reduced so was any interest in keeping it clean and open. When Jenkins died and left the town to his wife, a summer camp was opened along its banks. The ground was leased for several years, but after two seasons and mounting complaints about the lake's maintenance, the campers departed. A few local residents said the campers were frightened away from the water by the cries of dead slaves. Sixty men who helped Elijah Andrews, the town's founder and their owner, build the town's original forge in the eighteenth century had perished in a fire along the shore of the lake, but Mrs. Jenkins dismissed the talk as Piney superstition. With the camp's demise came a total disregard for the body of water. As long as it supplied enough power to turn the two antiquated turbines, nothing would be changed. The lifeline of the town had become an anachronism.

With the lake out of sight, the forest smothered everything. Traces of Worthing Mills had stretched along this road years ago. Kelly could see a green swath hundreds of yards in length as it paralleled the road to his right. All the trees and other vegetation were smaller there. The 1929 fire had taken this path and reached the town. The main building of the paper mill was burned. Worthing's prevention system of clear cuts and water towers had not been maintained, and the fire had crowned over the reduced obstacles. The pumps failed and the only thing that prevented the searing blaze from continuing through the property was a downpour. Another fire had raced toward the town from a different direction in 1917, but Worthing's defenses, along with a shift in wind, had saved the place. Townspeople wanted a series of hydrants installed and more efficient firefighting equipment bought, but their pleas never went beyond Mrs. Jenkins' deaf ears. Many said that she hoped for total devastation and a large insurance settlement. Kelly knew that disaster was inevitable. It would be fire, bankruptcy, or nature. Fire seemed the most fitting to him, but he expected death would take him before it happened.

Kelly stopped at the locked dump gate. A small tar-papered shack guarded the entrance. He looked at his small angular face in the mirror and readjusted his cap, drawing it down over his streaked black hair.

"Clevenger!"

The door opened and an old man stood in the entrance. He looked like he hadn't taken a bath for months.

"That you?"

"Who else would it be?"

"It's Wednesday, ain't it?"

"All day and I'm here with Widow Wescoat's garbage."

"How is she?" Clevenger asked.

"Still breathing."

"Do you know how I knew it was you?"

Kelly didn't feel like talking but went along with the man. "How?"

"I heard your brakes grinding when you stopped. Who else would let them go like that?"

"Come on. Open the fucking gate, man."

Clevenger stepped outside of the shack and fished for the key in his pocket.

"Gettin' hot," he said without direction.

"Why do you keep this place locked?"

"To keep things straight."

"Sure," Kelly commented as he inched the truck toward the gate. He stopped it when the bumper pushed on the fence.

When Clevenger reached the barrier, he hit the dented hood of the vehicle with the palm of his hand.

"Smart ass. Back this piss-poor excuse up, so I can get at the lock."

Kelly shifted the transmission into reverse, then first.

"You know if we didn't have this place you'd have to drive all the way to the township dump. But then again I suppose you'd just pile it in the woods." Clevenger fiddled with the key and lock.

"What's the difference?"

"That's what I thought you'd say."

"What do you do out here all day, wait for someone to come along so that you can give him a hard time?"

"I talk to fools like you and make sure no one uses the dump from the outside unless they pay a fee set by Mrs. Jenkins."

Kelly looked into the dump and his nostrils flared.

"What about the smell?"

"Get used to it." Clevenger grinned, revealing his few good teeth which were covered with tobacco juice. Then he opened the gate.

Kelly steered the truck past the fence. Gulls were everywhere. Red tails circled high above with a deceptive aplomb. Some of the garbage moved in the windless afternoon. His feet sank when they hit the layers of refuse. The town is beneath me, he thought. It would be possible to dig through the layers and identify them with a matching period and owner. People discard more when there's prosperity in a town, he surmised.

Kelly emptied the cans, not paying any attention to their contents, and instead watched the far edge of the clearing. He thought he saw two deer browsing in the shade along the treeline, but he squinted and they were gone.

When he returned to the open gate, he beeped. The door of the shack was open, and he could see Clevenger sitting inside.

"Time to lock up Fort Knox," Kelly yelled.

The man left his seat and walked to the truck, his feet banging against trash-littered ground.

"Any money to bet this week?" Kelly asked.

"Hell no. I lost it all on the Derby."

"I told you to go with the Admiral."

"You did." He rubbed his hairy ear.

"Come on, Clevenger. It's been a time. All the money you're making out here. What about the Louis fight?"

Clevenger started for the rusting gate.

"So you're not interested?"

"I'll let you know."

"Don't wait too long."

"I'll let you know," Clevenger repeated vexedly, waving his hand above his head.

Kelly returned to Wescoat's with the empty cans. He backed the truck into the yard using a service lane that ran behind the row of tenant houses. From there he could see the well-tended garden plots of the residents and noticed how much larger they had become. At one time, beyond the gardens, there was a low pasture where the townspeople grazed their livestock for free. Trees and bracken had overtaken the field, and a solitary cow meandered listlessly from one small clearing to the next.

"There he is Billy." Sammy looked through the screen door and away from the cooling pies made with the swamp blues they had gathered the day before.

"Jenkins' man?" his brother asked from the next room.

Kelly approached the rear of the house with two cans hoisted on his back.

"Mr. Kelly," the boy said.

The man tried to see who was calling him behind the screen.

"What do you need? Mother have something inside she wants hauled away?"

"No, sir," the boy said as his brother joined him. "We heard you were there when she went."

"The Hindenburg?"

"Yeah."

"I was."

They emerged from behind the door and stood on the steps in front of him.

"You boys are sure getting bigger." He put the cans on the ground. "How's everything?"

"Fine."

"Well, let me get these cans put back and I'll be out of your way."

"Do you have a minute or two?"

"We want to hear about it."

"It happened weeks ago, son. The papers and the radio have been filled with pictures and stories. I'm not sure that I could add much."

"But you're the only one we know who was there," the boy said quickly.

"Is that so?" Kelly leaned against one of the cans and folded his arms. "I guess a few minutes won't do any harm." He paused as if he needed time to recall events that had left his memory. "When she came into the Lakehurst Air Station, we were waiting. Everything was still. Really still. Each of us was handed a mooring line to steady her. She was enormous and floated up above us like a raincloud. Her engines were louder than I thought they would be. Throbbing. Making the air rumble. When she got to the mooring mast, they revved and it was deafening. Someone said that she was coming in too fast and that the captain had thrown the engines in reverse." He looked from one boy to the other. "A second later there was an explosion, and right after it a fire shot out near her stern. The flame went straight up as red as the Devil's tail. It looked like Lucifer himself. Then there was another explosion and this one shook the ground. I didn't move. The flames got white as the hydrogen started to burn, and they were so bright I thought I would be a blind man if I lived. Up above the ship, fire was suspended in the air. It was mighty peculiar. Now that I think about it, that was probably gas burning up there, too. That's what it said in the newspaper. Thick smoke started to pour from her as she fell. There were hundreds of folks screaming. Fire was everywhere. It was the inferno right here on earth. I don't know how anyone lived."

"Jeez."

"Some of the men who were holding on to the mooring lines began to run, but not me. I was so hot I thought I was going to melt." He turned his head. "See that red spot on my neck? The skin was burned there clean down to the muscle. I didn't even realize it until everything was over. It just stopped hurting me last weekend."

"Did you see any Nazis?"

"Lad, they were running all over. But not me. I held my post until the officer-in-charge relieved me. My hands were holding on so tight that he had to pry the rope out of them."

"Naw." Billy looked at his brother with amazement.

"And when I was relieved, I went straight for the wreck to rescue people. I pulled five from her. Four of them I had to carry on my shoulders. When I was real close, the flames were so hot that they burned the hair off my arms and the whiskers from my face. When I came home, I looked like I had just shaved. But I was lucky because some of the passengers were actually on fire, not just their arm hair, but everything."

"And what did they look like?"

"Oh son, you don't want to hear about it. You'd have nightmares for a year. I have them every night. It was something you wouldn't want to see again. You can be sure of that."

They protested, wanting him to reveal each detail.

"All right. All right. I'll tell you, but don't say a word to your mother."

They assured him, even though they knew they would

repeat his story.

"It was horrible. Once I was relieved I went in to help rescue people, like I said. After I carried the fifth person to safety, I turned back to the Hindenburg and then I saw him—the poor soul. He was running toward me." He hesitated, heightening the drama.

"And?"

"It was terrible, I tell you. Fire was climbing up his neck. His mouth was open so wide from screaming that I couldn't see his chin or nose or eyes—just one gigantic mouth in agony. I planted my feet and got ready to tackle him so that I could put out the fire. He dodged past me, and I saw that it was too late to save him. His hair was burning like a pine bough and his skin..."

"Mr. Kelly," a woman's voice interrupted from behind the door.

He stopped and replied, "Mrs. Wescoat." He lifted his cap.

"What are you filling these boys with?"

"Nothing, just a story about the Hindenburg."

"So I heard." She glanced at her sons. "You two shouldn't be bothering Mr. Kelly. He has work to do."

"I don't mind, missus. I had a few minutes."

"You've probably been bending Mr. Kelly's ear about that treasure of yours, too."

They looked at her through the screen.

"Treasure?" Kelly said inquisitively.

"We found it earlier today—Andy and Will and me and Billy."

"What was it, a gold nugget or an emerald ring?"

"No. It's a head," Sammy offered.

"A head?"

"Not a real one. It's stone," the other boy said. "It's from a statue of a woman I think."

Kelly's attention fixed on the boy.

"We found it up above the town in the river."

"Do you have this head?"

Sammy looked disappointedly at the ground.

"No. It's over Johnson's house. Will found it first, and then we dove in and got it with Andy."

"Did you find anything else?"

"No."

"That's too bad." He readjusted his cap. "But I'd like to see what you found."

"Will wants to sell it, I think."

"He said we would get some of the money for helping."

"You don't say." Kelly lifted the cans on his back, shifting the weight until they were balanced. "Well, I'd better get back to work. If you don't have anything more for me today, I'll be back next week, missus. You keep me informed boys. If you find any more treasure, let me know and I might buy it from you. And if your mother will let me," he paused as he dropped the cans into place, "I'll tell you about the day back in '28 when I saw Carranza's monoplane go down over behind Chatsworth."

FIVE

1990

Will saw her walking along the shoulder of the flat, straight road. When the truck got closer, she turned and stuck out her thumb. He hit the brakes, stopped a few feet past her, and looked through the rear window. She was in her early twenties and had black hair, which swayed from shoulder to shoulder as she jogged to the side of the truck.

The memorial stone rested on the bed. He was sitting against the passenger door with his mother next to him. His father drove the truck without speaking. None of them could believe that Andy was dead. Okinawa had claimed him, and they were a gold star family. His mother wanted nothing to do with citations or ribbons because she was heartbroken and angry, angry that her son was dead and that his body would remain so far from home. He had been reported as missing-in-action during the first day of the landing. His body was never recovered. The piece of marble would be the only thing in the cemetery at Worthing Mills. His father had said little about his son's death. What could be done? Andy's life was over. Will sensed that a small piece of his father's own spirit had died with Andy. And when Will's eyes gazed at the monument, he too felt the ache left by his brother's death.

On Andy's last weekend home before being shipped overseas, they had had a party—not a loud celebration—but a quiet, somber gathering of family and close friends. Will couldn't have imagined a worse idea. The house absorbed the solemnity of the occasion and moaned under the burden. A smell that reminded Will of death seemed to linger in the hall-

ways, and he couldn't get it out of his nostrils. Several times he left the house and went outside. It was October and the night air was chilly. He decided to speak with his brother about his fears and the dangers he would face, but Will realized how naive he was. Andy was already terrified and fought to keep himself from panicking. Andy's fiancee was there next to him, holding his hand as if that action alone would keep him with her. Will saw the fear in her eyes as well. But he never mentioned his apprehensions to his brother or his fiancee before Andy left for the Pacific.

"Where are you heading?"

"Up the road."

"I'm going four miles or so. I'll take you that far if you don't care."

"That's fine." She opened the door and lifted her slender, jean-covered legs onto the benchseat.

Will studied her for a second, thinking she was pretty. She looked like his ex-wife.

"Would you like a beer?"

"Sure."

He reached for a bottle and handed it to her.

"From around here?"

"North of here."

"Up above the development they're building?"

"Near there."

"What are you doing out here alone?" He pulled the truck off the shoulder.

"What is this, twenty questions?"

"Just trying to be friendly. My name is Will Johnson."

"April. But my friends call me Twister."

"Twister?"

"Yeah. You never heard of a twister before?"

"Like a cyclone?"

"A what?"

"A tornado."

"You got it." She raised the pony bottle to her mouth and drained it, then belched."

"Help yourself," Will said, motioning to the eight-pack

between them. "Been out there long?"

"Nope. It only takes a car or two, and then I get a ride." She opened another bottle. "A lot of guys think I'm going to give them a piece of ass or something."

"Oh."

"That's what they think anyway," she added pointedly.

"Kind of dangerous for a young girl to be hitchhiking."

"Listen Pops, that's my fucking business. I'll take my chances. Anyway," she said, reaching into her purse, "I always carry this." She pulled a pistol from her purse. "You see if some horny fucker gets weird on me I blow his balls off. You know?"

"Don't worry about me," Will answered, startled by her aggressiveness. "I'm not interested."

"You a fag?"

"No. I'm just trying to be friendly. I saw you walking along the road, and I thought I'd do the right thing."

"Bullshit. You saw my ass and thought you'd like to screw me."

"If that's what you think, fine," he replied not wanting to be contentious.

"Men are all alike."

"Oh, I don't know."

"Believe me. I know what I'm saying."

"Whatever," Will remarked, trying to distance himself from the woman's conviction.

"Let me tell you, I was down in Atlantic City yesterday and hanging out at a bar. A guy tells me that he'll give me some coke and a ride home if I stay with him. You know? He was good-looking and had a Vette, so I said to myself what the fuck. Everything was chill. We got wasted, did it—the usual. This morning we eat breakfast, do a joint, and start to drive. After ten minutes he stops and tells me to get out. He says, I'm late for work and this is as far as the free ride goes."

"Too bad."

"Not for me as much as him. When he pulled away, I blew his fucking windows out with this. She patted her purse.

"Hmm."

"So now you know it ain't for show."

"Yeah," he commented, glancing at her determined profile.

"I'm leaving you, Will," she said.

They had just turned off the lights. As his eyes adjusted, he could see her angular face next to him in the sparse light of the room.

"I can't stand this life anymore: living back here, doing without things, never going out except to that run-down bar. I'm suffocating. I want out." She started to cry, but that didn't alter the tone of her voice. "I don't understand you. You went to college. You're intelligent, but you have absolutely no ambition. Why did you bother?"

"I wanted an education."

"What about a career?"

"I wanted a feeling for the world, wanted to find my place in it. Knowledge was what I was after, what I needed."

She breathed impatiently.

"I found what I needed. I never wanted anything more. If I had, trade school would have been the place to go, I suppose."

"So you plan on working in the woods for the rest of your life?"

"I thought you knew that," he said, remembering her ready acceptance of his plans when they were younger. "We've been over this before."

"But this is the final time. Tomorrow I'm saying goodbye and taking Elizabeth and leaving this godforsaken town for good."

"There's another man," he said firmly, but without anger.

They paused, Will waiting for an acknowledgment, his wife waiting for her courage to build.

"He's a professional, a lawyer. So don't try to give me a hard time about Elizabeth. He's willing to adopt her. She's young enough, so when she gets older he'll be the only father she knows."

"And that's it?"

"Yes," she said firmly.

"I'll refuse to go along with it."

"You're only asking for trouble. You don't have any money to fight us."

"I love her and you, too." His voice began to betray the emotions he wished to deny.

"You haven't proved that to me. I've begged you to get us out of here to a real town before she starts school, but you haven't budged."

"That doesn't have anything to do with love."

"In my mind it does."

"I'm not going to beg you to stay, but you're not taking her with you."

The next morning she left, but without their daughter. Will didn't know what would become of his marriage or his wife, but he did spend the entire week doting on Elizabeth. Eventually, he was ordered to release the child to her mother. She had accused him of physical and mental cruelty. Her lawyer boyfriend had made the right calls, and Will's fitness to raise a child was doubted. He realized that he couldn't win and let his daughter go.

"So what do you do?" she asked, helping herself to another beer.

"Just about everything."

"That doesn't tell me much."

"Do you care?"

"No, not really." She offered a disinterested glance toward the passing trees.

"So?" Will grinned.

"I thought..."

"I work in the woods mostly."

"Sounds like a wild time," she said sarcastically.

"What about you?"

"Unemployed."

"There's plenty of work around."

"Haven't found anything that suits me." Her voice was defensive.

"What about school?"

"For what?"

"To find something you might be interested in."

"School takes too long. I need money now. The only problem is that all the jobs I've had pay minimum wage. It doesn't pay to work. So I have a system. You know? I take a shit job until I can collect unemployment. After my benefits run out, I take another shit job. It's perfect. Mom and Dad supply the food and roof, free of charge. I've got it beat."

"What about ten years from now?"

"Maybe I'll get a job working in the woods." She laughed, sizing him with her eyes. "Who are you to be lecturing me about work? Give it up. I don't see no Mercedes or any jewelry or nice clothes. You just have this hunk of tin and those crummy work clothes and that ratty jacket. Hell, this heap doesn't even have a decent radio."

"None of that matters. I mean in the long run."

"Right. Just like you don't want my ass," she exclaimed.

He could see that whatever logic he used the girl would circumvent it.

"I have to stop at Brown's store for a minute. I need a loaf of bread and a can of coffee."

"No problem."

"Thank you."

"Hey Pops, if you don't want me to ride just say so. You know?"

"Not a chance. I told you that I would give you a ride, and that's it. I don't want you lumping me in with all those other sorry bastards who want to take advantage of you. A free ride and free beer—that's what you're getting from me."

Once in the store's parking lot, Will left the engine running. His legs were stiff, and he limped for a moment as he walked toward the entrance. He spent a few minutes wandering around the store's three short aisles. Brown had rearranged his stock, and Will couldn't find his brand of coffee until Brown emerged from the back room and located the last dusty can. When he carried his bag outside, his truck and the girl were gone. Brown called the State Police and Will sat in front of the store, staring across the road at a cranberry bog where men in yellow waders directed walk-behinds over the shallow, berry-filled water.

They had walked several miles that morning to one of the most remote bogs in the area. Although summer was over, the air was warm by the time they scooped the first berries. Andy worked to his right, hunched over the dry field with his white canvas bag draped over one shoulder. He could scoop more than Will on most days. Often he would work through lunch, trying to surpass an old mark. He always wanted to better his past accomplishments regardless of their significance. If only you had a little of it, you would have been somebody, Will's former wife had said repeatedly. It was Andy's drive to set and reach goals that probably killed him, Will had always countered. When they finished for the day, they cashed in their tickets. The money never stayed with them long. A portion of it went automatically to their parents, and the remainder was spent on soda and candy or the movies if the opportunity to go to the county seat presented itself. Once they saved their earnings and went to a football game in Philadelphia. Will didn't remember the score or who won, but he did recall the rain and the mud. Whenever he watched a football game on television, he was amazed to see how clean the players stayed. Football, he would say to anyone who would listen at Tommy's, is meant to be dirty and tough, not glamorous. Most of the men who gathered to watch the contest would holler and tell him to sit down, which he usually did after repeating his previous remarks at least once.

Eventually, their days of working in the fields ended. Andy was nearly three years older than Will, and his interest in the opposite sex and dating interfered with their time in the fields and bogs. During the summers when blueberries were being picked, Andy would work a normal day, although he preferred to stand in the packing house with a pretty young girl rather than next to Will. During the fall when cranberries were being scooped, Andy's Saturdays were often spent with his friends instead of in the bogs. Frequently, he had a girlfriend to entertain. Will didn't appreciate the dichotomy in their interests until he grew older.

Sadly, the girl Will had chosen for a lifetime had left him. His daughter was taken from him. Now Elizabeth was married and living in California. He wrote to her a few times a year, mailed presents to his grandchildren, and even visited them one Christmas. Despite the attempts of his wife and her second husband, Will had remained Elizabeth's father.

"And you say that the keys were in the truck?"

"I've never done it any other way."

The trooper shook his head as he wrote. The radio crackled and he reached for the squelch.

"You shouldn't do that. This area isn't crime-free anymore."

"That's what I hear. Was it ever?" Will added.

"It was never a nursery if that's what you mean. What did the girl look like?"

"Attractive. About twenty-two or three. Long black hair which looked like it might have been dyed. Five six or so. Thin. Blue jeans. Carried a red jacket. She said her friends called her Twister, but her name was April."

"Anything else?"

"Said she lived north of here and had spent the night down the shore."

"That's it?"

"She had a twenty-two pistol in her purse. She didn't seem afraid to use it. She said she had shot out a couple of car windows this morning."

"Tough ass."

"I guess. She certainly thought so."

"Nothing unusual," the trooper observed. "I'm sure you've heard that school kids are carrying them now. They think it's cool. They want to be like the guys on television and not the ones that used to wear the white hats. You're lucky she didn't use it on you."

Will studied the dashboard for a moment.

"What happens now?"

"We'll keep you advised. More than likely from the description of the vehicle we'll find it abandoned. I don't think anyone will be interested in stripping it or repainting it and knocking the numbers off."

Will got out of the patrol car after refusing a ride. He

glanced across the road again and counted the men working the cranberries. The sky behind them was swirled with white cirrus clouds. A red pump house sat on the embankment behind the first bog and mirrored the crimson fruit that bobbed on the water.

"Any luck?" Brown said from behind the register when Will entered the store again.

"Hell no. He said that they would be in touch with me."

"What are you going to do?"

"Go back to Tommy's. Not much else I can do at this point."

"Why don't I get my wife to come out and I'll give you a lift?"

Will followed the shiny lid of the soda cooler with his hand.

"I don't think so, but thanks. I've had enough riding for one day. It's only a few miles."

"You sure?"

"I'll walk."

"Okay. Hope it works out for you."

"Yeah," Will replied as he left the store, carrying a loaf of bread and can of coffee in his bag. "Yeah."

After walking several hundred yards, Will began to think that he should have accepted one of the rides. He removed his jacket. His legs hurt, and the sun was hot enough to darken the color of his shirt with sweat. He looked at his boots as they kicked across the sand shoulder. They seemed distant. He heard a horn and raised his eyes to see his pickup pass. Defiantly, the girl gave him the finger and tossed an empty beer bottle at him. It struck the lip of the paving, and the glass shattered at his feet. He screamed and clenched his fist. But in a moment, his truck was gone.

S I X

1889

Around. Worthing felt it—
the wheels turning, the harness tightening, the gentle lunge
forward—once, then again. The dust rose through the turning
spokes and into the cab. He reached for his handkerchief
and held it to his face until their speed increased and a cloud
ballooned behind them.

The others didn't acknowledge the sudden jolt and made
no countermovement. The older passenger, a small, emaci-
ated man of about sixty, wore the same expression with
which he had descended the long gallery of the hotel and
boarded the jitney. The other rider, a young man barely beyond adolescence, mimicked the older man's countenance.

Before leaving the Pennsylvania hotel that morning,
Worthing had proposed to Elizabeth. He said that he loved
her and wanted her beside him. Unfortunately, he would
have to seek a divorce from Beatrice and that would take
time. He didn't mention that it might take more time than they
could imagine. To his surprise, Elizabeth felt that his love for
her was more important than the legality of a broken marriage. For a second, he didn't know how to respond. He had
dreamed of her coming to Worthing Mills that summer. He
wanted to flaunt his love for her, and if she agreed he would
make her his wife without a legal divorce.

Elizabeth refused to accept conventions that didn't suit
her. And she intended to be with him because she found
herself loving him; however, she did have reservations. He
was older—nearly twenty years stood between them—and
she wasn't convinced that this wouldn't cause problems in

their future. She didn't know much about him but felt as if she knew the most important things. She realized that the institution of marriage had ruined many apparently promising relationships. In the past, she had experienced one devastating breakdown of love just prior to marriage, but this was caused, in part, by her sense of ambition and adventure. She saw that a man like Worthing, a man she not only loved but admired and respected, might not come into her life again. Any doubts, she decided, must be ignored. She would alter her life willingly and accept whatever resulted. She felt like Nelly Bly setting out on a new exploit, not knowing where the next bend in the road would lead, but not letting fear or uncertainty restrain her from traveling it.

Worthing knew that his wife of many years would find his sudden romance entertaining. Samuel, she would say, you never cease to amaze me. Then she would throw her head back and laugh, thinking that in a week or two or possibly three he would forget about this woman. He knew that Beatrice was sitting with their son in that drafty mausoleum on the Maine coast. Snow was probably still falling with a springtime heaviness that created a dead hush—something Worthing dreaded. At times he thought it would suffocate him, but Beatrice could endure it for an eternity.

Nothing would move her from that house and the town where it sat, not even the threat of her husband leaving and moving hundreds of miles south. The two previous winters were endless. Towns were isolated; farms were cut off for days and frequently weeks; people were frozen to death. Even with this horror around them, he couldn't convince Beatrice to abandon Maine. His reasoning went beyond the weather and ended with sound business proposals. At forty-five, he needed a new challenge. His family had made money in shipbuilding. Worthing had made money in the manufacturing of machinery and had owned two mill operations. Now he wanted to buy a small mill town and develop it according to his own vision. He felt certain that Beatrice would change her mind and thought that once he located a property she would finally acquiesce. Just before he left Maine, she informed him that he was wrong, saying she would stay with "her people." She would die in that house. Their marriage, it seemed to him, had died there, too.

Originally, Worthing's energy was focused on business. He had traveled halfway across southern Pennsylvania. It was a matter of good business practice, he had told himself. He had been lured away from the other site—the one which before arriving in Pennsylvania he had decided to purchase. Knowing this, he still refused to operate on impulse and found he couldn't invest in that property before examining a possible alternative. Three weeks had passed since he had arrived at the hotel. The inspection of the business and its books should have required three or four days of his time, but something held him there in the lush spring of the surrounding fields, something that initially he wouldn't have believed.

During the first week, he thought that his reluctance to go hinged on his memories of the Civil War and of those days that had occurred not many miles south of the hotel. Sitting on the gallery in the evening with the cool fieldstone walls behind him, he stared into the night and puffed on his cigar. He rarely attempted conversation with any of the guests, although several made an effort to bridge his evening meditations. After the usual exchange of pleasantries he would fall silent, dropping into his mysterious revelry and driving them away with his brooding gaze. Impressed that he didn't want to speak, they became accustomed to his reticence and left him alone.

The war had entered his life when he was seventeen. He had enlisted with a Maine regiment without the consent of his parents and departed the state after a brief training camp. With this he left behind his innocence because within a month he was in Virginia facing others just like himself. Both sides possessed the same false hopes of honor and glory. He struggled to stay alive. Any idea of valor became secondary. Not only the dangers of battle threatened him. Unrelenting boredom, inadequate food, and poor sanitary conditions all wore on his well-being. As he watched men die, he realized without fanfare that war was a special brand of insanity created by noncombatants. He saw that he had been duped and that there appeared to be no escape. He thought about deserting but decided against it. Where would he go if he couldn't return home? Feigning derangement entered his mind. But what was more insane than the war around him?

One evening after a skirmish in which two of his friends were killed, he decided that a self-inflicted wound would supply him with a ticket home. He would return as the hero, wounded in the course of action. A wound, he considered, carried no shame with it. He would avoid a worse fate. But the possibility of an infection and facing the surgeon's saw made him reconsider. Remembering this moment always amused him because his ruse was quickly pushed aside and forgotten after two rapid promotions due to attrition. Responsibility entered his life. He wanted to protect the men he now commanded and began to advise a caution in battle which bordered on cowardice. They realized that he was trying to save their lives and most listened. This was his one great wartime feat.

And then there was his own son. Even at eighteen, he rarely left his mother's side. His son, if asked, would choose his mother over his father without hesitation. He was their second and only surviving child. His older sister had died just after her fifth birthday. Worthing, filled with bitterness after her death, wanted his son to be everything. Often he thought that this was what drove the wedge between them—a father's hopes for two children funneled into one. He wanted his son to have the same curiosity about life that he had had at the same age, but it never happened. His son was his wife's child and content to remain in their house while the town decayed around them. With so much excitement in the world, Worthing found this hard to tolerate. Worthing knew that at eighteen he should be living closer to where life was raw.

On the previous day, thousands had waited, ready to endure a mad rush to grab land in the Oklahoma Territory. Worthing imagined that he would have been there at his son's age to experience an unforgettable event, a part of the country's history. Each time he thought about his son in this way, his disappointment grew. It seemed that life's invitation to be tasted had been pushed aside by his son. Worthing wasn't even certain that if his wife relinquished her invisible hold on the boy that he would change. This caused still more frustration. When his son learned of his plans to purchase the paper mill and his intentions concerning Elizabeth Black, he might be lost to him forever. But Worthing was prepared to accept this. Worthing knew that Beatrice would attempt to increase her suffocating hold on their son once her husband's plans were revealed. Without his presence Worthing admitted that there was little hope for the boy, and this caused his feeling of hatred toward his wife to magnify.

Now it was Samuel Worthing who would refuse—refuse to return to Maine and continue with a marriage to a woman he had stopped loving many years before. This was the situation which he would leave behind. After years of consideration and pleading, he was going to make new commitments. He had promised her he would go alone. She had ignored him. He had waivered once and reconsidered, but now there would be no reversal. Worthing had located the ideal business: a paper mill set deep in the Pine Barrens of southern New Jersey. The town surrounding the mill was substantial but not overly large and consisted of a sawmill, a gristmill, the accompanying outbuildings, the mansion, tenant houses, a school, an old church, the company store, a post office, and one thousand acres of water, fields, and forest. He planned to expand the business, double the paper mill's output, increase the agricultural holdings, reopen the sawmill, and build several new structures. The town's name would be changed to Worthing Mills. It would be, if all of his plans and a few of his dreams were made reality, a stunning success—his magnum opus.

He had met a young woman, nearly twenty years his junior: an attractive (he would say beautiful), intelligent woman who moved in a man's world, determined and confident as well as clever enough to use a man's unfounded attitudes and beliefs against him. This pleased Worthing. At first, he hardly noticed Elizabeth, although he was surprised that she was the assistant manager of the hotel. He had passed her countless times in the lobby and in the large sitting rooms that straddled the front desk. A brief glance or a word was all she warranted. She was just another person, an employee. He acknowledged her but nothing more, or so he thought. Mixed with his thoughts of business and property and war came something undeterminable. Marked spots in his memory that should have been disturbing became infused with a feeling of calm. Initially, the reason for this was unclear. An evening or two passed before he noticed that his casual exchanges with Elizabeth were the cause of this unexpected peace. Worthing spoke to her more often until he felt comfortable enough to ask her to dine with him. Elizabeth accepted his invitation after a little badgering and a discussion with the manager about company policy.

From the moment she consented, Worthing knew that his life would change in some yet unknown way. This realization wasn't tinged with maudlin sentimentality, although it was totally unexpected. The feeling was, even with his implacable desire to question it, as definite as the sky above them. He was aware that this sudden rush of emotion could be misinterpreted, so he tried to check it. As they spent more time together and the weeks unfolded, it was evident that they were falling in love. This came as a shock to Worthing who saw himself as middle-aged and beyond the peculiarities of love.

Suddenly, during one of his long, solitary periods on the gallery, he divined the reason for their romance. She was everything that his wife had promised to be, but was not. Elizabeth was a composite of all he desired in a woman. At that moment, he knew that he would do anything to have her.

As they rode along the river and into the outskirts of the town, the traffic increased. When the jitney came to a halt, the dust returned and rose to his nostrils. The other men didn't move. It appeared that they would remain seated until he started for the platform. He could hear the hiss of the engine. The driver was whistling for a porter while trying to keep rein on the horses. Worthing tipped his hat, stepped down, and walked toward the train. He would be back again at the beginning of June. As he moved through the chaos of the station, he felt the odd sense of calm return. Elizabeth would become his wife regardless of Beatrice. The surrounding confusion would have normally caused excitement in him. But, after so much had happened, he was unaffected. After years of uncertainty, purpose had returned to his life.

S E V E N

1937

Agnes Johnson didn't have
the opportunity to search for the box containing her notes
and a collection of articles about the Worthing family until
late that evening. Her husband had worked overtime at the
machine shop, and they hadn't eaten supper until well after
seven o'clock. Afterwards, her sons began to help with the
dishes, but they could hear their friends playing kick-the-can
across the connected yards. She could see their anxiety grow
with each lost minute. Finally, she let them join the voices
that teased them as they echoed through the heavy dusk air.

Her husband was listening to the radio when she finished
in the kitchen for the evening. The boys were getting ready
for bed and she had a few free hours, although she rarely
had the energy to do anything by that time of an already
lengthy day.

"I thought it was in this closet," she said, closing the door.
"That's where I saw it last." She glanced at her husband in
the living room.

"Did you check upstairs in the empty room?"

"No."

"Most of the boxes in there haven't moved since we've
been married."

"I know," she said. "I've been meaning to do something
about that but..."

"We should fix that room up. Andy should have it for his
own. That's if we can find a place to store all of the junk up
there."

"The room needs more than that. Paint to start, and a

piece of ceiling plaster is on the floor." She paused at the foot of the stairs. "If you're willing to invest the money and time, I'll empty the room."

"We'll need a few pieces of furniture as well."

"True."

"Money is a little tight."

"Isn't it always?" Agnes said lightly as she climbed the stairs.

She had to move several boxes to reach the center of the room. One wall was stacked with containers of every size, but nothing was marked. It seemed to her that she hadn't planned very well, but the opposite was true. She had blueprinted every detail of her move from the day her husband had proposed. After thirty minutes, she found the box she was looking for. She kneeled on the floor in the dust and broken plaster to look through it and decided that the kitchen table would be more suitable. But when she stood at the table and removed the contents of the box, she was startled by the quantity of material that had accumulated. The events at Worthing Mills were at the forefront of the county news for years. Suddenly, she felt dwarfed by the simple task of sorting through the contents.

She was interested in the year when Elizabeth Worthing had been discovered in the middle of a sand road, the victim of an assassin's bullet. The county detective on the case quickly established that robbery was not the motive after he found nearly one hundred dollars in her purse. A love affair turned sour was the proclamation offered by him. And for most people in the county, the facts supported his conclusion.

Agnes tried to remember that day and her ride from the newspaper office, which was located in the county seat, to Worthing Mills. John Crawford, the editor, rode next to her. She was preparing for her final year of high school, and Crawford had agreed to hire her for a probationary period of one year. He seemed to doubt her dedication. But being a Lippincott carried with it certain responsibilities, at least as far as her parents were concerned. If Agnes wished to be a journalist, and she did with what she thought was her entire being, then she must be the best even though journalism was still considered a man's profession. Her plans included early recognition and fame. Her brother was attending law school and hoped to start his own practice in Philadelphia. Agnes wasn't interested in the law even though her parents had encouraged it, but she was fascinated with the people who broke the law. She wanted to observe and analyze motivations. She wanted to uncover corruption. She was a student of human behavior. Crawford had allowed her to pursue her dream. And she was determined to show him what she could do. *The Messenger* was the only respectable newspaper in the county. The trip to Worthing Mills was her first professional exposure to a murder. She was anxious, thinking that the death of Elizabeth Worthing might present the ideal opportunity to prove herself.

When they reached the town, people had started to assemble at the front gate of the mansion. An eerie quiet had descended on the town after the body was returned on the back of a collier's wagon. Faces were taut and confused. A predictable look of doom showed on some. They knew that Elizabeth Worthing had kept the town working, and without her nothing was certain. Their thoughts of company-insured security became an anomaly on that morning.

Following Elizabeth's death, many changes came and one of them resulted in the destruction of her statue. Now its head rested upstairs. In a way it was a return of her spirit. The town had rolled steadily downhill after the Worthings' tenure. Elizabeth's return, if only in memory, was too late. Nothing would change for the better in the foreseeable future, and Agnes freely admitted this.

So many problems had developed after the Worthings died that most residents stopped counting. The company's major difficulties revolved around water and fire. The potable water of the local streams and lakes had a brown tint to it. Although considered to have medicinal properties, it prevented the production of any paper product without a distinctive yellow-brown wash.

Agnes remembered the evacuation of all the women and

children during World War I when the first major fire roared down on the town from the northwest. The sky was black for miles, and breathing the air was nearly impossible. The wind was tremendous, but it shifted just as the blaze reached the cut surrounding the town, and the place was saved.

Within a year, the burned area was green again. Pine trees renewed their growth. But the town never recovered after that. The first fire wasn't the cause of its fall and hadn't contributed to it, but it was a marker. The new owner had already initiated the decline, and this resulted in an unstoppable downward spiral. The early signs noticed in 1909 by the Worthings were never heeded by the Jenkins family.

By the 1920's, a catastrophe was being manufactured under the not so watchful eyes of Anthony Jenkins. After reopening and reclosing the paper mill for the final time, no new, permanent employment was available. A reduction of employees took place. He wasn't interested in supplying work, only making enough money to break even. The concept of a mill town was dead in his mind. Houses were rented to anyone who could afford them regardless of their affiliation with Worthing Mills Incorporated.

Many families turned to seasonal work and stayed in town. In the spring, they gathered sphagnum moss for florists. In the early summer, they picked wild blueberries and huckleberries. When cultivated blueberries started to appear, they picked them, too. Later in the summer, peaches and vegetables were harvested. In the fall, cranberries were scooped. The winter brought charcoaling and cordwood cutting. Before Christmas, they gathered pine cones, holly, laurel, boughs of pitch pine, and mistletoe. Grave blankets were made as well. All of this was supplemented by hunting, trapping, and odd jobs. Some even built sneakboxes and railbird skiffs or made whiskey. Families who lived in the area did what was required. It was a hard but good, peaceful life for most who stayed in the town, even though many were not employed full time by the company. No one made more money than it took to live, but the desire for material goods wasn't great. Travel to any sizable town was reserved for special occasions. With the Depression still raging around them, there was little urge to venture into the larger world. Their isolation seemed to protect them. At one time, it had been Samuel Worthing.

During the Jenkins' time at Worthing Mills, the social events there hit a new high. What Anthony Jenkins lacked in business savvy, he made up for with lavish parties thrown during the holidays and summer months. The mansion had a billiards room, bowling alley, card room, and a monumental ballroom. Guests never failed to find entertainment. His banquet-sized dinners became legendary. He knew no limits. If his guests desired something, he bought it. Bootleg gin flowed during Prohibition. Many guests stayed for days and found the setting of Worthing Mills quaint and rustic. The lake added to their amusement and a naked romp in the water at the evening's end became customary.

Many town residents were thankful for even seasonal employment, but they resented the money being spent by Jenkins. They thought the money should be invested in the town and its future. But Jenkins was unconcerned. Their prosperity wasn't important. It became evident that Anthony Jenkins had purchased the town to use as a retreat where he could bring guests. As long as the town paid for itself, regardless of the size or nature of its businesses, everything was fine. His two sons eventually left the family for college and married soon after completing their degrees. Their interest in the town was nil. With the death of Anthony Jenkins came the end of the majority of the parties. Although most of the extravagant social functions ceased, the money saved was never invested in the town except for increased agricultural holdings which only supplied temporary, low-paying work. All of the excess funds were absorbed by the battery of lawyers who helped the dead man's wife manage the operation. Olivia Jenkins became a spectator of not only the town's demise but also her own. Then, finally, her sons interceded, but it was too late.

Agnes remembered how it looked. When she was young, she had fantasized about living there. When fire threatened to destroy it, she thought her beautiful town would disintegrate. The Worthings had created her dream as if they were aware of her specifications. Her mother would visit Mrs. O'Malley, a family friend, and bring Agnes along. It was, Agnes had decided, straight out of a fairy tale. The scent of the air was like an exotic perfume to her. The surrounding forest was filled with enchantment. She imagined that the future would find her there dressed in expensive gowns and jewelry, living in the mansion with the man she loved. Only part of that dream came true.

She held a note about County Detective Nichols in her hand. He repulsed her with his arrogance. At times, however, she envied the man. He triumphed without effort. His success rate was astounding—too astounding for her taste. Even with his infuriating behavior, he was one of the best county detectives in the state. His advice was sought on numerous occasions. Commendations were frequent. His behavior was considered to be aggressive by most people, although not many of his detractors were women. Nearly thirty-five years had passed since the day he had started to work for the county. When he retired, a legacy of solved crimes would be left behind. Only a handful had slipped by. One of them was the second biggest event to happen in the county for forty years.

"What are you doing out here?"

"Thinking. Sorting through this mess." Agnes touched the papers on the table.

Her husband placed a hand on her back.

"Recalling those days of chasing down a lead?"

"In a way."

He reached for an article on the table and studied it.

"This all happened a long time ago," she said, stretching her arm around his waist.

"It wasn't that long ago," he responded, "or we're getting old."

"It feels like forever."

"You did spend years at it. You almost managed to avoid me."

"Not true."

"You married late."

"I wanted to be a successful writer. I wanted a career."

"And?"

"I got the career, but the great writer part eluded me. But I do have you and the boys."

"I'm glad you didn't stick with it a few more years. It would have been awfully quiet around here."

"Everything worked out. My mother was convinced I would die a spinster or get killed sticking my nose into someone else's business for the paper."

"I wasn't." He kissed the top of her head. "Things have changed around town. It was quite a place, wasn't it?"

"Yes. Yes it was."

They looked at the yellowed clippings for a minute.

"Well, I'm ready for bed."

"I'm tired, too," Agnes returned a handful of papers to the box.

"Don't stay up too late."

"I won't." She hesitated. "You know, Paul, I would like to see the spot where the boys found her."

"Why?"

"No reason. I mean...maybe I just want to scratch my curiosity."

"It's the reporter in you," her husband remarked.

"I guess."

"Still looking for skeletons?"

"You know better than that," she responded with a smile. "I'll be up in a few minutes."

Andy could hear the steps creaking as his father climbed them. Andy couldn't sleep and propped his head up with his folded pillow. The light from the window fell on the bureau where she rested. He could see her features clearly from his bed and tried to imagine her alive. He closed his eyes and tried to see her, but Kate Harris appeared instead. His eyes opened and he listened. His father was in the bathroom. Andy heard the medicine cabinet close. Water ran for a second. The door opened, and his father walked down the hall to his bedroom. Andy could hear his brother snoring lightly in the bed next to him. He looked at her head again. The room was black except for the spot beneath the window. She is beautiful, he admitted to himself, just as his brother had exclaimed. When his eyes closed, the other woman appeared. He watched for a moment and felt himself move. He was alone with her again just as he had dreamt twenty times. Another minute passed, but she didn't leave him. He reached under the sheet and touched himself.

EIGHT

1990

Before traveling a mile, Will was exhausted. The beer had made him drowsy, and each foot felt as if weights had been attached to its sole. After another hundred feet, he stopped and looked down the razor-like road behind him. Heat waves streamed from the asphalt. He sat on the grassy mound that abutted the shoulder and was littered with beer cans. Five minutes passed. I'll have to take it a mile at a time, he thought. A car appeared, popping up over the horizon into the dehiscent haze. He watched it draw closer. Instinctively, he stuck out his thumb, and the black four-door screeched to a halt. The tinted window came down with a mechanical hum and music poured from the inside, blasting the air around him.

"Where are you going?" the driver said, turning the radio down.

Will tried to see inside from where he sat, but his eyes couldn't reach into the cool, dark interior. He pulled himself to his feet.

"Tommy's Bar. Down the road two miles."

"That's chill." The driver adjusted his sunglasses, looking at himself in the rearview mirror. "Let's do it."

Will got into the car. As he touched the door, the window closed. He dropped his jacket on the seat beside him.

"Nice car."

"Just picked it up this morning," the driver said with a sniffle.

"Lincoln?"

"Yeah." He readjusted the radio to a low roar. "Kind of

warm out today."

"Don't I know it," Will said, sliding his bag to the floor in front of him.

"What were you doing out there?"

"Damned pickup was stolen a little while ago."

"No shit."

"A young lady by the name of Twister."

"No shit."

"I thought I'd walk to my friend's place, but I guess the sun was too much for me. And my legs aren't what they used to be."

"I know what you mean. I've got problems like that, too. I've got to wear these glasses or my eyes swell up. You know? Hell, I don't even take them off at night. Fluorescent lights even hurt them."

"Really." Will touched the upholstery and said, "Must have been expensive." He noticed the man was sitting on an enormous pillow which made his legs dangle from the seat's edge. The tip of his right shoe barely reached the gas pedal.

"Not too bad."

They left the mansion just after ten o'clock. Mrs. Jenkins sat next to her driver. Will sat in the back with Peggy Cushing. The interior smelled of leather, and he relished it, inhaling deeply as they drove toward the school. Occasionally, the scent of Mrs. Jenkins' perfume would waft to the backseat and smother the smell of the interior, but the memory of it lingered in his senses until the intrusion dissipated. They were being driven to the county seat to compete in a contest. Will and Peggy had been given an award for scholastic achievement. They would compete with other eighth graders for the chance to represent the county in a state-sponsored event. Will couldn't feel the road beneath them. The car was quiet; no sound invaded the passenger compartment. He had been told that this was a rare honor. Mrs. Jenkins offered her services infrequently, and Will wasn't sure why she had volunteered this time. He glanced at Peggy Cushing, who seemed just as flabbergasted by the experience, and grinned. Mrs. Jenkins coughed, raising an embroidered handkerchief to her red lips.

Her hat jiggled on her head. He wondered, as she coughed a second time, if the fox would drop the tail from its mouth because of the vibration in her heaving chest.

"What's your name?"

"Will Johnson."

"Lou, Lou Torelli."

Will extended his hand. The other man's hand was damp and didn't grasp Will's large hand firmly.

"Where are you heading?"

"A.C." Lou touched his nostril with a small knuckle.

"Haven't been there for at least thirty years. I hear it's changed quite a bit."

"You're kidding? That's where it's slammin'—casinos, bitches. You name it."

"Maybe I'll go someday. I don't get outside much though."

"Definitely."

Will tried to determine Lou's age but couldn't decide whether he was twenty-five or thirty-five. His sunglassses hid half of his tiny face.

"Yeah. I'm heading down to A.C.—the city by the sea. I'll play the wheel some. You know? And then I'll find a good lookin' bimbo. And then it's wham bam. You know?"

"Like I said, it's been years."

"I tell you, Will, I'm going to ask her to marry me."

"Larry, you're crazy. The girl is thirty years younger than you."

"She loves me. I know she does. The last time she danced at Tommy's she spent three-quarters of the night wiggling around my barstool."

"Don't you think it had something to do with those twenty-dollar bills you were stuffing into her G-string?"

The truck hit a bump and the headlights danced above the road for a second. A doe froze on the fringe of the brush.

"She's a big one," Will said, pointing.

"Hell no," his friend answered, ignoring the deer and Will's observation. "When they closed, she came over to me and said, 'Anytime you're ready, baby.'"

Will laughed.

"That doesn't seem funny to me."

"You're too much, Larry."

"She's not the run-of-the-mill type. Remember Masaryk? He was drunker than ever, almost passed out, with his head on the bar. Every time she danced past him he'd raise his head and say, 'The bitch is good. The bitch is good.' After he said that a few times, I whacked him. She saw it and realized how I respected her. When we get hitched, I want you to be my best man."

Will was still laughing and tears started to collect in his eyes. The truck shuddered when it struck another bump.

"I'll tell you what," Will said, trying to control his laughter. *"Give me the money you plan on ramming down her pants tonight. I'd say the last time you gave her about two hundred dollars. I'll put the money in her G-string, and if Masaryk says something I'll tell him to shut up. Then we'll see who she pays attention to. By the end of the night, she'll be whispering in my ear, 'Anytime you're ready, Will. Anytime.'"*

"You can't be that old," Lou said raising his eyes above his sunglasses. "I'm going to bag it before I'm forty, man. I don't want to be some old dude in a wheelchair. Live fast and hard. That's my motto. Seize the minute. You know?"

"I'm not in a wheelchair yet."

"You're lucky then, or you haven't lived very much." Lou drummed his hands on the steering wheel. "Hey, does this place have any good scotch?"

"As long as you don't ask for anything too dear."

The car hurtled along the road, speed obscuring the scenery, disallowing any clear view of what passed. Will studied the reflection of Lou's face on the window next to his head.

"That's it?" Lou pointed slightly with one of his fingers.

"Yes," Will said as the sign appeared in the distance, just visible as it protruded from the treeline.

When they entered the parking lot, the younger man said, "Is this place safe?"

"Safe? What do you mean?"

"My car will be okay out here?"

"Of course," Will said, thinking that he wasn't as certain

as he had been before that afternoon.

"You're sure?" Lou asked again with a sniffle. "I mean, it's insured and everything. But I have some stuff in the trunk."

"No problem," Will reassured.

They sat at the bar and ordered two drinks. Dunphy was alone, and Tommy hadn't checked in. Will told him about his truck, and the bartender shook his head in disbelief. Reaching for a bottle, Dunphy mentioned that his friend's car had been stolen from his driveway in Tabernacle two weeks ago.

"Thanks, my man," Lou said when Dunphy placed his drink on the bar in front of him. He readjusted his sunglasses. "This place is different."

"How so?"

"It looks like something out of a movie. You know? Old. No women. No music playing. A little more than an hour from here things are really hot."

"We have a jukebox," the bartender said.

Lou turned sideways on the stool and said, "So you do. Any good jams on there?"

"Jams? What in the hell..."

"Music, man." Lou looked at him incredulously. "Rock and roll. Tunes." He picked an invisible guitar. "You know? Shit."

"I don't think so."

"Tell me one thing, my man," Lou asked. "Have you ever been to A.C.?"

"Many times."

"Recently?"

"Last month."

"All right." Low slapped the counter. "Tell Will here about it. It's fucking awesome, right?"

"You're wasting your breath on Will. He's not into gambling and women and drinking. If he's not in here sipping a beer and losing at pool, you'll find him back in his ghost town staring into the woods or reading a book."

Lou raised his eyebrows and looked at Will.

"Jesus dude, you're unreal. I mean don't you get itchy?"

Will didn't respond.

"You can make a fortune down there," Dunphy offered. "Or lose one," he cautioned.

"I could use the money. I'll admit that," Will said. "I'll have to buy another truck if they don't find mine."

"Shit, yeah," Lou added.

Will watched Lou as he sipped his scotch. He was a double of Henry Atkinson's boy who was in federal prison for counterfeiting. His expressions were the same, and his gestures matched Atkinson's. After finishing high school, Henry's boy had left the Pines to live in the city. Money became a problem. He discovered that the skills of his youth couldn't be used in the city, and his high school diploma had little value. Eventually he found a way of making all the money he needed with the aid of several new friends. For a few years he was a wealthy man, although no one knew that his wealth was bogus. His arrival in his hometown every few months and on holidays was celebrated as if he were a knight returning from the Crusades. He had made it in the outside world, in the fast lane. Now he marked his time on a calendar with green ink.

The telephone rang, and Dunphy walked to the end of the bar to answer it.

"Like I said, this place is really something," Lou said, moving on his barstool. "It gives me the creeps."

"Why?"

"I can't explain it. It just does. You know? *Twilight Zone.* Fucking weird."

"Maybe you should take your glasses off. It's dark enough in here. You must feel like you're in a closet."

"No way, man. I told you the light hurts my eyes."

"But..."

"I'll be okay." Lou finished his drink and looked at the clock as the second hand sweeped backwards.

"So what do you do for a living?" Will asked, wondering how someone his age could afford a new Lincoln.

"This and that."

"Oh."

"I'm what you would call an entrepreneur. I buy stuff and

resell it for a profit. Before that, I did a lot of things. You know? I worked in a bar, played drums in a band, sold used cars for a year, fooled around with photography—nudes mostly."

"College?"

"No. I make more money than most college graduates do in ten years." Lou rolled his empty glass on his paper coaster. "You?"

"Four years. University of Virginia."

"What for?"

"History, literature, philosophy."

"Ever make any real cash?" Lou emphasized the word real.

"No."

"Told you. It's not worth it."

When Dunphy returned he said, "That was Tommy. He'll be tied up for the rest of the day, but there's no problem with using the twenty-four footer. He said he'd see you tomorrow morning and that he'd bring his boys with him."

"Did you mention that it's final?"

"Yeah."

"He suspected that they couldn't be stopped?"

"That's what he said," Dunphy replied.

"I guess I'll hit the road then. No use in hanging around here until supper." Will stood. "Lou, it's been a pleasure."

"Where you going, Will? Let's have another drink. Chill out, man. Why don't we do some tequila?"

"I..."

"I'm buying."

"I have a few things to do back home. I left my jacket and bag..."

"Hey, that can wait. You have the rest of your fucking life to do things. Have another round. My treat." Lou glanced at the clock again. "We're on a roll, man."

Will sat on the barstool again and looked at Dunphy who was already searching for the bottle.

"How far do you live from here?"

"A couple of miles."

"And you were going to walk? When I picked you up, you looked pretty sad, man."

Will was silent.

"We'll do some tequila. Then after we're feeling fine," Lou stopped to sniffle, "we'll hit the road and who knows? I'll give you a lift."

"I suppose there's no harm in it."

"Fuckin' A, dude. Fuckin' A."

Vandals had visited his house early one morning. Will had slept at Larry's house because they had been late getting back the night before. The next morning was cold and rain was falling. His body didn't want to move. As long as he stayed in one place he could avoid pain, but when he tried to change positions he thought his stomach would rise to his head. They had stopped at Tommy's after driving to Waretown and back to hear some local musicians play. Friends appeared and rounds were ordered. The next morning Larry cooked break-fast, and Will tried to eat. He succeeded in swallowing an egg and a cup of coffee along with four aspirin. When he reached his house, it was mid-afternoon. He knew immediately that something was wrong because the front yard was filled with ATV tracks, and Maggie was barking from inside the locked tool shed. The front door was open, creaking on its hinges as the rain and wind blew around the porch. Inside, several pieces of furniture were broken. His portable television, which he never watched, was gone along with his parents' floor model radio. His guns had vanished as well. When he entered the kitchen, he found that all of his mother's dishes were smashed on the floor. He sat at the table and surveyed the damage. For a second, he was ready to search the woods for the people who had ransacked his home. In his anger, he spotted one unbro-ken plate that had escaped destruction. He seized it and hurled it against the wall.

"Leave it," Lou told the bartender, flipping him a twenty-dollar bill.

"So what do you think, my man?" Lou said after several shots.

"About Atlantic City?"

"You got it."

"How much money do I need," Will asked, noticing a

numbness in his mouth. It had been years since he had drank tequila.

"That depends."

Will dug into his pocket, pulled out his wallet and counted his money as Dunphy watched.

"Lookin' good."

"One hundred and eighty dollars," Will said.

"That should do it. You'll walk out of the casino with a pile of cash. I guarantee it. No sweat, motherfucker."

"Yeah, no sweat," Dunphy repeated sarcastically. "I wish I could come but duty calls. He gestured to the empty bar. "After-work crew comes in soon. I'm the only one here."

"You're sure?"

"Can't make it. I need the job."

"But you're in?" Lou emphasized as he looked at Will.

"Hell yes," Will said, finishing another shot and inserting a slice of lime in his mouth. "Should we go now or have another?"

The other man looked at his watch, avoiding the clock behind the bar, then said, "Let's do it. We have to drive down there. I have a couple of packages to drop off at an associate's house. Then we'll hit the Boardwalk and the casinos."

The two men slid from their stools. Lou spun his seat with one hand, then stopped it with the other.

"You two have a good time. And Will, you watch out for those wild women in A.C. They bite—hard—at least that's what I've heard."

"Damn right," Lou remarked. "And I should know."

Will wasn't convinced that he would enjoy himself as much as the other men professed, and he suspected that he would leave the city with less money than he had in his pocket now. The day had been marked with bad luck. He found Lou amusing and hoped that their trip would help ease the disappointment, which if allowed to run its normal course, would be with him for weeks. His mind was not as sharp as he would have liked, but after drinking tequila and beer for the better part of the day, he was in better condition than he would have imagined possible. He was ready to visit the city that had received so much attention since gambling had been legalized. It had been allowed to decay for years after its golden era. Gambling had been dubbed a windfall by many while others thought it had created a postmodern Gomorrah. Some claimed it was a social disaster and had failed to meet expectations which included the promise of better days for its many poor residents. Now Will would see what he could for himself.

NINE

1909

Green crossed the street, skipped over the trolley tracks, and got into the car. His eyes followed the long tangent of brown telephone poles, which carried seven and eight sets of wires on their cross members, as they moved away, diminishing up the avenue.

"Well?"

"He's not there."

"Checked out?"

"No. The clerk said he usually leaves after breakfast and comes back early in the afternoon. Rarely speaks. Wears a cape or something of the sort."

"Is he registered as Anderson or Zauber or..."

"Zauber."

"We'll wait." Nichols looked at the two uniformed men in the backseat, their brass buttons and insignia framed by the deep blue of their jackets. "I suspected this would happen. He's full of surprises. He isn't even supposed to be alive. She was seen with him a few times over the past several months. A man who works at the mill saw her down here last month. He even recognized Zauber. Said it took him a while, but he remembered his face. Zauber goes back to when Worthing bought the place. He stayed there, at the Worthing house, years ago. He got sick and was there for months. Fellow said he thought our man was a mystic or one of those traveling faith healers. I checked around and found a little information. After he left Worthing Mills twenty years back, he disappeared. Some of the locals said that old Sam had him bumped." He gazed at the entrance of the hotel, noting the activity around its doors. "I didn't believe it. The locals thought there was something dirty going on between them—Mrs. Worthing and Zauber. Evidently, the authorities down in Mexico found his body in a cave. They said it was Zauber. Couldn't really identify him physically—he had been ripped apart by animals—but they found a few papers. It seemed like an open and shut case." Nichols looked at his evenly trimmed fingernails. "If there was foul play involved, they would have never found his murderer, never in a million years. That was the end of him, or that's what everyone thought. He probably had a con going and set some poor bastard up. So here he is, and it's murder this time."

"Can't be sure," one of the men mumbled.

"What do you mean? He's guilty all right. I saw her body. They found it in the middle of a road only a few miles below Worthing Mills. She was seeing him. We know that. Why, I don't know. It's not as if she didn't have more important things to worry about."

"The first Mrs. Worthing," Green added.

"That's going to be history soon. I can't understand what would possess a woman like Elizabeth Worthing to get involved with this fellow. But then again, who can understand what motivates women?"

The others agreed.

"Here was a woman who owned a company and the whole damn town to boot. Of course, you have to discount the fact that her husband never legally divorced his first wife. She did marry him regardless. And she proved that she could run a business without a man. Although, if you want my opinion, the boys at the bank were giving her assistance along with Sooy, her business manager. I heard this morning that the place just went in the red last month. I wasn't startled. How could a woman run a company the size of Worthing Mills and get away with it for long?"

"Anything is possible," said one of the men in the backseat.

"Maybe. But look at this mess. Obviously, she didn't handle her affairs very well. I'm not sure we'll ever know exactly what happened, but I do have a theory." Nichols waited for a sign of interest from his companions. He glanced at his fingernails again.

"Well?" Green asked.

"Zauber was working a scam here. He comes back into the picture after he discovers that Sam Worthing is dead. He figures that—and this is supposing that Zauber did know Elizabeth Worthing in an intimate way—here is a chance to cash in. A woman who has inherited a fortune and one that he's known sexually might, in a moment of weakness, consider marriage. He thinks that she will welcome his help. A widow who has to make difficult business decisions is a perfect mark. So by offering his services, he helps himself to her money. Who knows if he planned on sticking around after he got his hands on it. Now remember, this was at the outset. Well, Zauber discovers a rather distressing fact. Worthing's will is being contested. Elizabeth isn't home free. He has to make a decision. Should he continue? Should he hang on? He decides that he's in for the duration. How long could it last—six months? Well, we know that it's been at least that long. At first, he finds that she is pleased with him. As time passes, though, she starts to get bored. Two days ago she finally tells him that she has had enough. Zauber is a foreigner and dangerous as well. She realizes the first and suspects the second but dismisses this, never imagining that he would murder her. She doesn't know that he is wanted in two states for fraud and in Texas for questioning about the murder of a Mrs. Velacott, another widow with money. When he hears that she is leaving him, Zauber panics. He doesn't want his whereabouts revealed. They've argued about other men. He's lost his temper once and hit her. When she ends it, he threatens her with more of the same. If you knew her, you'd see that this was a challenge. She tells him that if he bothers her she'll report his whereabouts to the police. She leaves the hotel after this. Zauber knows exactly which way she'll travel. He takes a different route, gets ahead of her, pulls a tree limb across the road, and waits. When she appears—bang. She's dead."

"It sounds like you have this cracked," Green said cautiously.

"I think so."

"Has to be good for your career. You haven't been at it for many years."

"Can't hurt," Nichols admitted.

"This would be a peach, prominent widow and all."

"That's if I'm right. Everything's falling into place. From the time we got the call about her body until now, it's been hard to believe, but true."

"She appointed a Board of Trustees in her will to oversee things. I heard something about a cousin as well," Green added.

"That won't last long. The court already appointed a trustee of its own. Beatrice Worthing or her son will be in that mansion within a month. Elizabeth Worthing held her off. What's the sense now? Let the first one and her boy have the place. If I had a chance at it, I'd be in the courts, too."

"Doesn't it seem odd that Zauber stayed around?"

"Who knows what's going on in his mind? He probably figured on at least a week. If anyone else tried to put this together, it would take that much time. That's the type of character he is—calculating. Remember, she kept this as quiet as possible. She didn't need any scandals at this point. She probably wouldn't have said anything to the police for that very reason. She really couldn't say a word about this arrangement, although evidently Zauber wasn't so sure. I managed to ferret out the facts—a piece here, a piece there. For the amount of time she spent here, I couldn't believe how little there was. Really just the fellow who saw them together. She met Zauber every weekend, sometimes in the city and sometimes at a farmhouse she owned. That was the most convenient for her but risky because it was so close to Worthing Mills."

"Sounds like a time."

"Sure. Give me a chance and I..."

"Don't kid yourselves boys," Nichols said to the men in the backseat. "She moved in affluent circles. She belonged to the Chatsworth Club. Just about every big shot in the state or any one traveling through stops there. For all the dirt that I've uncovered, you still can't say much about her. Of course, she was used to getting things her own way."

"I know the type," Green said. "She sounds like the woman my wife would like to be. She likes to run things, and when she gets together with her mother, look out." An over-loaded trolley, clanging as it passed, interrupted him. "They're a pair." He paused, brushing his moustache with one finger. "You married Nichols?"

"Not on your life. Between work and my women, I don't have time for a wife."

"Stay that way. It changes when you get married. Your time isn't your own. Your entire life will belong to her, and believe me it's impossible to beat."

"You don't have to worry. It'll never happen. I'm not the marrying type. I believe you though. It seems like a mean dog waiting to be kicked. I look at it this way. Worthing was married to two women, and they were fighting over everything he owned. His only son was locked outside the cat fight. God could only say why he married another one after finishing with the first, but I've heard that some men can be cured of almost everything—drinking, smoking, cursing, gambling—but not marriage. I'll do everything in my power to stay a bachelor."

"Good luck," Green said solemnly. "Look at Danny back there. He's going to take the fatal step next month. A young fellow like him with all these shaking asses walking around town. Shit."

"You don't..." Nichols twisted to look at the man behind him. "Of your own free will?"

"Yes." The young man was uneasy.

"No hidden reasons?" He looked at Green. "What about it Danny? Nothing baking in the oven?"

"I love her."

"I'll bet you do."

"I've tried to warn him. Hell, any day of the week all you have to do is go up on the Boardwalk. Women flock to the piers and the amusements. They hang over the railing, tossing money at the sand artists, or they're right down there on the beach with half their clothes off. They're screaming for it."

75

"A man in love is blind," Nichols said halfheartedly, scanning the sidewalk above the hotel.

"I think so. I told him to join Perry and take a trip to the Pole. That would cure him. If he came back still in love, she wouldn't want him."

"Why?"

"It's cold up there. Things freeze."

"Or he could wait for a rainstorm then stand around Captain Young's villa with all of those imported Florentine statues. Remember that lightening bolt between Adam's legs?"

Everyone laughed except Danny, who tried to ignore the negative remarks.

"Well good luck to you. I won't say that I envy you, but I hope you find what you're looking for." Nichols stopped and focused his eyes on a figure that rounded the corner a few blocks from where they sat. "There's our man."

"Where?"

"Up the street."

Green searched the space between the buildings. Twenty or thirty people walked along the sidewalks. A group of tourists, many of them carrying small valises, emerged from the hotel and waited for the beach jitney. In the distance, he could hear the faint, static growl of the ocean.

"Which one?" Green strained his eyes.

Nichols pointed and said, "It's him." His pink arm was heavy with flesh.

"How can you tell? He's over three blocks away."

"Believe me." He started the car. "Let's take him before he reaches the hotel."

Nichols drove around the block. The two men in the backseat were ready. It was Zauber. Green still couldn't determine how Nichols identified the man from such a distance, but that wasn't important. When they reached him, the two uniformed officers were behind the man in a second. He didn't resist and acted as if he expected them. Only a moment passed before he was in the backseat between the two uniformed men. As Nichols pulled the car away from the curb, Green tried to ask Zauber a few questions, but he remained reticent and uncooperative until they reached the county jail.

TEN

1889

Elizabeth heard the church bell ringing long before they reached the town. She was astonished that nothing was visible; the paper mill described by her husband was over fifty feet high and three hundred feet in length. It didn't rise above the scrub pines, but now she realized it was their density not their size that prevented a glimpse of the building and town.

They crept along the sand road, and except for the occasional strain of the carriage, nothing but one lone heron could be heard as its call intermingled with the pealing bell. Laurel bloomed around them, and the white and pink flowers contrasted sharply with the dark, vertiginous pines. All of it was new to her, but it seemed very comforting: the continuous stretch of pines mixed with oak and laurel, meandering brown streams and white sand roads slicing through the forest, the serrated tops of cedar trees as they rose above the green blanket. It was not the typical deciduous forest of Pennsylvania, but something different. There was an enigmatic stillness that hinted they were insulated from the dangers of the larger world.

The lake appeared to the left: the source of power for the mills, stretching a mile or more back into the pines before it disappeared in a ring of knotted cedars. Suddenly, the sound of rushing water and the low booming of the paper mill filled the air as if the forest had blocked the sound purposely until they were in sight of the mill. On the right, through a gap in the trees, she could see it now: its sandstone walls rusty in the noon sun, the white cupola crowning its cedar-shingled roof.

He clasped her hand, recalling the first moment that he had seen it. Somehow it was perfect. Before he inspected the books, before he let his foot touch the sand, he was convinced that happiness might still be his. Now he realized that his initial trip to Pennsylvania was fated. He didn't travel there to examine another set of books or to face harried, desperate owners but to discover the final, missing element and carry it back with him to this isolated place.

"Yes," she whispered, sensing that he was anxious to hear her thoughts. "It's exactly as you described it."

"Peaceful."

"Yes. And beautiful."

"I'm glad." He was relieved that she seemed at ease, if only with her first glance.

They crossed over the sluice and turned hard to the right onto the main street. The white-shuttered, dark brown, tenant houses appeared. People waved from their fenced yards. Then the gas lamps commenced on each side of the street—black iron posts placed about every seventy-five feet. He had mentioned the lamps and the octagon-shaped stone building that housed the gas machine. It was peculiar, she thought, that the owner would go to the expense of installing the machine to produce the gas for streetlamps when financial catastrophe loomed over the town.

"You're not disappointed?"

"No."

"Any regrets?"

"No." She squeezed his hand, knowing that behind his cautious actions was a man who hoped to find support as well as love in her.

They moved past the first row of tenant houses, all as neatly kept as he had described. She knew that he would not accept less. He wanted people to take notice, believing that their recognition would go beyond the physical accomplishments there. Social reform was one of his concerns. Even though reform was nothing unusual in New England, several of his business colleagues felt his ideas went too far. Many thought that the worker should be used and replaced like machinery. But at Worthing Mills, the workers were now supplied with homes and ground for gardens and livestock. They weren't forced to buy goods at inflated prices in the company store or to use a script system, a change which would have been abhorred by the former owner. Production goals, along with bonuses for meeting those quotas, were put in place. Ownership of company stock was permitted. He shortened the workday and told anyone who would listen that if employees were treated with dignity their performance would be better. This, he added, was only common sense. He wanted Worthing Mills to become the standard for the region so that his peers couldn't separate his theories from the town's successes.

They stopped in front of the mansion: a white, two-and-a-half-story house surrounded by a variety of trees and boxwood, brick walkways, and an imposing wall. As she traced the property with her eyes, her ears were still impressed by the deep, pulsating mill machinery echoing through the streets and yards of the town. She marveled at the intricate ironwork at every break in the mansion's wall. She was startled by the house's immensity. The rest of the town had a functional simplicity about it, but the owner's house was not only large but extravagant, what Elizabeth might call ostentatious.

Between the open iron gates stood the staff and many of the workers from the paper mill. They cheered when the carriage stopped. Elizabeth sensed a strong affection for her husband, even though he had owned the town for a short time, even though many in the region had strong Southern sympathies during the war. He was a savior of sorts. The town had faced bankruptcy and the auction block. No options existed except a new owner willing to pump capital into the ailing operation. A decade of bad management by the son of the former owner had forced the town to the brink of an abyss. Before the previous owner, there had been several men who had operated iron furnaces, sawmills, and a variety of other enterprises on the site. Some had made fortunes while others had lost everything. Worthing appeared at the final knell, just before the burial, and handed the town a reprieve. Now the paper mill was running twenty-four hours a day.

As she stepped down, she couldn't help thinking that they respected her husband and knew that the best days were ahead of them. The driver, a young man named Martin, held her arm and guided her safely to the ground. Worthing followed, watching her graceful movement from the carriage. He was amazed by his audacity and good fortune.

"Allow me," he paused, reaching for her hand, "to introduce all of you to Mrs. Elizabeth Black Worthing, my new wife."

A mixture of greetings rose from them.

"I would introduce each of you personally to Mrs. Worthing, but we are rather tired. However, we do plan on staying in Worthing Mills for quite some time."

Another sign of approval sounded from the group. A few approached the couple and offered their congratulations while others returned to work, knowing that they would have an opportunity to meet Worthing's new wife in the next few days. The newlyweds were escorted into the house by Mrs. O'Malley, a short, heavyset woman, who possessed a command over the house staff, and it eventually became apparent to Elizabeth, the entire town.

The interior of the house wasn't in good repair. It was obvious that work had to be done. The need for wallpapering, painting, and some refinishing struck Elizabeth's trained eyes immediately. Her husband had mentioned several items before their arrival, saying that they would be left to her. She didn't object, knowing that he wouldn't limit her to domestic duties. Once finished with the house, there would be other tasks. She wanted to open a lyceum in town, start a weekly newspaper, and even get involved with the daily operation of Worthing Mills. But for the moment, she would be content to fulfill her husband's request. She wanted to please him as well as herself. She was confident that she could do both and not neglect either set of needs.

The idea of being married appealed to her. Several members of her extended family had died only days before when the Conemaugh flooded. Her mother and father had been dead for close to five years. Alone, she had found her way in the world but knew it could be a hostile place. She needed that refuge where one could rest and gather strength for the next confrontation. Now she felt that place embraced her.

Beatrice Worthing wouldn't be pleased with her husband's decision. He had told Elizabeth about her and her determination to stay in Maine. He spoke about their lack of love. They hadn't shared the same bed since their son was four. It was illogical to continue living in the same situation because of a few words mumbled over a Bible. Elizabeth realized that Beatrice could decide to make public the fact that her husband was now a bigamist. The consequences of this were uncertain. Whatever happened, Elizabeth knew she would continue to love him and be his wife.

Samuel Jr. presented another problem. His father was greatly disappointed with him. Elizabeth understood that this wasn't an unusual problem—a father failing to understand his son's refusal to conform to his own plans, and a son astounded that another person, regardless of lineage, could have such plans for him. These differences might be smoothed over in a few years, once her husband saw that his son wasn't a reflection of his father but an individual with different needs. Someday, she hoped, the three of them would be friends.

During the next month, Worthing began several improvements at the paper mill. He wanted to increase immediately the output of the mill by fifty percent, expanding its tonnage from just under one ton a day to a ton and a half. This required two steps. The first was more power. The main race was widened and deepened at its beginning then narrowed near the paper mill itself. The nature of the surrounding land allowed a head of just over six feet. Additional manpower from neighboring towns was hired to complete the project. Once the word spread men filed into town, alone or in groups of two and three. Most were locals. Drifters appeared on the odd day and Worthing, willing to give all men a chance, hired them without hesitation. The second step in achieving increased production was additional machinery. Much of the equipment needed to be upgraded. Another papermachine was purchased, and an extension was constructed to house it.

He wasted no time in making decisions. Once he saw what was required, he set about obtaining it.

In order to bring about many of the town improvements, he reopened the sawmill and hired proggers and other lumbermen. With a thousand acres of forest around them, it made little sense not to have his mill producing lumber. Cedar and pine were at a premium. Eventually, he would begin selling lumber on the retail market. Worthing was spending more money than it originally cost to purchase the property, but he knew that problems left uncorrected would hinder future progress and profits.

New tenant houses were started. With increased productivity came more employees who needed homes. A dormitory for single men was constructed. Many new workers brought wives and children, so the town school was enlarged and a new teacher hired. Worthing was appalled that several of the children who lived in Worthing Mills couldn't read or write. The new instructor was given a house behind the school. Township and state tax appropriations paid for some of this, and Worthing absorbed the remainder.

A number of other problems plagued him. The town's population had increased to well over two hundred. The company had too many employees and subsidiary operations for him to oversee personally. He needed a business manager who could handle day to day affairs while he worked on specific projects. He found him in a town twenty miles away, working for a glass manufacturer. A good salary and a new home for his family were offered, and within a short time Randolph Sooy was a Worthing employee.

Although it would have to be produced in town, electricity was another thing that he saw in the company's future. He had the water power to generate it but knew that a total transition would be costly and time consuming. It would be years before power was brought in from the outside. The nearest sign of modern civilization was nine miles away, and this was only a train station where his products were delivered by mule-drawn wagon and shipped to the cities on the eastern seaboard. So much in the town was still done as it had been one hundred years before. He knew that electricity would have to wait.

While her husband was busy with the mill complex and town, Elizabeth was occupied with the main house and Mrs. O'Malley, who knew the town's history from its beginnings. Elizabeth was entertained by her stories, although she wasn't convinced that all of them were true. If she questioned something, the woman would insist on its accuracy.

"And that's the truth, on my father's grave," she swore.

"Slaves?"

"There were thousands of them in the state."

"And the founder of the town, Elijah Andrews, owned sixty of them?"

"There was money being made in iron. The Richards family, Quakers they were, made a fortune back in the last century. Then they lost it. Andrews wanted to build another forge; actually he built four of them. So he drove the slaves back here to put it up. They say that the slaves came from his father-in-law's plantation in the West Indies. Andrews was in the British Navy down there, back in the last century, before the Revolution. Met his wife in Antigua."

"What happened?"

"Well now, Andrews returned with his wife and the slaves. He built forges and became an ironmaster and a plantation man. But his money ran low, and he was forced to take on investors. When he built this place, the slaves died in a fire, locked up in a building they had made with their own hands. You can still hear them sometimes. If you take a canoe out on the lake at night, you can hear them even better. I've heard them myself. They say it's their death chant."

"Lucy."

"Missus, I wouldn't lie to you about something like that."

"It's just another story that someone invented for children."

"You'll hear them if you go out there. I swear on my mother's grave."

Elizabeth shook her head and said, "What happened to Andrews?"

"His wife died on the same evening as the slaves. Some

folks said it was their revenge. Andrews lost his drive after that. His heart was broken. Without his business knowledge, things began to fall apart. His partners were city men and didn't want to live in the Pines. Debts mounted. Andrews went to the West Indies to settle his wife's estate. By the time he reached Antigua, her money was gone. Creditors and lawyers took most of it. Her family took the rest. Andrews never returned to the Pines. He stayed in the Caribbean for two years; then he traveled to North Carolina where he opened a little country store. Evidently, he couldn't return because the Pines reminded him of his wife. Within a year, he was dead. His interest in this place and in the other forges was purchased by William Richards. And the Richards family knew how to make money. They supplied the Continentals with munitions. For seventy-five years, they made money in iron, lumber, paper, and glass. That was until the Pennsylvania iron and steel industry, along with bad management, ruined them just before the Civil War. It's been down hill around here ever since. That is until now. Mr. Worthing is a godsend, he is."

Their conversations broke the tension that Elizabeth had sensed after her first days in town. Lucy O'Malley was over twice her age and was used to doing things her own way. She had been in charge of the house staff for several years and soon discovered that Elizabeth knew exactly what she was doing and could run the house alone if necessary. After a week the tension vanished, and Elizabeth was firmly in charge without causing any animosity between them.

Every day something arrived from the train station, carried by the wagons as they returned from delivering products. Elizabeth felt that her husband was accustomed to a certain quality of furnishings and knew that he would be entertaining customers. Her purchases weren't excessive, and she didn't make expenditures without his knowledge. From her experience at the hotel, she knew how to work through a problem to find the best solution. If she saw that a price was too high or quality poor she would tell the retailer, and if he was resolute she would seek another. Her determination not to be cheated impressed both her husband and Mrs. O'Malley.

This woman, Worthing often said to Lucy O'Malley, could run this entire operation and do it well. She'd probably make more money than me.

His faith in her grew with each job she approached. There was little reason to doubt her decisions because he generally agreed with them. He began to discover new qualities in her that he didn't know she possessed. This delighted him since he had become somewhat of a pessimist because of his experience with Beatrice.

Invitations to attend Independence Day celebrations arrived at the mansion from several families. One of them came from another man new to the region—Prince Mario Ruspoli, an attaché at the Italian Embassy in Washington who owned a home on Lake Shamong, several miles north of Worthing Mills. A club was being built on the lake by the Prince and other investors, including Vice President Morton. It was said to be a copy of the Duke of Devonshire's country manor, Chatsworth, in Derbyshire, England. Once finished the nearby town of Shamong Station would be known as Chatsworth. The Pines reminded the Prince of southern Italy. Elizabeth was intrigued by this, but her husband was convinced that once the clubhouse was completed there would be many opportunities to meet the Prince and his friends.

Another invitation came from a local politician, Thomas Cramer, jokingly nicknamed Landslide Cramer, because of his one vote victory in a recent election. Cramer was a farmer who had made a small fortune in the cranberry business. Worthing knew that he would have ample chance to meet Cramer as well. Worthing had political ambitions, too, and could easily imagine his evolution from successful businessman to state politican and reformer.

Worthing refused the invitations because he and Elizabeth hadn't been on any kind of honeymoon. They didn't have the free time to tackle the trip he envisioned. He had promised to take his wife to Europe once the company was running properly. They both knew that a trip of that length was a few years away. So a short holiday in Atlantic City was arranged. It was not far from Worthing Mills, and the city was becoming a magnet for the country's most influential people. He admitted to Elizabeth that it would be a relief to get away for a few days, and she agreed. Several things had to be done before they could leave, however, and it seemed to Elizabeth that there was twice as much to accomplish in the few days before they left than during their entire time at Worthing Mills.

E L E V E N

1909

It was a day for great accomplishments. An airplane bearing two men remained in the sky for over one hour. Albert the First became King of Belgium. And Beatrice Worthing succeeded in making Worthing Mills her own.

By the end of the month, Samuel Worthing Jr. arrived in Worthing Mills, the only son of a man who had been obsessed with the town for fifteen years. In adulthood he had grown to resemble his father: tall, square-shouldered, a thick head of red-blond hair. He came to see the place he had never visited. His mother had taken control of the company, and he would oversee its daily operations. This was her plan. Leaving Maine wasn't his decision, but his mother insisted. She had become, it seemed to him, as unpredictable and overbearing as his father had been. But he hadn't objected more than twice. Once on the train his curiosity quickened, and he began to look forward to the experience his mother said had been denied him for too long.

His first glimpse of Worthing Mills wasn't what he had expected. His mother had damned the town, his father, and Elizabeth Black so many times that any mention of the place caused her to conjure gloomy, nightmarish images. The heat was unbearable, she said. The mosquitoes were bigger than butterflies. The people were backwards and married their own relatives. Her list was endless. With this in mind, his initial reaction to the town astonished him. He was delighted. It reminded him of a small New England village, but the surrounding scrub and bogs gave it an exotic flavor. The air was heavy with humidity as well as the scent of pine and was balm-like for someone used to Maine seabreezes. Within a few hours, he began to understand his father's fascination with the place.

He found Sooy to be very supportive. Worthing knew nothing about the business, the region, or the nature of the employees. Sooy was willing to spend the time needed to acquaint him with the operation and answer his questions. The employees, after a natural hesitance, were openly relieved that the battle for Worthing Mills was over and their futures more secure. Everything progressed according to plan until Samuel Worthing Jr. revealed his mother's first request.

Beatrice Worthing wanted her husband's body returned to Maine where it would be placed in the family plot. She would lie next to him when her time came and could no longer bear the thought that his body rested next to his wife—that whore, his mistress—as she referred to Elizabeth. While alive her husband's infatuation couldn't be corralled, and her attempts at creating a scandal had been ignored by him. It was true that she had met the news of his affair with laughter. She assumed that it would be short-lived. She thought the woman wouldn't be able to keep up with her husband. He would tire of Elizabeth after he became satiated with her body. She predicted that within two months he would sell the mill and return to Maine. After six months had passed Beatrice extended the time to one year, thinking that she had miscalculated. When the year ended, she started to realize that her husband might remain with Elizabeth Black, although it took another year for her to admit this openly.

Beatrice had resolved, with her Yankee obstinance, that she would never agree to a divorce, and if still alive at the time of his death she would contest a will that gave Elizabeth anything. There was only one thing left to do now that Worthing Mills was won—separate them. Her final revenge would be to deny her husband his eternal resting place next to Elizabeth Black. She told her son about her resolution on the morning of his departure. He didn't object. After so many years of torment, he wanted to make his mother happy. He saw that it was her revenge; it was something she had to do, and he would oblige her. He even considered his own feelings, recalling the letters from Elizabeth asking him to visit and his refusal of the requests which was colored by his mother's displeasure and his own anger.

He went about his task quietly. He wasn't convinced that many people in the town or county would support his mother's wish. There was a loyalty to his father and Elizabeth in the region. The people respected them and considered their relationship valid although slightly irregular. His father had provided the area with opportunity. Once he died, Elizabeth carried on with admirable efficiency.

A small white church, its simple wooden edifice punctuated by matching but separate doors, sat next to the graveyard. On the morning of the exhumation, the laborers, who had been assembled by Sooy, expressed their doubts about the plan which further confirmed what Sooy had told him.

"Sir, if you'd permit me to say something."

"Go on." Worthing replied, knowing what would be said. "That body can't be moved."

"Mr. Sooy has mentioned his doubts to me."

"Well, Mr. Sooy is right. I helped build this grave. It ain't ordinary. Old Sam Worthing...I mean your father, had specific orders about his casket and burial. His grave is more than a hole in the ground with a coffin in it. And when his wife, his second wife that is, died, she was made part of it."

"Yes, Mr. Sooy informed me."

"You know then that the caskets..."

Worthing grew impatient and snapped at the man. He had heard the stories about the grave and dismissed them as false because they were too fantastic to believe. He suspected that the townspeople wished his father's body to remain in Worthing Mills. They had taken custody of his earthly remains partly because of affection and partly due to superstition. Once his body was gone, the locals said, the town would fall from the prosperity that his father had brought. But the son refused to believe it.

After three days of digging, pounding, and cursing, he learned the truth. His father's casket was constructed with a series of perforated iron plates. Iron bars passed through the casket at various points. All of the space inside and around the casket was filled with concrete. The top plate allowed the iron bars to protrude over five feet toward the surface and concrete had been poured over this. Elizabeth's tomb was constructed in the same manner. The bars from his father's casket on the right side passed through her casket. Concrete and iron bound them together in death just as love had in life. Defeated, the vanquished son had to send a telegram informing his mother that her demand couldn't be met.

He was depressed for several days afterward. His mother had made plans for a service and had informed her friends and relatives that her husband was finally coming home. He knew the embarrassment she would have to face and decided to do something about it. He went to the county seat and purchased a casket which he filled with sand. The casket was put on a train. He paid everyone who touched it, hoping that they would keep it to themselves. He wired his mother and said that after a second attempt the casket had been freed but had to be replaced because of damage. It would be in Maine within a few days. It was a minor triumph, but he felt vindicated and knew his mother would, too.

He gazed outside from his bedroom window and wondered how many times his father had stood in the exact spot. He could see across the enclosed garden and the statue of Elizabeth to the south wall of the paper mill. The sound from the mill was constant but not annoying. At that instant, it seemed to stand for everything in which his father had believed. It was persistent and domineering but forgiving as well. It is a good thing, he thought suddenly. Mother is happy and her honor has been reclaimed. She thinks she is victorious. No excuses will need to be offered. But father didn't want to leave this place. He loved Elizabeth. He had to. No one constructs a grave like that unless his heart is committed. Now everyone is happy. Father stays here. Mother has him in Maine and owns Worthing Mills. Elizabeth had it while she lived, just as he wanted. And I'm here where I think he wanted me to be. He paused and considered what he had been thinking. What will happen to me? I'm only here because of her. I didn't want to come. I didn't want anything to do with him or this place. His eyes found her statue. He had looked at it many times and had studied her features. He had glanced over his shoulder more than once, feeling that she was watching him, waiting for him to move, waiting to approve or condemn his actions. His imagination frequently ran away from him, but he couldn't quickly explain the seduction of the place or the woman. Her presence hovered above the entire town. Even in death she appeared to be the owner of the place, he thought, and he began to believe the local superstition.

Within a few days, he had resolved to stay. He would try to get his mother to visit but guessed any attempt to do this would fail. He decided that overseeing the business would be good for him. In the past, the company had been profitable. His mother had expressed distrust concerning key employees, but he saw only loyalty to the company in their actions. His future would be made if he remained. His father would have approved of this after disapproving so many times. For a second, he thought he was trying to make amends. But he dismissed the idea. He had stood fast over the years and had refused to meet him on his own ground. Now he was there and felt the magnitude and power of his father's achievement. He was his logical successor. Even his mother had said this. At first, he didn't believe it. His father was bigger than life and had accomplished great things at a young age. As his son, he was afraid of failure. He knew that he could never equal his father's achievements. But his father was gone, and without him there would be no competition. Samuel Worthing was part of local legend—the man who saved an entire town. His son could only bask in the reflection of his father's legacy.

It was night now—humid and still. He could hear the carpenter frogs in the blue-black light. One rasping note was followed by an echoing rattle. He glanced away from the walls of the house and garden. The mill windows twinkled through the branches of the catalpa and ginkgo trees. He could hear laughter drop from a window somewhere in the town and fade into the omnipotent hum of machinery. A nighthawk plunged through the air toward earth causing a sharp bang. He was alone and finally at peace.

T W E L V E

1990

"How long have you lived down here?" Lou said.

"All my life except for college."

"You're retired now?"

"Semi-retired, you could say." Will suddenly thought his own voice sounded tired and foreign.

"What did you do out here?"

"Outside work mostly. Trapped. Spent a considerable amount of time clamming and oystering over on the bay. Gathered orchids and sphagnum moss for florists. I collected and popped my share of pine cones. Cut wood. Even made a little charcoal and some clear. I've picked a lot of blueberries and cranberries. At one time, I was a broker."

"Any money in that?" Lou noticed men working a bog as the car passed. "In cranberries, I mean."

"Yeah. But the money is in owning the bogs not in what they're doing. Big cash outlay though. A century ago most people thought you couldn't cultivate them at all—wild was the only way they would grow. But a bog has to be ditched and turfed. Everything has to be cleared away. The land has to be level. You need to build a reservoir and dam. You have to set out the vines. If you have a good season, there's money. If not, there's always next year."

"Fucking crazy. I like my money fast. Those bastards have to wait and worry and wait some more. Not me." Lou adjusted his sunglasses, sliding them against the bridge of his nose.

"There's a difference though. They get a way of life with their business, and that's enviable in this world."

"Couldn't handle it." Lou's fingers drummed on the steering wheel.

"Do you think we could turn the music down a little?" Will asked, knowing that he would have a headache before long.

"No problem," Lou said, adjusting the volume control. "Don't you like jams, man?"

"Depends."

"Suit yourself, dude." Lou sniffled." I mean we all got our preferences.".

Will watched the landscape rush by. The car was quiet and moved effortlessly down the road, but when he glanced at the speedometer it read eighty-five.

"Do you always drive this fast?"

"Fuckin' A. I like to feel like I'm a bullet or in the cockpit of a fighter jet. You know? It's great just flying along like this. She really rides good, doesn't she?"

Will eased the Chevrolet out of the lot. It was their first new car. His wife was ecstatic because the automobile represented something more than reliable transportation to her. She imagined it spoke to people when they passed and said this is what a successful man drives, and I'm married to one. He had had a good year as a cranberry broker and had managed to save enough to purchase the car with cash. All their money went toward the car. Their lifestyle was as frugal as ever. They owned a small house which the former owners were glad to be free of when they decided to leave Worthing Mills shortly after World War II. The previous owners were part of a trend that continued unabated until Will and his mother were the only residents left. The majority of the homes had collapsed from decay or had been destroyed by fire. When his wife left him, he closed their house and moved in with his ill mother until she died in 1973.

When they arrived home, his mother and father were waiting on the porch. He saw that his father disapproved of the car and remembered how many times he had said not to buy a new car or truck because of depreciation. Buy it two or three years old and you'll save a bundle was always his advice. His mother was used to her husband's ways and made a fuss over the car, commenting on the color and the interior and even the tires.

PINELANDS

Will's wife had pleaded with him to buy it. We don't need it was his first response. But after weeks of pestering and finally demanding that it be purchased, he conceded. He realized that his wife had an insatiable urge to be someone. When she went to the store in a new car, she was convinced that people would pay her homage. That was what she thought. The first time she appeared at a gas station with the vehicle the attendant asked her if the Johnson family had started a new business. The sudden question perplexed her for a moment, which was long enough for the man to answer his own question. 'Robbing banks,' he said, laughing. This ended most of her illusions that a 1955 Chevrolet coupe would turn many heads in the Pines.

"Which way do you plan on going?"

"Right down to the Pike and then straight on into the city."

"There's a shorter way," Will said.

"How much?"

"Twenty minutes, at least."

"Seriously?" Lou looked at himself in the rearview mirror. "Well man, show me the way. The faster we get there the sooner we can get in on the action."

"You'll want to turn left about two miles from here."

"Just tell me when," Lou said rolling his head from side to side in time with the music. "Hey man, what about a beer?"

Will reached for the six-pack on the backseat and handed him a bottle.

"To a big night," Lou said as he toasted them.

Will raised his beer in compliance.

"To a big night," he repeated, not knowing what the evening would bring but finding the possibilities enticing.

"I hope you win enough to buy another pickup."

"I'll second that."

"You only had liability on it?"

"Even that was outrageous."

"I know what you're saying, man. Take a stab at what I pay to drive this baby on the highway?"

"Eight hundred."

"Try thirty-one hundred, dude. Thirty-one hundred fucking beans."

"You're bullshitting me," Will commented.

"Not a buck."

"Why so much?"

"Oh, I've had a couple of accidents. One time I was driving under the influence, if you know what I mean."

Will turned his head toward his window. The outside world passed without definition. A knot tightened in his stomach.

"Anyone hurt?"

"Five people in one accident, but I was okay. No biggy. I mean no one bought it. The last time I ran off the road and hit a tree. I totaled the car, and that broke my heart. I was destroyed. You know? A brand new Caddy—I really loved that car." Lou paused and exhaled loudly as if he needed time to reflect. "But what the fuck. Here we are in a new set of wheels and heading for the city by the sea."

"True." Will looked for the dilapidated building that marked the intersection of the road which they would take as a shortcut. "Do you see that old schoolhouse on the left?"

"Where?"

"About two hundred yards ahead. You can only see its roof now."

Lou leaned over the steering wheel until his nose was an inch from the windshield. His pillow started to rise behind him but returned to its original position when he leaned back against the seat.

"Yeah. I got it."

"Make a left after it."

"No problem."

When they reached the intersection, the car made a wide, swerving arc which scattered gravel and sand away from the tires. Will thought they would slip off the road into the drainage ditch so he braced himself, but the car grabbed the asphalt and bolted down the empty road. Lou hadn't touched the brake pedal.

"Kind of fast."

"You only live once, Will. Did you get a rush?"

"You could call it that."

"A tingling sensation that moves up your spine and into your head and makes your eyes bulge for a second?"

"I think it moved into my pants instead of my head."

The other man smiled and said, "You're too fucking much, too fucking much."

With each passing mile, the road narrowed. Random potholes became constant, then the rule. After the third mile, the road surface was obliterated by deep ruts and unrepaired spring heaves. Lou slowed the car but still insisted on driving twice as fast as he should.

"You're tearing the front end apart by hitting those holes like that," Will remarked after striking his head on the liner a second time.

"It's still under warranty. Remember I just picked it up. Anyway this is man over machine or should I say Lou over machine. You know? I'm in control of this car. If I let it control me then I'm fucked."

"It's your car."

"Fuckin' A. And I won't let her forget it."

The road changed to gravel, and the contrapuntal banging coming from beneath them changed to the static grinding of stones being rapidly moved by turning wheels.

"Are you sure this is the road?"

"A few miles of this and we hit tar again," Will said.

"It's sure deserted out there. Where are all the people?"

"Nobody lives back here. This is state forest."

"Can't blame them. Too goddamned quiet. Probably animals out there, too. No streetlights. Look at it, man. It gives me the creeps."

"Twilight Zone?"

"You got it."

Will leaned back and enjoyed the things Lou disparaged. Fall leaves brightened the ever-present green of the pines.

"Do you live in a place like this?"

"It's quiet if that's what you mean."

"But you're moving, right?"

"Not because I want to."

"Bank?"

"State," Will said, correcting the man. "And the power company. Rights-of-way."

"All the same fucking thing, isn't it? Banks and down the line."

"I don't like to admit that. Old Byrne wouldn't have allowed it," Will mumbled.

"So, you been in the house long?"

"My entire life practically. They manufactured paper in the town at the turn of the century. It had a store, church, school—everything you'd need. My father worked in a machine shop there."

"No shit."

"Nothing left now. Ruins. My house."

"Just like a ghost town out West?"

"Pretty much, except my ghost town isn't surrounded by hundreds of square miles of desolation. I have millions of people breathing down my back."

The road changed from gravel to sand. The undercarriage of the car responded with a cool, dull ring.

"You want to keep moving through this. If you see solid ground drive on it," Will warned.

"That's what they call sugar sand," his father said. "It's softer than mud."

"Is it deep?"

"Son, you wouldn't believe how deep it is. If I drove through that patch instead of around it on the cut-off, we'd sink down over the windows."

Will didn't believe his father and said, "Dad."

"Years back when they brought the salt hay to the mill in wagons, the teamsters had to go around the sugar. There was one fellow who wasn't from the Pines and didn't believe it was very deep. One evening he was coming back to town with a full load. He was leading four wagons. When they reached this one particular spot the man in the wagon behind him yelled to go around, but this fellow was stubborn and didn't listen. He screamed to the mules and snapped his reins. In they went and in a second they were gone. The sugar had swallowed every-thing—wagon, mules, salt hay and driver. The other men

couldn't do anything to help. He was never found."

"You're making that up."

"Nope. It's God's honest truth."

"Watch out, Lou." The car started to veer sideways. "Keep moving. It's really deep here," Will said as the other man tried to correct the sudden drift. "Don't overdo it or we'll get stuck."

The car pitched obtusely to the right as Lou hit the accelerator. The engine vibrated and the front end lifted for a split second; then the tires settled into their own unforgiving ruts.

"Shit," Lou said, pushing the pedal again with his extended toe.

"No use in doing that. You'll only dig us in deeper."

"Great. Fucking great." He slammed the dashboard with his clenched hand. "What are we going to do? We're in the middle of nowhere." He looked at Will. "This was you're fucking idea. You know? Now what?"

Will lowered his window and looked outside.

"Do you have a shovel in the trunk?"

"A shovel? What in the fuck would I have a shovel back there for?" Lou asked emotionally.

"To dig us out."

"Right."

"We dig or walk. If we walk, it could take a few hours before we get a ride, find someone with a four-wheel who is willing to help, and then get back here. But if we dig, we'll be going in less than thirty minutes."

"You think we can do it?" Lou looked through his window at the ruptured ground.

"Do you have a jack in the trunk or is that optional equipment?"

"Should be one."

"Let's get on it then."

Lou opened the door and put his foot on the sand.

"Jesus Christ!" he screamed, retrieving his leg and closing the door. "There's a fucking snake out there!"

"Did it bite you?"

"I don't think so. God that was close." He laid his head on the headrest and snorted deeply. "Probably a rattlesnake.

Aren't there rattlesnakes around here?"

"Not really. Around Mt. Misery maybe. Could have been a whomper."

"That's Rattlesnake Ace from over in Upton," Andy said. "He's been catching rattlers for years. He sells them to museums and zoos and shoemakers. Look at his face. He even looks like a snake."

"What happened to his teeth?"

"They say that snake venom made them fall out. I heard that he let snakes bite him, so he would become immune to their poison."

"No way."

"He got in a fight once with one of the Ridgeway bunch. A man bit him and drew blood. Later that night on the way home, the man died because Ace's blood is like snake venom. Some people are even afraid to shake his hand because they think his sweat has poison in it, and it will get into their pores."

Will got out of the car and walked around to Lou's door. A snake coiled away toward the base of a Virginia pine.

"Just a corn snake son. Nothing to worry about."

The electric window came down.

"Is he gone?"

"Yep."

Will circled the car. The sand wasn't as deep as he had thought. They raised the rear of the car slightly on the jack and cleared the earth away from the undercarriage. Will inserted several tree limbs under the car before gently letting the vehicle off the jack. They repeated the process for the front end. Before starting the engine, Will walked ahead and surveyed the condition of the road.

"Better let me drive, Lou," he said. "One burst and we'll be free of this hole, but we have another fifty feet of soft shit to go. You get behind the car and rock with me. When I go, you push hard until we're out."

A minute later they were sitting on the far side of the furrowed sand.

"Do you think you can get us through the last mile, or do you want me to drive?"

"I can handle it," Lou responded coolly. "But I need a joint." He opened the glove box. "What do you say, man? Do you want to smoke a bone?"

Will didn't expect the offer.

"I don't know," he answered, unsure if he should accept the invitation. He looked sheepishly at the dirt on his jacket.

"Come on, dude. This is primo weed. Have you ever had any?"

"Sure," Will said. "Plenty of times," he added, purposely lying.

"Let's do it then." The younger man lit the joint and inhaled deeply.

Will observed him closely, noting each movement. When Lou passed him the joint, he took it.

"You only live once," he said, mimicking the other man.

"That's right," Lou replied, trying not to let the smoke escape his mouth.

Will took a long drag and held it in his lungs.

"Good stuff," he mumbled, handing the joint back to Lou. "Fuckin' A."

Lou returned to the driver's seat after they finished and drove to the paved section of road without stopping. He accelerated once the asphalt was beneath the car, and within seconds they were moving at seventy miles an hour over the uneven surface.

"So what do you think?"

"About what?" Will responded lethargically.

"The shit, man. Isn't it primo? It's excellent shit."

Will wasn't clear about what was being asked for a moment but finally deciphered it.

"Primo. It's fantastic," Will said, not convinced that he felt anything more than light-headed. "What about another beer?"

"Now you're talking, my man. Now you're fucking talking."

Will pulled a bottle from the container and decided that their predicament of a few minutes ago had been very funny. He started to laugh; his mouth felt like it was made of rubber.

"Here you go, dude," he said to Lou as he handed him the bottle.

THIRTEEN

1937

Kelly hadn't been to the county seat for twenty years. He enjoyed the isolation of his cabin and liked to say that he depended on or needed no one, although he admitted to himself it wasn't true. The town had grown over the years. The trolley cars were gone. More houses and people crowded around the downtown. He didn't recognize one person on the streets and remembered a time when his business brought him into contact with many well-known and wealthy residents of the town. A car almost struck him as he absentmindedly crossed the street in front of Nichols' office. When he reached the glass door of the building, he saw his image and resolved that he looked different from the townspeople who seemed to be watching him and making comments to their friends. It was as if they knew he wasn't meant for the place. He felt awkward and nervous. The harsh, threatening noises of the street bothered him. Before entering the building, he considered returning to Worthing Mills. He adjusted his cap and tried to look past the glass door. Then a young man emerged and nearly knocked him down.

"Mr. Nichols?" he asked the first person he saw inside.

"His office is upstairs."

"Is he in?"

"Don't think so," the woman said as she walked by and ducked into a doorway.

He couldn't help thinking that he should have telephoned instead of driving to the town. He walked upstairs. A secretary sat in an alcove at the rear of the landing.

"Is Mr. Nichols in?"

The woman looked grudgingly away from an open magazine, the pages fluttering into place on their own. She was startled by his sudden appearance.

"No."

"When will he be back?"

"Not sure."

"Could I leave a message?"

"Name?" she questioned, reaching for a pencil.

"Kelly. Martin Kelly."

"Message?"

"Could you ask him to call me or come down to my house if he has the time?"

"Number?"

"I don't have a telephone."

"Figures," she grumbled, moving her eyebrows.

"The office at Worthing Mills will know where I am if he calls. If he decides to come down, he knows where I live."

"I'll give him the message." The woman returned to her magazine as he left. One of her fingers mechanically reached for a piece of hair and began to twirl it.

"What did she mean by figures?" Kelly asked himself softly as he descended the stairs.

He could hear people talking in several first floor offices as he entered the hallway, but no one acknowledged his movement through the building. With a few quick strides, he was standing on the sidewalk. Across the street a group of young children caught his attention. He hesitated as he tried to hear their playful exchange which was framed by the squat, castlelike county jail behind them. His eyes drifted from them to his truck.

"Excuse me," someone said from behind him. "You're blocking the door."

"Sorry," Kelly stuttered, moving to the right. He reached instinctively for the door, but the man had already grabbed the knob himself.

Kelly was glad to leave the town. His last visit to the county seat was to see a woman. He had known her for years, and she had kept her door open for him without qualification throughout their undefined relationship. Whenever he was near the town, he would stop to see her and inevitably stay the night locked in her grip. She worked in the town's fish market and was a widow. She bathed in lemon juice every evening, but he could still smell the pungent fish oil on her skin when they made love. One night, a night that he slept in Worthing Mills, she fell in her bathtub and drowned. He remembered her funeral and the sudden pang of sadness he felt as her coffin was lowered into the earth. He drove past her small yellow bungalow on the outskirts of town and beeped the horn. For a moment, he thought he saw her standing in the garden next to the house, her slender form hunched over a flower bed. But then he saw that the yard was empty and flowerless.

As he drove, he lifted a pint bottle to his mouth and let the liquid slip by his lips. He thought about the other woman, the one who had caused his trip to the county seat. He had lived a crazy, haphazard life and was thankful when the Chatsworth Club fell to a forest fire. The time spent around that club had made him a considerable amount of money. A fair sum was still buried near his cabin. He had more than he would ever need and worked only to keep his mind and hands occupied. He was sorry for many things in his past and had tried to atone for them over the years. He gave money to the church and volunteered his time. If he was able to help someone, he did and prayed that his actions were noticed.

Now she had reappeared. She brought back old memories and anxieties. He had started to worry incessantly, from the very moment of his discovery of her new life. He tried to recall it, thinking about its dimensions and how the face looked—her face. With each mile, he only desired to see her more. His memory wasn't as precise as it once had been, but he did recall how the marble seemed to possess a silk-like smoothness under his fingertips. Her discovery alarmed him; over the intervening years he had presumed that she was forever buried. But he was mistaken. By the time he reached the lake outside of Worthing Mills, his rekindled memories had turned into a determination to see her.

He tried to think of some kind of pretense concerning his need but dismissed the idea. Agnes Johnson would have to accept the fact without any excuse. She'll understand my curiosity, he assured himself. I'm an old man looking for my past, trying to remember where I walked. She won't object.

Kelly stopped at the Johnson house. After knocking on the front door then walking around the yard to the kitchen door, he decided that no one was home. He peered through one of the kitchen windows, but the head wasn't in the room. He walked methodically around the house and gazed through each first floor window, hoping to glimpse her, but his search was fruitless. He considered breaking into the house but ruled that out. His truck would be seen by someone, and with his luck he would probably be caught inside.

His desire to see the face of Elizabeth Worthing forced him to circle the house a second time. He pressed his nose against the screens and studied the contents of each room again, making certain that the head wasn't there. He spent a long time on the front porch, peering into the living room and noticing a variety of books, toys, and furniture scattered around the room.

"Could I help you, Mr. Kelly?" a voice next to him said.

He jumped as Agnes stepped back.

"I'm sorry, Mrs. Johnson." He turned to face her. A black smudge covered the tip of his nose. "I thought someone might be home."

"I am now."

"I don't do this kind of thing normally you know. I mean looking through people's windows." He smiled, not wanting to offend her.

"No, I imagine not."

"I guess you'd like to get inside." He moved away from the front door which was next to the living room window.

"I do live here."

"Yes, missus, I know that."

She grasped the door knob and said, "What is it that you wanted?"

"Me?" he responded clumsily.

"You're the only one here." She opened the door.

"I've come about the head."

"I see."

"And I..."

"You want to buy it?"

"I wasn't planning on it but now that you mention it."

"You'll have to speak to Will."

"He found it?" Kelly asked, knowing the answer.

"Yes." She motioned for him to follow her inside.

"What do you think it's worth?"

"Depends on the buyer. Why are you interested?

"Sentimental reasons."

"Oh." Agnes glanced around the room. "But you were the one who destroyed it."

"Yes, missus, but that was my job."

"Were you especially fond of her?"

"In a quiet way, you might say."

"A secret love?" She sat on the sofa, noticing the disheveled room around her.

"No. I admired her. I didn't realize it then, but after she was gone I did."

"Do you remember when she was killed and when her son disappeared? I spoke to you a few days after that."

"Yes, missus."

"You knew where the head was all along."

A vague look covered his face. He followed the line of the floorboards.

"It's been a long time. I couldn't tell you exactly where the spot is now. Twenty-eight years have gone by. The woods have grown." He wanted to change the direction of the conversation. "I'll bet your boy is proud—finding it and everything."

"It scared him half to death. He thought it was real. He was swimming with his friends and Andy. He must have been six inches from it to see it so clearly in that iron water."

"Something like that could scare a boy I'm sure." Kelly scratched his head. "Where did you say he found it?"

"I didn't but I think he said about three miles above town near a flooded spong."

"Over the years it must have moved quite a distance then. Don't see how that's possible. Maybe someone else found it and moved it to where your boy saw it. I know it was more than three miles from here."

The conversation stopped. Kelly wondered if Agnes would let him see her. He counted the beats of the ticking mantle clock for a few seconds. She started to stand.

"Would you mind terribly if I took a peek at the head. It's been years. I'd like to see it again."

"Well..."

"You're certain it's Elizabeth Worthing?"

"Positive."

"I'll only be a minute; then I'll be off."

She considered what he had asked as he waited impatiently for her response.

"It's upstairs in the boys' room. I don't think there would be much harm in it. Turn right at the top of the stairs, and their room is on the left. It's probably a mess."

"Thank you, missus."

The room was flooded with light. Each beam was filled with motes that were suspended peacefully in the still air until he opened the door. The particles moved rapidly for a moment, violently transferring positions and then resettling into a different beam but a familiar pattern. The head sat near the window, serene in the room's silence. When he entered, his eyes traced the wall to his left and moved in a clockwise direction, following the contours of the room and traversing the space until he saw her.

"Mother of God," Kelly said quietly. He couldn't move and felt as if his feet were nailed to the floorboards. An ice-cold buzz filled his ears, and for a moment he thought the sound originated from somewhere in the room. The light illuminated the discolored stone head from behind. "Elizabeth." He was there the day she arrived with her husband. She reminded him of everything that was painfully lost years before.

In her face, he saw what he had been and never would

rise above. She had survived, unblemished by all that had happened, tranquil and even forgiving. It was as if someone had taken a stick and had drawn a circle in the dust around her and then had spoken an incantation. He faced her now just as he had done on that first day at the train station when he was still young and eager to make his great fortune in America. He hadn't seen the flaw in his dream until she was gone, and he found himself trapped in a life that offered no alternatives beyond what he already had. He had tried to live according to his dream but had failed miserably. However, she was triumphant. She had endured and won the battle thrust upon her by another's fear, something that was beyond her control. He sensed that she was with him in the room.

"Mr. Kelly?"

He heard her voice above the incessant buzz and stepped closer.

"Mr. Kelly?" The voice was louder. "Mr. Kelly!"

"Oh, Mrs. Johnson," he said with embarrassment. "I thought..."

"I didn't mean to interrupt you, but I thought something was wrong. You've been up here for..."

"No," he said, moving past her into the hallway. "Nothing's wrong. I'll be going now. Thank you." He paused at the top of the stairs. "I'm interested in buying her if your son would like."

"I'll tell him."

Kelly left the house quickly. A feeling of dread overcame him, but he couldn't explain it. He had felt a bittersweet euphoria in the room. Now he imagined that Death itself was in the cab next to him.

FOURTEEN

1909

It wasn't long before Beatrice Worthing issued another demand. This time it concerned the statue of Elizabeth. On the morning the message arrived, her son was busy with Sooy. The paper business hadn't been profitable since his father's death. The ancillary businesses had been supporting it since 1905. An ongoing discussion about the size of the paper operation and the quality of the paper which was used primarily for wrapping and heavy board backing was coming to an end. Expansion into other types of paper production wasn't feasible because of the tea-colored cedar water used. A variety of solutions existed, and Worthing knew that without the paper mill as the hub of the company the entire town would suffer. The idea of a cohesive mill town wouldn't last long without the one central business. The sawmill produced a large quantity of board and shingle, but it wasn't enough to carry the town as his father had left it. They were expanding their bogs so that cranberry production could be increased. A small glassmaking operation had been added by Elizabeth. But all of the solutions pointed to the downgrading of the paper mill's importance. Worthing saw that a way of life was at risk. If Worthing Mills ceased to function as a complete mill town, it would be one of the last in the region to do so.

It was after lunch, when he was alone in his room, that he first opened the message. He had waited to read it but knew that the telegram was from his mother. Destroy the statue, was all it said. He looked through the window and surveyed the blooming green space until he found it. He didn't know how his mother had learned of its existence, but her desire was clear. Worthing understood her obsession but didn't sympathize with it. She wanted to eradicate any sign of Elizabeth Black from Worthing Mills. If she had visited the town, his mother would have realized that it was impossible. Elizabeth's influence was everywhere. The mansion would have to be gutted; the garden would have to be plowed under. The town would have to be destroyed and rebuilt. He thought that Carthage had fared better than Worthing Mills would after an attempt to erase her presence and influence.

The idea of destroying the statue troubled him. He had tried on more than one occasion to imagine Elizabeth. He started by reconstructing her physical appearance and placing her in the Pennsylvania hotel where his father had stayed. He wondered exactly what his father had said to her. It was increasingly difficult for him to believe that she was only interested in money as his mother continued to say. He heard himself asking questions about her and listening to the answers as a child would after hearing a fairy tale. He followed her movements through the years, piecing together information until he felt as if he had known her. The house was imbued with her spirit. A portrait of the woman and his father hung over one of the first floor fireplaces. It was a powerful rendition of a couple who stared back at the viewer with defiant, proud eyes. In the evening, he would catch their indomitable look and was stunned. They seemed to possess no trace of compromise, no hint that the world had been resistant to them. He found himself respecting them. He left his personal memories behind and tried to see them as one of the workers had. It was then that he knew his mother had been wrong. Elizabeth Black didn't have the face of an opportunist. She was free of any dependence on a man, even one with money. Survival was second nature to her. She was a compassionate woman. He was sorry that she was gone and that he hadn't met her.

Worthing regretted not accepting their numerous invitations. His anger and his desire to please his mother had sustaine 1 his rejections. He wanted to make amends but only his mother was left, and she was intent on obliterating any trace of what appeared to be the happiest years of her husband's life. Eventually, his mother would have to accept the fact that her obsession was an impossibility. He would act one last time for her and considered what he would say if another request came. The employees and their families were offended by her previous demand. Hard feelings would affect their loyalty to the company. If nothing else, he thought, she will understand this.

He didn't know who to ask about doing the job so he solicited the advice of Sooy, who in turn recommended Martin Kelly. Sooy's face showed what Worthing thought was displeasure when the nature of the work was mentioned. Sooy didn't object verbally but paused a minute as if to contain his dissatisfaction. He wondered what Sooy thought and if the destruction of the statue was the cause of his annoyance, but he didn't ask. The less said about this, Worthing considered for a minute, the better. Then he dropped the thought.

It was late morning when Kelly arrived. Worthing was sitting in the far corner of the garden reading the newspaper. He heard someone whistling on the other side of the wall. When Kelly entered through the rear gate, he saw him immediately. Kelly was in his thirties, walked with short rambling strides, and didn't seem to be in a hurry to speak to him. He gazed around the garden and noticed the other man.

"Morning, sir."

Worthing folded his newspaper and stood. He was nearly a foot taller than the man whom he had observed working around the mansion's grounds on a previous occasion.

"I have a job for you."

"Yes, sir."

"Did Mr. Sooy tell you?"

"No. He only said that you wanted to see me about some work."

Worthing found that interesting. Maybe he had underestimated Sooy's displeasure. Maybe this was so distasteful that Sooy didn't want to discuss it because Kelly might have refused.

"It's the statue."

"Statue?"

"That statue," Worthing said, pointing across the grass and flowers.

Kelly faced it. Sunlight struck his face. He instinctively raised his right hand and pulled the brim of his cap onto his forehead.

"I'm sure that you've seen it many times."

Kelly didn't answer.

Worthing repeated himself.

"Yes, a hundred times at least."

"Well, this is what I want. This afternoon bring the truck and a sledge along with some chains. I want you to pull it from the pedestal and break it apart."

"Why, sir?" His voice was faint.

"That's my business."

"I suspect so," Kelly said quietly.

"And after you've destroyed it, I want you to load it on the truck—every piece of it—and take it to the river. I don't want you to tell anyone exactly where you're going. Do you understand?"

"Yes."

"When you reach the river—make it several miles from town—I want you to dump it in the water. Make sure that it's deep. I don't want someone finding it, even by accident."

"That will be the end."

"Excuse me?"

"The end. There won't be anything left."

"You'll be back at two o'clock?" he said, ignoring Kelly's last remark but wondering if his mother would actually succeed in eradicating the memory of the woman with this final action, not within the confines of the town, but within her own mind.

"Two o'clock," he said, still sounding faint and uneasy.

"I'll be waiting."

"Yes, sir." Kelly didn't turn away from the statue.

"That's all."

The man stepped back slowly and disappeared through the gate. Once outside of the wall, Kelly didn't start whistling again.

Worthing returned to his seat and opened the newspaper. Kelly looked like he had seen a ghost, he thought. He was distant and Worthing wasn't sure that Kelly heard half of what he said.

Lunch was served in the garden that afternoon. One of the house servants, a young, attractive girl in a blue and white uniform, set the table and Worthing made advances toward her as she moved near him. When his meal was in front of him, his attention shifted from the giggling woman, who re-entered the house, to the statue. He felt sorry for Kelly, but Sooy said he was the best man. He would stick with him. Kelly would destroy it. Worthing didn't find any joy in the act. The statue, like the painting, had captured his attention. It spoke to him, but beyond his exaggerated perceptions, he wasn't sure what was being said. He had realized one thing on his first day there and found it to be more true as time passed— Elizabeth Black was a beautiful woman.

After lunch, he returned to his newspaper and its endless stream of bad news. Most of the world didn't seem to intrude on Worthing Mills. He thought of it as an evolving oasis. The only recent transgression had been Elizabeth's death, and the accused was being tried within a week. The county detective on the case was sure of his guilt. The people living in Worthing Mills had already convicted him. He thought about attending the trial but decided it would be in bad taste. But his curiosity about Zauber was great. The relationship that had developed between a man known as a self-proclaimed mystic and possible con artist and his father's second wife intrigued him. How could she be taken by him? he wondered. He didn't want to believe that she was an ignorant victim of his charms. There had to be more to it. But the complete truth, he reasoned, would probably never be known.

Zauber hadn't said a word since his apprehension. He refused to cooperate in any way. It was rumored that he hadn't eaten since his arrest. When Worthing saw his picture in the newspaper, he thought him enigmatic—a Svengali. His appearance was totally different than his father's had been except for an intangible quality flowing from his charismatic eyes. He could see the man had the power to draw people to him just as his father had and decided that Elizabeth could have been influenced by this. But he wasn't certain, and with Elizabeth dead only Zauber knew the answer.

At two o'clock, Worthing heard the truck approach the rear of the garden. Kelly appeared and opened the other side of the gate. He backed the vehicle to the statue. Worthing remained seated near the garden wall, which was now darkened by shade. He didn't speak to the man, thinking that he would prefer to be left alone. He decided that Kelly had an affection for Elizabeth and had possibly denied it until faced with the destruction of her effigy.

Kelly went about his work methodically, attaching a double set of chains to the rear of the truck and the statue. He checked them more than once before returning to the cab. The chains tightened when the truck lurched forward. The statue rocked on its base. The truck moved again and the statue fell forward, hitting the edge of its pedestal and one of the columns that held an arbor above it. There was a grating sound, then a solid crash.

He turned the engine off but remained in his seat as if he were waiting for something. Worthing could see that the statue had cracked in several places. He expected Kelly to move, but the other man was still and stared across the garden.

After a few minutes passed, Worthing left the cool shade and crossed the lawn. He called to Kelly, but he didn't answer. Again, Worthing supposed that he hadn't heard him or that he was troubled by his actions. Worthing studied the remains of the statue at the rear of the truck. It was in several pieces. One of the arms was broken. The head sat to one side. A break separated the trunk. He searched the bed of the truck and found the sledgehammer under a tarp. He grabbed it and looked at the other man's head.

"Kelly?"

The man raised his hand slightly as if to signal that he was all right.

"Kelly. Time to get busy." Worthing raised the hammer above his head and struck the marble which broke cleanly.

He lifted the hammer again and brought it down. Another break inched its way across her chest.

Kelly moved after the second swing. He left the truck and walked along its side toward Worthing.

"You've decided to end your nap I see," Worthing said, bringing the hammer down a third time.

FIFTEEN

1889

Samuel and Elizabeth were driven to the train station a few hours after their luggage had been deposited there. Although only morning it was warm, more like afternoon with its dead pause. They were glad that a trip to Atlantic City was measured in hours rather than days.

They stayed at the Traymore, a cottage hotel with green lawns that touched the Boardwalk and sand beach. It wasn't a large hotel with hundreds of guests, and Worthing was grateful. He relished simple pleasures and wasn't interested in socializing. With the piers and amusements so near, as well as the crowds swarming around new attractions and improvements like the electric trolley on Atlantic Avenue, he wanted to be able to draw away from the confusion and find a little peace. The wide lawn of the Traymore allowed guests room to stroll without forcing them to venture away from the property. Diamond Jim Brady and his cronies wouldn't be found at the Traymore. It wasn't considered glamorous enough. Years later the Traymore would grow to fourteen stories and six hundred guest rooms. Sanford White, the hotel's architect, would be murdered there by Evelyn Nesbitt's jealous husband. In the winter, guests would ice skate on its parking lot. But Samuel Worthing wouldn't be impressed or intrigued by these occurrences because what he sought was tranquility.

Elizabeth had planned a schedule for them: up early and a brief swim before breakfast—it was recommended by medical authorities that ladies stay in the ocean for no more than three minutes and Elizabeth purposely ignored this—then breakfast on one of the Traymore's porches overlooking the

Atlantic and Boardwalk, and afterwards a short walk. In the afternoon, depending on the heat, they would explore the city or swim and relax at the hotel. They frequently stopped at the Saratoga Water Stand and drank the mineral water, which was touted as a cure-all, or sarsaparilla, a new beverage popular with children. The evenings were devoted to dining, reading, walking, love, and sleeping. He fell into her regimentation without any problem, and after two days confided to his wife that he had never felt better, at least not since he had been a boy.

Several times during the long afternoons they went to one of the entertainment piers. Occasionally, they listened to music played by bands hired to attract customers onto a specific pier. On other afternoons, they enjoyed the amusements—the carousel, the games of chance—or the food stands which sold everything from saltwater taffy to complete meals. Often they acted like newlyweds. For Elizabeth it seemed natural and expected. But her husband felt his past haunting him as he tried to be as carefree as his wife. After years of a sour marriage, he couldn't help being slightly antagonistic about the love that tried to overwhelm him.

One afternoon they stopped at a music hall to hear Zauber. He was an adherent of New Thought Mysticism which was undergoing an enormous surge of popularity in the country. He was a tall, gaunt man with a long black beard and dark hair that fell in unruly curls on his shoulders. He wore no shoes or hat. Someone said that he was from Denver while another said he was from Europe because he heard a soft, benign accent that was barely noticeable. In the hall, Zauber spoke for thirty minutes and expressed to the audience his feelings about the nature of life and love.

"Without love in one's life only hate is left. Only hate can fill the void left by a transitory love," he said in a tone that suggested his message of a new utopia founded on love was without flaws.

His eyes danced around the room, fixing on each person and pausing for several long moments to study the most attractive women there. He asked once for donations—funds to be used for the founding of a school where people would learn to love. After his presentation, many people formed a line to receive his blessing or advice with the knowledge that a donation would be offered as payment. At times, Zauber dropped to his knees in a trance. Someone said that his touch had the power to heal. Worthing listened closely but couldn't hear what was being said to the individuals. The people standing before Zauber at these moments seemed to comprehend and digest the man's words and nod repeatedly. Tears and a thank you generally followed this exchange. Whatever was being said, Worthing couldn't find a crack in his performance. The trances seemed genuine, but Worthing was still skeptical.

"The faith healing must be a sham," he whispered to Elizabeth.

Zauber had a command of the language and created an atmosphere conducive to the nature of his performance. Worthing's suspicions grew when the supplicants dropped money into a golden bowl near the podium before returning to their seats.

"I'm going to let him cure my stiff neck," Elizabeth said with a playful light in her eyes.

"You're not serious?" he asked but saw that she was already standing and ready to approach the line with a devotional air. Her sense of humor amused him. He noticed that by the time his wife reached Zauber some of his previous exuberance was gone, and he looked as if each new encounter continued to drain him.

"Your concern?" the mystic questioned.

"My neck."

His right hand touched her neck. She could feel an unusual concentration of heat which seemed to come from his fingers.

"I feel it. It's locked inside." He closed his eyes. "It's crying out...trying to escape..." He trembled. "I see..." He dropped to his knees, clutching her waist. "The man, the older man..."

She knew that he had studied the audience closely.

"He's married...to..." He paused.

"What are you saying?"

He looked up at her; his eyes were filled with tears. "I'm

sorry. You must help. You must desire more. Your mother. Her death—she wants..." He rose slowly. His robe unfolded and his appearance changed instantly from that of vulnerability to one of dominance. He smiled and closed his eyes again. "Love. Love is the only answer, the only thing that can save you. Only you can change that, only you."

She stared at him, not knowing how to respond. She wondered how he knew about her mother or Samuel. Why did he begin to cry when he held me? she asked herself. How is love going to save me? She couldn't answer any of these questions and sensed that he wouldn't accommodate her inquiries at that moment. Others waited behind her.

"Thank you," she whispered, walking toward the golden bowl. She reached in her bag and noticed that the pain in her neck had vanished. Some coins slipped from her hand into the bowl.

"What did he say?" Worthing asked when she returned.

"He tried to tell me that you were married to two women, I think."

He laughed and said, "So I am."

"He mentioned my mother. It sounded like gibberish," she added. "Although I'd like to speak with him again in a different place—the hotel maybe."

"I'm sure that could be arranged for a deposit in that bowl of his." He touched her neck. "And the pain?"

"Gone," she replied vaguely. "I wonder what he was suggesting?" She straightened in the chair.

"It was probably just nonsense," Worthing assured her. "Anything for money."

Light filled the page of Hardy's novel as she turned to the next. They had dined earlier that evening and afterwards had decided to relax on the upper gallery of the hotel. Worthing sat quietly watching her. He remembered those nights not so far in the past when he fought the imbroglio that his sudden feelings had caused. He lit a cigar, ceremoniously drawing on it until smoke obscured his features. The constant drone of the ocean reminded him of the paper mill and the amount of work waiting for him. He had tried to forget about the business for a few days and enjoy his time alone with Elizabeth. And she purposely hadn't mentioned any aspect of it to him, knowing that this time alone would be their last for several months.

"Isn't this...," he offered without thought.

"What?"

"The mill. I hope everything..."

"Sooy would have sent word."

He hesitated, still watching her through the smoke, then said, "You're right."

She looked at him and rested the book on her lap for a minute.

"I don't think that there will be any problems. And we'll be home in a couple of days," she added.

"True."

There was silence again, except for the sea. Dusk fell quickly into twilight; the scent of the salt water rose as the light diminished. Around the hotel, lightning bugs showed their yellow flux. The world seemed to fold over them. She stopped reading, although there were lights along the gallery, and she could still see the pages of the novel.

"Samuel." Her voiced drifted in the darkness.

"Yes."

"This night." She arranged the material of her skirt where it fell across her legs. "I want it to stay like this."

"Quiet?"

"It's not the quiet I think as much as the peace of this place in the evening when the guests are relaxed and tired. You can hear them speaking in hushed voices."

"There's still a lot happening out on the Boardwalk."

"But when you pretend that we're the only people here and think that those hushed sounds are part of the ocean and the night, and then you listen to our voices and think we're part of it, too. We're beyond the here and now suddenly." She halted, trying to recognize exactly what her senses were trying to tell her. "It's almost as if something is attempting to say, this is what eternity is like—not death, but peace, peace with remembrance, with you, together."

"I hope you're right." He touched her as he had done so many times since they had met. Sometimes he thought his reaching for her was only to reassure himself that she was real. "You mean the world to me, Liz," he said tenderly.

On the previous evenings, they hadn't said more than five words to each other. They felt a certain amount of respect for the other's unpronounced moments. Any discussion or exchange of thought was usually followed by a quiet period as if they were considering and reconsidering the words waiting to be spoken. Their only disagreement at that time involved children. She wanted to wait until she had a chance to explore the possibilities created by her marriage. He was anxious, thinking that his days as a patient father were numbered. Elizabeth understood his reasoning, and he respected her feelings. Their contention over this didn't result in bitterness but in a compromise. They would wait three or four years. By that time, Worthing Mills would be secure, and Elizabeth would make her place there.

"Samuel. I'd really like to talk with him again."

"Zauber?"

"Today, when he touched my neck, I had the queerest sensation. I can't explain it really. He mentioned my mother. I feel like he knows something that I need to know."

"Why don't we have him over for a drink? If he does that is. He'd probably be interesting for an hour or two. I'm sure we can arrange something."

"Then you wouldn't mind?"

"Not at all." He rolled his cigar between his fingers. "We'll send him a note first thing tomorrow morning. But don't put too much faith in the fellow."

Elizabeth had already started to think of the possibilities, of what he would say. She had overheard someone at the hotel say that a man had been stalking the beach at daybreak, wearing a robe and nothing else. The woman thought he was a foreigner who was performing somewhere in the city. Elizabeth suspected it was Zauber. Who else would walk the beach at sunrise wearing a robe? she found herself asking.

"That's a good idea...first thing tomorrow."

"He may not accept."

"Granted."

"If he doesn't?"

"Well," she pondered.

"Make another trip to his lecture or whatever you'd call it and approach him. A promise of a small donation might persuade him. I imagine that he needs the money," Worthing chuckled, "for his school."

"Yes." She didn't notice his shift in tone and suddenly felt removed from the conversation. "I think you're right, a donation." Her voice weakened.

"What else would he accept as payment for his time?"

She didn't respond.

They left two days after the holiday which was celebrated lavishly in the city. Parades filled the morning hours; picnics and athletic contests started around noon; speeches began shortly after the contests and carried people into the evening when fireworks were launched seaward from oceanfront locations, creating a display that stretched for a mile along the coast. Within two months, this festive day would be forgotten. A hurricane would savage the place, leaving much of the city under three feet of water, the sea swelling to meet the bay somewhere near Georgia Avenue.

Elizabeth was happy with their short stay. She wished to see more of the world and knew that this trip was only the beginning. She felt uncomfortable admitting to people of her husband's social standing that she hadn't been to Italy or France or California. Her husband sympathized with her uneasiness and reassured her that they would remedy this.

Worthing had few complaints about the trip but was particularly annoyed by people who asked Elizabeth if she was his daughter. He assumed that he was showing his years. If not, he reasoned, why do people automatically assume that I am twenty years older? After this he decided that it was Elizabeth who, when standing in a certain light, appeared to be eighteen or nineteen. He admitted to himself that he might pass for forty or even thirty-eight, but with this in mind he still would appear to be her father. To add to this, they had met two couples who had made his acquaintance previously. At first, this struck him as odd because they both were from Boston, but considering Atlantic City's growing reputation he realized that it should have been expected. The first couple did not seem to recall that Elizabeth wasn't Beatrice, so he left them to their unclear memories. The second couple, especially the woman, remembered meeting Beatrice and were surprised to meet, in her place, a woman many years younger and considerably more attractive.

"How do you do," the woman said stiffly after the introductions were freshened. She paused as she glanced from Elizabeth to her husband and then back to Elizabeth. "My, how you've changed."

"Pardon me?"

"You've changed or my memory has completely failed me. We first met Samuel in Portland about a year ago."

"I'm sorry?" Elizabeth knew what was coming but refused to be flustered.

"It must be my memory. Have you been using one of those youth cremes? It's done marvels for you. You look twenty years younger."

Elizabeth held back, gauged her response, and decided to tell the woman exactly what she thought.

"Over thirty years if you're comparing me to yourself."

The woman's husband smiled as he looked at Worthing. His eyes said everything. It was a subtle compliment that some men share in situations which don't normally warrant discussion about women. Worthing immediately noticed this and accepted his offering. The woman huffed once after Elizabeth's remark and was escorted away by her husband.

Elizabeth knew that the woman's behavior was defensive. In Elizabeth, she saw cause for alarm. If Samuel had managed to change wives after being married for so many years, what about her own bored husband? Could he replace her with another wife? The woman feared a challenge, even an indirect one, because she suspected that she couldn't compete on any field other than time spent in service—a service probably resented but not denied.

"That was marvelous," Worthing said after they were out of earshot.

"I'm glad you didn't mind, but she was a bitch."

"Yes, she was." Worthing searched for the woman, but her husband had ushered her outside.

"Let's go back to our room."

"Fine. I've had enough for one evening." She clutched his arm. "These games are so insipid."

They walked along the Boardwalk toward their hotel, both hoping that all adversity would draw them together rather than apart. Only one obstacle seemed to stand in their path at that moment and ironically it was the object of the earlier exchange. How would they convince Beatrice to relinquish her hold on him and some of his assets? He was willing to pay her handsomely for consenting to a divorce, but all his money might not satisfy her. She had no desire to remarry or see other men, which made her apathetic at best in accommodating her husband's pleas.

The Boardwalk was filled with embracing couples, groups of young women, and loitering bands of men who rested on benches or against railings. Many men talked about baseball and Shibe Park in Philadelphia or about the upcoming fight in Richburg, Mississippi, between Sullivan and Kilrain. Others watched the young women as they strolled past in small defensive clusters, their long skirts rustling under the soft glow of the Boardwalk lights. Several rolling chairs were pushed past them, their white wicker seats engulfing the older occupants whose legs were covered with plaid blankets. Their wheels caused a vibrating, hollow sound to emerge from the wooden planks beneath them.

Zauber was contacted before they left. When his message arrived, it stated he wasn't available until the following week. Too late for us, Elizabeth thought when she read it. She decided that he would be an interesting speaker at one of the events she hoped to organize in town. The offer of a contributing audience was something she thought he wouldn't refuse. She had persuaded her husband to construct what she called an Opera House for musical performances and speakers in her lyceum series. She thought cultural events in Worthing Mills would benefit everyone. And Worthing knew that her managerial skills would need occupying. The house renovations would be finished in less than two months and her need to keep busy impressed him. A note was sent to Zauber proposing an engagement. A day passed and for a time they thought he had decided against their offer. Finally, they received his reply accepting the proposal. He couldn't give a definite date but felt that it would be sometime in August. This was too early for the Opera House, but arrangements could be made to supply a suitable stage for his presentation. Elizabeth replied quickly that a week's notice would be needed. She wondered, as she wrote the message, if he remembered her. Her interest in the man didn't seem abnormal to her. There was simply something that she felt he knew, something that she needed to be aware of.

A wave of relief overcame her when the final agreement was made. After examining her feelings, she dismissed them as a reaction to the success of the trip and not to the completion of the arrangements with Zauber. Elizabeth's belief in clairvoyance was shakable, and Zauber's talents as a mystic were unproved. He was, however, a mesmerizing speaker and for now this seemed to be enough. The people of Worthing Mills would enjoy hearing one of his lectures.

They left the city on a brilliant, cool summer morning. A steady breeze blew out of the northwest. It was the type of day that made visitors wish they had another week of vacation left, but the couple knew an inordinate amount of work waited for them at home. Only one message from Sooy had been received, saying that all was well. Worthing appreciated Sooy's competence. The lack of messages filled with questions had allowed him to relax, although the town was constantly in his mind, crowding his thoughts and pleasures.

SIXTEEN

1990

Ｔhe trailers started to chop, and they released the younger hounds. The men listened for a minute and tried to anticipate the direction of the chase. The dogs packed up quickly. The men started their pickups, and Will broke away from the rest and drove east, thinking that once the fox reached the low ridge he would turn toward him rather than follow the crest. Stan kept his head partially outside the window, straining to hear any alteration in the pack's direction. The truck rocked wildly and jolted the two men inside. Will dropped the transmission into neutral and let the engine fall to an idle as the truck plunged across the blinding white sand. The yelping was growing louder. The fox had avoided the ridge and now had turned toward them.

"He's coming our way, Will. Take this right."

Will steered the pickup onto the overgrown fire lane that appeared too narrow for the vehicle to enter. The oak saplings and small pitch pines slapped its sides. He slowed for a second. Behind them he could hear the other trucks whining as they tried to cover lost ground.

"Another fifty yards," Stan said, still hanging from the open window.

The fox was close. The hounds' chop was frantic. Will drove another few yards and then the fox appeared, springing from the brush and hitting one sand track of the road which he followed for ten feet. He leaped over the raised, weed-choked center strip onto the other track and, in an instant, he plunged into the woods again. Within a second, the frenzied dogs exploded out of the woods from four or five closely spaced *points, crossed the road, and disappeared in the cover of the opposite side.*

"He's going to double back on them. There's a swamp down there in that bottom," Stan yelled, waving one of his hands. "Go straight. Go straight. We'll spot him again on the backside."

"See that clearing on the left?"

"With the chimney standing?" Lou said.

"An old jug tavern was there a few years back before it burned to the ground. It had been open since the Revolution."

"No shit."

"I used to go there on occasion when I was a young man."

"Any action?"

"On weekends. They had a band on Friday and Saturday nights. That was a tradition that went back over two hundred and fifty years. Men from the iron forges would congregate there a long time back."

Lou glanced briefly at the site.

"Used to make shot and cannon for the Continentals in those forges. Kettles, skillets, and firebacks as well."

"But what about the action?"

Will could see that Lou wasn't interested in what he was saying.

"Quite a lot. Fights every night, if you wanted. Pretty women."

"All right."

"I remember going in there alone many times and leaving with one," Will exaggerated.

"No shit," Lou paused. "We'll score tonight. You can bet on it.

Will doubted him and said, "We'll see. If we don't, that's fine." He rested his head on the upholstery.

"You can count on it, dude. Leave it to me. I haven't come away empty handed yet."

The causeway crossed the tidal salt marshes and the intercoastal waterway to Atlantic City. Billboards flanked the road, most of them directed west toward the arriving cars. Will could see the high-rise casinos across the flat, pungent wetlands. The buildings held a north-south line on the horizon that blocked any view of the ocean, which had become so polluted that health advisories filled the radio and television airwaves each summer.

"I've done a bunch of duck hunting along this coast. It's on the flyway," he commented, sensing that Lou wasn't listening and was probably lost in thought as he contemplated the next few hours.

"There it is, my man—the city by the sea. It's a fucking beautiful sight, ain't it?"

Dombeck stood in front of his cedar-shingled house as Will's father parked the truck in the dim light before sunrise. He was ready to go out to the blind and wasted no time getting them, along with the stools, into his small garvey. Dombeck was a recluse who made his living as a guide, sneakbox builder, and decoy carver. When hunting season was over, he remained in his weatherbeaten shack, without interruption, until the next hunting season brought new demands for his services. Will's father had known the man since he was a young boy. Over the years, Dombeck had become his father's friend. He didn't act as their professional guide. They could shoot ducks on other parts of the bay as well as inland on the bog reservoirs and freshwater marshes. Will's father associated hunting ducks with the old codger's company. The guide's normally withdrawn, abrasive personality became animated and congenial during their visits. Will found his companionship and knowledge of wildlife and hunting fascinating. His brother admired Dombeck's carving and the old man, reacting to Andy's interest, gave both of them a decoy which Will still had, packed in one of the boxes that would be moved to the gun club.

"I have to make a trip to Eddy T's place before we hit the casinos," Lou said when they reached the city. "He lives away from the boards. He likes his privacy." Lou turned the car south after several blocks passed. Men gathered on a corner, laughing and sipping from bottles in paper bags. A young woman, her clothes covered with grease, limped through the trash along the curb. Her face grimaced as she waved her arms frantically at an unseen adversary. One low, hoarse groan emerged from her mouth. The men ignored her until several rats sprang from the garbage the young woman disturbed. The men scattered into the street for a moment. Lou nearly hit one of the men as the man tried to dodge a fleeing rodent. "Son of a bitch," Lou mumbled as he yanked the steering wheel to the left.

Will wasn't surprised to see that the city hadn't changed appreciably, at least the section of town where Lou drove, since his last visit with his mother on her birthday. The beach had been crowded and the boards offered a good vantage point on that day. Gambling was far in the future, but the city was still alive and thriving along the beach. He bought her a box of fudge. She didn't want anything else even though he had offered to buy her a present in each store that they entered. They ate dinner at a Boardwalk restaurant and watched the yellow electric tourist train pass by the windows as it cruised the entire length of the wooden structure. Beyond the Boardwalk, most of the city was rundown and dangerous. Many buildings were vacant. On that day several years before, it seemed to him that Atlantic City was divided into two very distinct towns. The affluent, who controlled the Boardwalk and its businesses, had no presence in the other Atlantic City, preferring to live in places like Margate. The poor and the retired and the service employees owned, rented, or controlled the rest of the town. They had little money and less influence in the affairs of the city. Poverty was their sole franchise.

"It's not different," he finally said to Lou as he turned another corner.

"What do you mean?"

"All the money that's being made and look at this place," he said, thinking about the hype surrounding the casino industry.

Two rows of empty houses slid past them. Garbage littered sidewalks and gutters. A mangy dog rooted through a swollen, black plastic trash bag.

"This part of A.C. is a slum, man, a real hole. You have to watch your ass down here or you might lose it."

"Just like the casinos?"

Lou didn't answer.

"Your friend lives down here?"

"Not far. He does a lot of work in the area. He's an entrepreneur like me."

Lou drove through an open gate and stopped before a closed garage door. Above it there was an apartment. He blew the horn. The window blinds parted above the door; then it slowly opened.

"Pretty nice," Lou said.

"Just like a prison."

"You'd better wait outside man. Eddie T gets a little nervous around strangers." Lou looked at Will. "He's paranoid, man. I don't know why."

"No problem," Will said as he left the car. He stood outside the building as the car entered the empty space.

A door opened in the back of the garage and the larger door slowly closed behind Lou's car. A man emerged. Will could vaguely see him through a small, soot-covered window in the center of the garage door.

"Eddie T," Lou said as he adjusted his sunglasses and got out.

"Hey man. Jimmy Jones. What's happening?"

They shook hands and Eddy T noticed Will who had remained beyond the window of the closed door.

"Who's the old dude outside?"

"That's Will. He's cool." He motioned to Will to move away from the window. "Don't worry, man. He don't know what's going down."

Will looked at the thin man with a diamond in his left earlobe and a shoulder holster strapped to his left side. He felt a warm flush of blood under the skin of his face as Eddie T glared at him. When Lou signaled, Will gladly moved away from the building which had the stale smell of chemicals around it.

"Did you bring it?" Eddy T said anxiously to the other man.

"Would I let you down?"

Lou walked to his trunk and produced a heavy package wrapped in plastic.

"Top grade?"

"Fuckin' A." He sniffled. "And I have a bonus for you," he said, leaning the large parcel against the wall. "Voila," Lou exclaimed as he removed a box the size of a cinderblock from his car.

"Going to be a hot time in A.C. tonight," Eddy T said.

"I told you."

The other man clapped his hands. Overhead, a woman screamed.

"Motherfuckers look out," Eddy T pronounced as he removed an envelope from his back pocket. "Here's the green, Jimmy."

The woman's voice cried out again. This time Will could hear the word Eddie as it echoed down to the garage and out into the barren lot around the building.

"Damn woman," Eddie T said, shaking his head. "She wants something. What can I say? I told her to chill but..."

"Thanks man," Lou said. "Exactly?"

"Huh?" Eddie T was preoccupied now.

"Money?"

"Yeah. What you told me."

They shook hands. Eddie T raised his eyes to the ceiling.

"Next week?" Lou questioned.

"I'll be waiting."

Before Lou passed the fence, he stopped the car and Will returned to his seat. Lou removed the envelope from his pocket. He discarded the paper cover and fanned his face with the bills.

"Looks like a lot of cash."

"Not bad for a day's work."

"Did I hear him call you Jimmy Jones?"

"Yeah. That's my business name, like a stage name. You know? All my friends call me Lou. Only my business associates call me Jimmy." He glanced at Will as he returned the money to his pocket. "Let's do a little before we hit the casinos."

Will opened the glove compartment.

"See that small box in the back? Take that out."

Will followed his instructions.

"And take some more ganja out, too. That's what you were going for."

They smoked the joint, and Will began to feel it work inside him. The sensation was pleasant, and it drew him away from Lou and the city.

"Now the surprise, my man." Lou opened the box. A mirror was glued to the reverse side of the lid. He removed a vial, tapped some of its white contents onto the mirror and divided it into fine lines with a razor blade. "You have a dollar bill?"

Will removed one from his pocket.

"Roll it into a tube and snort a couple of these bad boys."

"What kind of shit is that?"

"Coke dude. Cocaine. You know? Haven't you ever seen good ole snow before?"

Worthing drank Peruvian Coca Wine habitually. When the mansion was still standing but vacant, Will and his brother found several unopened bottles stacked in a corner of the basement. The labels were dust-covered and stained, but the printing was still legible. Worthing considered it a cure-all and found its charms irresistible. On his deathbed, after being gored by his trained moose, Bully, he asked for a glass of the wine but before the maid brought it, he died. Death could have been held off by the wine, he probably thought, as his spirit left the mansion. His physician would have disagreed but had failed to prove medical science could do any better.

"I don't know."

"It won't hurt you," the younger man said impatiently.

Will's head was heavy. Lou seemed far away. His voice was an octave higher than it should have been.

"Toot. Toot. Put that bill up your nose and do a line."

Will leaned forward and drew it through his nostril. He felt a tingling sensation that made his eyesockets slightly cold, then numb.

"Do the other one, dude, on the other side."

He snorted the second line through his other nostril. The sensation spread across his face, and his entire body reacted with a joyous surge of energy.

131

"Well?" Lou said as he took the mirror and prepared two lines for himself.

Will didn't know what to say. The only comparison was that of an orgasm, but the immediate aftereffects of the drug entering his system were more invigorating.

"Good," Will finally said, realizing that his description was inadequate. "Really good."

"We'll take some into the casino and do a toot before we start playing." Lou snorted the lines he had created with somber efficiency. He let his head fall back. "Just what the fucker ordered." He glanced at Will. "You ready, dude?"

SEVENTEEN

1937

Agentle wind blew off the ocean when Nichols left. As he glanced out across the blue-grey ocean through the car window, it ruffled the white hair around his temples. He had combined an official trip to the southernmost tip of the state with a brief three-day vacation. He enjoyed the town, and the privacy it offered added to his pleasure. In the past, several trips to another coastal town had nearly ended in disaster. Its proximity was too close to where he lived and worked. Too many residents of the county—people who were important to his survival—vacationed there. With the constant fear of outside intrusion, his relaxation was ruined. He needed to feel secure about his privacy. Cape May was more distant. People tended to mind their own business and respect the affairs of others. It didn't possess the frenetic magnetism of Atlantic City, but he cared less about that as he grew older. This small town was a more secure arena for him. Over the years no one ever mentioned seeing him there, although he did know two people who spent every August in the town. Rather than break his association with the place, he simply avoided it during that month.

With less than one year left before retirement, he could ill-afford a scandal. He was sensitive to rumor and back-stabbing as well as any subtle shifts in the attitudes of others. He kept alert but detected nothing abnormal. His private life—not the one he had created for the benefit of the public but his real private existence—remained his own. He did his best to create the illusion of an eternal and grateful bachelor, a man who was satisfied with his singular life.

His knowledge of county affairs helped secure his privacy. Dirty politics existed. County government was a victim of nepotism and favoritism. He kept tabs on county officials and employees from the most important to the least significant. If necessary, he could have half of them arrested. For years he had managed to evade the scrutiny of various county sheriffs. Luckily, Nichols wasn't an elected official. His expertise had not only allowed him to capture felons but proved to be invaluable when dealing with other county law enforcement people. Once he had caused one overly zealous sheriff to lose his job. Leave the capital crimes to me, Nichols told the elected officials, and I'll make all of us look good. Corruption was the natural state of man, he told himself. He availed himself of it. Those who knew anything about the county and its workings realized that Patrick Nichols was a power to be avoided.

He had worked for the county for almost thirty-five years. He considered himself to be the best detective the state had but looked eagerly forward to the day when he could walk away from the position and into retirement. The lack of activity retirement would bring might not suit him, but the idea of endless free days without a time clock and the responsibilities of his job appealed to him. He knew people who had waited until they were ill to quit working. Within a year they were usually dead. This option wasn't attractive. If he got bored, which he doubted, he would open an investigation service and be highly selective about the cases he accepted. But that was left to the coming years.

He wouldn't stay in the county or state but not because he harbored animosity toward the people or place. He was admired by many residents. Much of the region appealed to him. He liked driving down through the farm fields and into the Pines where he had his hunting cabin. His desire to leave was caused by his need for a warmer climate. His shoulders ached when the cool, damp winter arrived. Colds plagued him, and the weather of Florida appealed to him. He thought about the place until it had assumed mythological dimensions. At times, his mind was filled with thoughts of that state and nothing else. His work seemed secondary. His few colleagues meant little to him. Only Florida mattered.

In that place, he felt that he could live as he wished without being troubled about his reputation. He hoped that his public life—the success and fame—would survive his retirement, intact. But the narrow path he had followed to establish and build that image had to widen, regardless of the consequences at home. His few pleasures had to be hidden, and he was tired of the charade. He knew that his fantasies couldn't be acted out on a stage, but after four visits to Florida he found life to be more accommodating there, especially in the resort communities.

His years had been spent alone. He had built his career out of a broken childhood filled with abuse and sadness and had become, over time, one of the most productive detectives in the state. There had been little time for diversions. Traditional arrangements didn't suit him, and he had managed to make peace with his sexual preferences. Unfortunately, middle age was ending and old age loomed ahead of him. He yearned for companionship. So he dreamed of retirement and escape, counting the days of his last year as if they were part of a prison sentence, knowing that the end of it would give him his freedom. It would be a return to his early days when he was reckless, when he stood shoulder to shoulder with the most influential citizens of the state at the Chatsworth Club and didn't hesitate to indulge himself in the pleasures he desired.

Murders, robberies, and kidnappings had occupied his years. As they occurred, he solved them with an ease that looked like the machinations of a sorcerer to many. His name became known throughout the law enforcement community. His advice was sought after, even though his methods were frequently labeled as unorthodox, and he had been accused of using criminal tactics against suspects. It was true that he beat, blackmailed, and deceived criminals as readily as they would him if given the chance. Everyone was fair game once a crime was committed. He had sidestepped severe censure. Catching and convicting felons, it seemed, appealed to the citizens more than the legality of the methods employed to do so. On several occasions, he had found a not too guilty party to fit a difficult puzzle, even though he knew that the suspect's part in the crime was questionable. Usually the suspects came from the local pool of petty criminals. Defense lawyers pried at the evidence, but the jury generally convicted the accused. He could arrest anyone, he thought at one time, and make the charge stick, even without actual wrongdoing. He always prevailed, and the jury and their fellow citizens slept better at night knowing the county's roads were safer. Discounting his unusual methods, the percentage of crimes solved by him was the highest in the state, and he took pride in this.

Only one major mystery went unsolved during his years in service. He had thought about it at least once a week for twenty-eight years but couldn't do anything to unravel it because his hands were tied. This great conundrum would remain just that. He couldn't approach it, and his knowledge of it was the proverbial thorn in his side. Samuel Worthing Jr.'s disappearance from Worthing Mills was permanently consigned to the back of his file cabinet. If he moved to solve it, the achievements of a lifetime might be extirpated. He had underestimated someone who knew too much about him, and he had lived to regret his oversight. The entire population of the county, with the exception of a very few, didn't see any deficiency on his part. This helped ease his frustration. Worthing had simply disappeared without leaving information or clues. Nichols had thought about creating a workable solution, but it was of little use. He resolved to face his one great failure.

Eventually, speculation and gossip answered the question without prompting by him, but it had nothing to do with the correct solution. The theory satisfied most people. A woman was involved. Worthing desired her but she was unacceptable to certain members of his extended family, who were intractable in their opinion of the woman. A grim determination existed in Worthing's mother as well. Her son must marry someone of his own class without concern for love. According to her, that would come in time. Their elopement was a flight toward anonymity. The woman had convinced Worthing that a total break was best. Their love would thrive once they were free of outside pressures. The man had access to a fortune and knew that his family would never accept the woman he loved. They vanished, and the family insisted that the love affair never existed.

Nichols accepted the theory, at least publicly. Privately, he stated it wasn't true. The simplest answer was often the right one, but not in this case. It was feasible, he admitted, but no proof could be found. Once he acquiesced officially, the county breathed easier. As the years passed, nothing new developed. Most people either forgot or died or believed the theory to be correct. As the mystery became more and more an event of the past, it appeared that no one except Nichols remembered the occurrence.

As he drove, he fantasized about one final case—a crime of such complexity that it defied explanation. The riddle would appear sphinxlike to the general population, and he would be the only one to see the less-than-obvious solution. He wouldn't fear failure and savored the thought of the governor asking him to head a special task force to solve other crimes. That won't be necessary, he would say, because he could handle it alone. He saw the honors accumulating and demands requesting another five years of service. After a suitable period of consideration, he would accept the honors but refuse to stay for another five years, even if it happened to be at the state level. Keep in touch, he would tell them and they would. Whenever another crime of great magnitude baffled everyone, they could call him in Florida.

His daydream was interrupted by the scorching heat. Once he was off the coast the breeze ended and the unrelenting sun grew even more intense. He rolled down all of his windows, but the air entering the car only turned hotter. The sharp wind that circulated around him felt like a wall of heat released from a just-opened oven door. He was soaked with perspiration, and he could smell the usually comforting odors of his flesh, although he found no relief in them. He moved his heavy, pink body on the seat, recalling his younger years when he could handle the burden of being a few pounds overweight. Finally, Nichols reached his county. The air is cooler here, he

thought. But the change in temperature didn't last five minutes. The heat intensified everything around him, making him
think that his progression was toward a more significant kind
of heat, even though he was traveling north and was surrounded by forest. He longed for a coastal seabreeze, tall ice-
filled drinks made with rum or gin, and someone to understand him. But he found no solace in the thought. The remainder of his trip back to the county seat was spent in ungodly
heat which had turned his black sedan into a furnace.

EIGHTEEN

1909

When Agnes heard from a family friend employed at Worthing Mills that Samuel Worthing's son hadn't been seen for almost two days, she left the office immediately. She didn't wait for Crawford to return because she saw this as something that couldn't be put off. As the paper's deliveryman drove Agnes south toward the town, she thought that Crawford would be angry with them for not waiting but knew it might be hours before he returned. She was anxious to prove herself. If she could uncover something of value, he would be impressed and might agree to hire her permanently once out of high school. She held the blond hair away from her seventeen-year-old eyes. She knew that Worthing hadn't been in the county for more than a month. The developments at Worthing Mills had been of interest to her throughout high school. She had met old Sam Worthing and his wife and had witnessed their burials. She watched incredulously as the son arrived and attempted to exhume his father's corpse. Now he had disappeared, and as far as anyone knew he hadn't returned to Maine or been called elsewhere on unexpected business.

She hoped her impetuous behavior would benefit her. As she rode, her thoughts retraced all of the facts that Crawford would call relevant. Worthing's son was accepted by the community. There had been no layoffs, but rumors had been circulating. Business wasn't as good as it had been when his father was alive. Many thought the paper mill was in danger of being closed. The attempt to remove his father's body hadn't been met with approval, although most viewed this as part of a vendetta by the son's mother. When he failed there was a sigh of relief, and the matter was forgotten. It was said that he feared his mother, and to appease her he sent an empty coffin to Maine. Agnes had no proof but liked to believe that it was true. She saw the action as a partial victory for a son who was reportedly only a weak reflection of his father. Agnes had decided that Beatrice's husband couldn't be blamed for leaving her and becoming a bigamist. But his son was another question. His business acumen was in doubt. People wondered if he would be clever enough to keep the entire Worthing Mills complex in operation.

They parked on the main street near the business manager's office. She knew Mr. Sooy's daughter and thought he would be a good starting point. Ordinarily, she wouldn't have approached Sooy or any other person of his importance, but as a reporter she felt that access to people was a right guaranteed by the nature of the profession.

"Agnes. What brings you to town?" he asked when she entered his office.

"I'm working for the paper now."

"Oh." His body stiffened.

"I'm here about Mr. Worthing."

"Senior or Junior?"

She frowned. She didn't want to be treated as anything less than a reporter.

"You're the second person today."

"Who else has been here?"

"Patrick Nichols."

She let the corners of her mouth fall.

"What's wrong?" Sooy said.

"Did he have any information?" Agnes asked, ignoring Sooy's question.

"Just what I told him. As far as I can see, there isn't much more available."

"I'd like to know as well."

"For the paper?"

"When was he last seen?" She removed a small notebook from her purse as she spoke.

"Two days ago, just after lunch."

"Where?"

"The garden."

"By whom?"

"Martin Kelly."

"Is this Kelly available?" Agnes asked.

"He's working in town."

"Is there anything else?"

"Well, Worthing came to me a couple of days ago. He had received a telegram from his mother. This was after his attempt to remove Sam's casket."

She nodded.

"Beatrice Worthing had another idea. She wanted her son to destroy the statue of Elizabeth. She wanted to eliminate everything associated with her, but that's beside the point. I told Mr. Worthing that the best man for the job was Martin Kelly."

"What was to be done?"

"Mrs. Worthing wanted the statue disposed of. Kelly came by the office to pick up his orders, and I told him to go over to the mansion and see Mr. Worthing."

"And he did?"

"Yes." Sooy moved a few papers to a corner of his desk.

"And the statue?"

"Martin said he spoke with Worthing and was told to come back at two o'clock with the truck, sledgehammer, chains—everything to do the job. When he returned at two o'clock, Worthing was in the garden reading the newspaper. Kelly destroyed the statue, loaded it on the truck, and left."

"Worthing was still in the garden?"

"Yes."

"Did Kelly notice anything unusual about him? Did he say anything? Give him any sign that something was wrong?"

"Not that he saw."

Agnes let a small stream of air escape through her teeth. She wasn't uncovering anything of value. Nichols was already snooping around. All of this would be common knowledge before long. Her only option was to find Kelly and pray for a lead.

"You said that Kelly is around town?"

"He's working behind the mansion."

"All right."

"Maybe he'll say something that I didn't pick up—you being a reporter now."

"Yes." She replaced her notebook.

"Agnes."

She looked up from her purse.

"Good luck."

She walked toward the mansion and noticed that some of the tenant houses had lost their well-cared-for appearance. Several yards were overgrown with grass. She crossed the green lawn that bordered the mansion wall. Before she passed through the gate, Nichols appeared on the front porch of the house. They met just inside the wall.

"Miss Lippincott." He lifted his hat slightly.

"Detective," Agnes replied with the same sarcasm that she heard in his voice.

"Out chasing the Jersey Devil again?"

She hesitated and then said, "No, I think I've found him."

He smirked.

"I'm surprised that Crawford lets you out of the office alone." Nichols smiled. "A young lady shouldn't be out on her own tracking down dangerous criminals. You never know when that Hoodle Doodle's going to swoop down and..."

"Mr. Crawford sent me because I can handle the assignment."

"Is that so. My mother always said that young ladies should get married and raise a family."

"I wasn't aware that you had a mother."

He smirked again.

"Mr. Nichols, you're not proposing to me?"

"If you're looking for Martin Kelly, he's in the garden behind the house."

"Why would I be looking for him?"

"Because you spoke to Sooy, and he told you that Kelly was the last person to see Worthing."

Agnes didn't like Nichols and she didn't care if he knew it. She felt he was arrogant and wanted to control everyone around him. She knew that he hated the thought of not being informed of every piece of news, gossip, and scandal in the county. Unfortunately, he will be around for many years, she thought. Many important people in the county seat were very impressed with his performance. With their support, his position was guaranteed. And if she planned on working in the area, Agnes knew she must make an attempt to tolerate him.

"Did he have anything interesting to say?"

"He didn't have much to offer."

She folded her arms, waiting for his next sentence, but he simply returned her gaze.

"Do you want to tell me exactly what he said, or should I speak to him personally?" she finally asked.

"I don't usually share information. Crawford will tell you that. But just this once I will. Kelly only had one thing to say actually. He was working in the garden and saw Worthing reading. He left after he finished the job."

"The statue?"

"It's gone."

"Nothing more?"

"No," Nichols said curtly.

"Is he a suspect?"

"I wasn't aware that a crime had been committed."

"Did he speak to Worthing?"

He shook his head and started to walk away.

"Good day, Miss Lippincott." He touched his hat. "And remember what I said about my mother."

Agnes still wanted to speak with Kelly. She didn't trust Nichols, although she had no reason beyond his arrogance for feeling this way. Intuition was what she attributed it to but wouldn't admit it, at least not professionally.

Kelly was removing weeds that were growing along the base of the garden wall. His back was facing Agnes when she approached him.

"Mr. Kelly."

He flinched and said, "My God, girl!"

"I'm sorry." She extended her hand. "I'm Agnes Lippincott and I work for the newspaper."

"I'm not interested in a subscription," he said.

"I'm not selling subscriptions."

He looked at her, puzzled by her presence.

"I'm a reporter."

"You don't say?"

"I'd like to ask you about Mr. Worthing."

The skin around his eyes tightened; then he said, "Don't know a lot."

"You were the last person to see him."

"That's what they tell me."

"I spoke to Mr. Nichols, and he said that you were breaking apart Elizabeth Worthing's statue while Mr. Worthing was reading the paper."

"That's right. Over on the far side there."

"Was he here when you finished?"

"I think so."

"You didn't notice?"

"I don't recall the last time I glanced over there. I don't remember if I looked when I was leaving for the final time or when I was nearly finished."

"Why?" Agnes was persistent.

"I'm not in the habit of being nosey. I leave that to women and reporters."

She didn't like the insinuation and wanted to say something, but she stopped and remembered what Crawford had told her—stay calm.

"That's all I know, missy." He turned away from her toward his work.

Before leaving the town, Agnes visited Mrs. O'Malley, who had retired the year Worthing died. Afterwards, she worked for Elizabeth Worthing on special occasions until Elizabeth's death. Samuel Worthing had given her a small house to live in because of the years spent with the family. From the second-floor sewing room, Agnes could see Kelly working in the garden.

"And what did he have to say?"

"Nothing really, just that he was working on the statue."

"A disgrace that is."

"The statue?"

"That woman was a saint. She loved Mr. Worthing and he loved her. It was a present."

"Beatrice Worthing wanted it removed."

"You'd think her son would have put an end to that foolishness." Lucy O'Malley was angry.

"The woman is bitter."

"The woman is filled with hate. After so many years. Mr. Worthing had no love in his heart for her the day he arrived and even less than that on the day he died." She made the sign of the cross.

"It's gone now," Agnes said, watching Kelly through the pine boughs.

"Do you know anything about Kelly?"

"He's a troublemaker. He lives in a cabin outside of town, and people say that he throws his garbage outside. They say its piled against the walls."

"Why a troublemaker?"

"Lazy. He's always roaming around the fields and bogs joking with the females."

"That's all?"

"Drinks."

"No problems with the police?"

"Not that I know of. But I did hear that he was involved with the I.R.B. back home."

"But nothing here?"

"No."

"I ran into the glorious Detective Nichols a few minutes ago."

"What did his excellency have to say?" the older woman said, examining her needlework.

"Nothing really. He said that Kelly saw Worthing last and that he didn't know anything more."

"I thought that was probably Nichols. Could tell by the tone of his voice, even though I couldn't hear a word of their conversation. I came up here at the same time Nichols entered the garden, what I could see of him that is. I didn't have my good glasses with me. I misplaced them yesterday. But I watched what I could see for a few minutes; then I left the room to get my scissors. When I came back, he was still talking to Kelly. At one point, he waved his arms in the air."

"How long was he there?"

"I sat down and started this. Ten minutes later I got up to stretch my legs, and he was just leaving."

"Was he mad?"

"I couldn't say, not without my glasses, although he wasn't waving his arms anymore."

"So he talked to Kelly for more than fifteen minutes?"

"I'd say closer to twenty minutes."

"It probably doesn't mean anything." She turned away from the window. "Nichols isn't the type to reveal everything. What he said to me was an edited version, I'm sure. It's unlikely that they were arguing. Nichols was probably testing Kelly, thinking he knew something. Maybe Kelly was being hard-nosed with him." Agnes drew her conclusion with the same words she thought Crawford would have used.

"Possibly."

When Agnes entered the office, her boss was playing with a stack of papers on his desk. He didn't seem to be upset, but when she sat at her desk he kept his eyes lowered.

"I'm sorry, Mr. Crawford."

"About what?"

"Going without you. And telling Shinn that it would be okay."

"I would have liked to come."

"I couldn't wait.'

"That's a good sign."

"Good?"

"Curiosity," he answered. "Without it you can't be a reporter."

"You're not mad?"

"Of course I am. This could be big. Who knows what might develop." He grinned.

She was relieved.

"What did you find out?"

She told him about Martin Kelly and the destruction of

Elizabeth Worthing's statue. She mentioned the slight discrepancy between what Nichols had told her and what she had discovered in Lucy O'Malley's sewing room.

"What do you think?"

"I'm not sure that it means anything. Actually, I doubt it really. Kelly has worked for the Worthings since Sam bought the town. If there had been a crime committed, Nichols would be the first one to want his picture in the paper. If Kelly was involved, Nichols would have thrown him in jail. He wouldn't miss a chance to stand in the limelight, especially so soon after the disappearance."

"You're right."

Crawford placed his feet on one corner of his desk.

"What do you want me to do?"

"Since you left me behind, I guess that means you should stick with it. Try to find out if Worthing was seeing a woman or if he has done this sort of vanishing act before—in Maine or wherever."

NINETEEN

1937

Kate watched the boys playing in the yard. Andy had climbed a mulberry tree and was shouting to his brother on the ground below. Will stepped back and circled. His brother was hardly visible in the green-black shadows of the branches. Andy shouted again, wanting Will to climb the tree, but the younger boy refused.

Earlier, Agnes had shown her Will's discovery. She mentioned that Andy thought the head looked like her and said she agreed. But Kate wasn't convinced and didn't see any resemblance at that moment. As she followed the boys' movements, however, something clicked. She saw it. The similarity was there. Before, when their parents left, she went upstairs with the boys to look once more. Andy was certain about the likeness which Kate now saw more readily. She didn't realize that those few minutes in front of the stone face had swayed her. It was as if a fuse was burning slowly inside her. As she stood to call the boys, she willingly acknowledged it.

She caught her reflection in a mirror and saw, in the dwindling light of dusk, that it was true. She lifted her chin, assuming the haughty angle of Elizabeth's pose. The deepening light accentuated her most prominent features. She drew her thick brown hair into a bun. Her face was almost lost in the increasing darkness. She switched on a light and let her hair fall, thinking how ridiculous she must look. Me and a thousand other women in the county, she thought. Agnes looked more like her, and Sarah Haines could be her daughter, she decided.

Outside, Andy was still in the tree. Will was throwing stones at him. She called to them, telling Will to stop and both of them to come in. They protested but knew that their mother wanted them inside not too long after dark. Andy clambered down out of the gloom to meet a final stone thrown by Will. It struck him on the thigh, and he chased his brother into the house.

They listened to the radio for an hour as the town was engulfed by the humid night. When they happened to glance away from the living room through the screen door, they could see individual lights through the trees. The town was quiet except for the periodic cry of a baby and the ever-present sounds of the woods. The program ended and it was time for bed, but they weren't ready to sleep. Kate wasn't surprised when they asked for a story. She had stayed with them for years and had watched them grow. When Kate was younger, she imagined that she would have a family some day. She enjoyed being with children and always looked forward to watching the Johnson boys. Kate had known Agnes and Paul before their children were born and felt as if she were part of the family. She remembered Agnes when she was pregnant with Will. Her pregnancy had been a difficult one, and Kate spent weeks living in the Johnson house, caring for Andy and Paul.

At the library Kate catered to the visiting school children, answering their questions, hovering over them and directing their work and interests like a concerned mother. As she grew older, motherhood seemed to move away from her. There were no eligible or desirable bachelors in her life. Her love for Andy and Will grew stronger, almost as strong as a mother's love for her own children. It was true that they were rambunctious at times, but this only helped to endear them to her. Soon Andy would be mature enough to look after his brother when his parents weren't home. Kate knew that she would still be welcome, but she suspected that her relationship with the Johnson family would change in the near future.

Before she agreed to tell any particular story, Andy ran into the kitchen for a candle and matches and Will turned off the lights. They were at her feet on the living room floor within seconds. Andy handed the candle and matches to her.

"And what do you want to hear?"

"The Dancing Bandit."

"No, the Jersey Devil."

"What about Fiddlin' Sammy? I haven't told you that one for a long time." She lit the candle. "Is that all right?"

They agreed as they arranged themselves on the floor.

"Okay. Now be quiet. Hear that breeze blowing outside?" She looked toward the door. The yellow light illuminated one side of her face.

"I hear frogs."

"And crickets and a baby."

"You're not listening hard enough."

The wind blew gently. One of the trees creaked, and a branch scraped the roof.

The boys didn't speak.

Then the wind swelled with one lengthy crescendo. Tree limbs rattled and the house responded with a shudder. A door slammed upstairs.

"It was a night just like this. The wind was blowing, but not very hard. Every once in a while, it stirred for a minute and sent shivers down your spine. You could hear, if you listened closely, the dead calling. They're out there now, calling to us from the lake and the graveyard where it's black as tar.

"Sammy Giberson was over at the New Gretna Inn. You know how Fiddlin' Sammy was always looking for excitement. Well, on this particular evening Billy Denn was at the very same inn. The two of them decided to have a contest. Now if you know anything about Fiddlin' Sammy, this wasn't unusual. He loved contests and this night was no exception. Billy Denn played his fiddle and Sammy danced. Then Sammy played and Billy took his turn on the floor. They were drinking applejack but didn't get the palsy. Each time the fiddle changed hands, the playing and the dancing got better. This went on for hours. Everyone thought that the contest would end in a draw, but Billy Denn started to weaken. He was a few years older than Sammy and couldn't drink as much. Finally, after the dancing became too fast and wild, Billy quit. He was tired. He conceded that Sammy had won. When Sammy heard this he said, 'I'm so good I could beat the Devil himself.'

"Later that night Sammy was walking home. He couldn't see ten feet in the darkness. After traveling several miles, he sat down on a gnarled windfall to rest. He could hear the wind shifting and getting stronger. All the trees in the Pines seemed to bend and groan at the same instant. He looked down the road and saw a man standing at the edge of the blackness. 'Who are you?' he shouted. 'Who are you?' the stranger replied. 'I'm Sam Giberson.' 'I understand you think that you can beat me fiddling.' 'What's your name mister?' Sammy asked, fearing that he might be in trouble. 'I'm the Devil and you'd better start playing, or you'll be coming with me. I'll name the song and you'd better know it.' The man stepped toward Sammy, blocking the road with his huge body. Sammy could see horns protruding from his head. He reached for his fiddle and began to play the tune requested by the Devil. Sammy realized that if he lost the contest the Devil would take his soul. When he finished, it was the Devil's turn. Sammy named a song and the Devil played it. The whole forest sang with the Devil's notes. Fiddlin' Sam wasn't one to be intimidated though. Back and forth they went. Each tune was finer than the last and more rare. But Sam matched the Devil song for song, note for note.

"This went on until the sky started to lighten. The Devil wasn't about to stay around through the day, so he asked Sammy to play a song that hadn't been heard for a century. It was an obscure tune and the Devil didn't think Sammy had heard of it, but he had. While Sammy played the piece, an idea popped into his mind. He would trick the Devil and win the contest. When Sammy finished the piece, his turn to name the next song came. He said, 'Play me the Air Tune.' The Devil stared at him and couldn't believe the request. He had never heard the Air Tune. He hissed and hollered and stomped around the road. Then he asked to hear it. Fiddlin' Sammy performed the Air Tune for the Devil and with that he won the contest. Of course, the reason the Devil had never heard the song was because Sammy had invented it right there on the spot. Each note he played was pulled directly from the air.

"The Devil agreed to make Sammy the best fiddler in the Pines. He granted him a magical power. After that night, Sammy could make the fiddle sound like two musicians playing at the same time. People said that it was the Devil playing a duet with Sammy Giberson, and everyone said that Sammy had sold his soul to the Devil to become the best player in the Pines."

The boys fidgeted for a second.

"Did you know him?" Will asked.

"No," she answered, laughing.

"What about the Bandit?"

"Yeah, let's hear about the Bandit."

"You mean old Joe Mulliner. There's not much to say about him. His gang roamed the Pines during the Revolution."

"But what about his ghost?"

"You both know he was an Englishman who robbed people and burned their houses to the ground. He wore a sword and carried a brace of pistols. Some folks say he was missing an ear. Others swear that he was missing a hand. But everyone agrees that he was a bloodthirsty murderer and a robber. They say that in one night he robbed and killed twenty-seven people. I'm not sure if I believe that, but I know he was a wicked man.

"He had one unusual weakness though—he liked to dance. Whenever he heard music, all his ideas of robbing and murdering went out the window. He would go into the tavern or house where the music was being played and dance all night with the prettiest girl there. Once the authorities figured this out, they set a trap for Joe Mulliner. They waited outside of a local jug tavern where music was played every night. Eventually, Joe Mulliner appeared with his men, and they were ambushed. Several of his men were killed, but Joe Mulliner and three others survived. They were tried and hanged. People came from miles around to witness his execution. Some of the prettiest girls in the Pines wore black after his death. They say many girls who danced with the Bandit fell in love with the man, and their hearts couldn't forget him.

"This is where the frightening part enters the story. Joe Mulliner loved to roam the banks of the Mullica looking for unsuspecting victims. When you're out at night, especially down on the Mullica, be careful. Some people claim they've heard a galloping horse and wild laughter behind them when they're hurrying through the woods to get home. The noises would get closer and closer until they thought the horse would trample them. They jumped out of the way only to see darkness pass them and the noise fade in the distance. But it wasn't the horse or the laughter that was bad. It was the air. Even in the middle of the summer when it was steaming hot, the air was ice cold, like death. They say that it's the air from his grave, and if you breathe it you'll drop dead right where he passes you. Just last year I heard of a young boy who breathed the air when Mulliner rode by. When the commotion started behind them his father warned, 'Hold your breath.' The boy didn't listen, and they buried him the next day."

"God," Will exclaimed.

The candle flame grew brighter; then it shrank in size until the room seemed to consist of only a chair, table, and three people huddled together.

"One more," Andy pleaded as if the variation in light increased his desire to hear more.

"Yeah. The Jersey Devil."

"Yeah."

"Well?"

"Just one more," Andy said looking up at Kate's face. "Just one, Miss Harris."

"Okay." She leaned forward. "But I don't want any complaints after this. You two have to go to bed. You know what happens if Sam Worthing or his son comes around and finds boys still awake when they should be asleep?"

Will slid his finger across his throat.

"That's right. You know they keep an eye on the town and when something wrong happens they..."

The wind roared again. The boys tensed for a moment as the frogs and crickets grew louder. The candle flickered once; then the flame disappeared. Kate ignored the lack of light.

"Now. The Jersey Devil. It was way back in the early part of the 1700's. Mrs. Leeds, who had twelve children, was in the process of having another, and she wasn't happy about it. She cursed the unborn baby and its father and said that the Devil should take it. She didn't want anything to do with the child. When the baby was born it was a boy, and the midwife gave him to Mrs. Leeds to hold.

"It was midnight and a great storm had blown in off the ocean. Thunder and lightening crashed outside. Rain and hail came down so hard that the roof sounded like it would fall under the pressure.

"As soon as Mrs. Leeds touched her son, he began to change. First his head stretched to the shape of a horse's head, and his soft pink skin turned leathery. Then bristles of stiff hair appeared. Instead of having teeth like a baby or a horse even, he grew long, pointed fangs. His body started to grow, and within a minute he was bigger than a man. His feet turned into hooves and his hands became claws. Enormous bat wings sprouted on his back. A long forked tail grew from him and began to flail around the room, striking the screaming women. Then the beast went up the chimney and out into the night sky.

"The thunder boomed outside. Rain pelted his wings in torrents. Hail the size of oranges rolled off his back like grains of sand. Each time lightening came, you could see his hideous shape against the rain clouds. But he wasn't afraid. The Devil loves bad weather because it scares people, and when people are afraid that's when he can do the most mischief. He flew over the Pines and suddenly his stomach growled. He was hungry. He looked down into the trees and saw a house with a light on. His body grew rigid, and he swooped down the chimney into the lighted room. Two boys were inside, awake. Their mother and father didn't know it. They thought the boys were in bed, asleep. In one big gulp, the Jersey Devil ate both of them. They didn't even have time to scream. They were gone in a second, and so was the Devil. He scrambled up the chimney and back into the night."

"Have you ever seen him?"

"No. But I saw some tracks when I was a little girl. Someone said they were his prints in the woods."

"Was it him?"

"Half the state thought so. It was in 1909 or 1910. I don't remember exactly. They said he was out looking for something to eat."

"Boys?"

"And girls and cows and dogs and parents. Anything and everything that had red blood."

"God," Will said.

TWENTY

1990

The valet drove Lou's car to the line of vehicles waiting to enter the garage, and the two men stood facing the casino's entrance. Will was impressed by the opulence of the building. His hand automatically brushed the front of his poplin jacket, smoothing its wrinkles. A few blocks before the Boardwalk the town had started its transformation. The derelict buildings were gone. Garbage didn't overflow onto the streets. People no longer stood in the gaping mouths of musty doorways. Within a block of the ocean, the change was complete. The forlorn desolation of the other areas seemed inconsequential, especially for the people who swiftly passed through it in locked automobiles or casino buses. Men and women paraded in and out of the entrance as if they were dignitaries.

The Boardwalk, which fronted most of the casinos, was filled with hotdog stands, T-shirt emporiums, bars, and novelty shops. Junkies huddled in small groups, scheming about the night's rich victims. Hookers strutted under the watchful eyes of their pimps and the tourists. Panhandlers looked for their next free meal or bottle. Pieces of paper blew lazily down the wooden walkway. Music blared from five or six locations. Will could hear the thump and rattle of amusement rides located on a distant pier. Below the Boardwalk, the ocean pounded the beach, depositing everything from medical waste to raw sewage to large chunks of styrofoam on the sand. This is theatre, Will thought. Pure entertainment. Luxury cars were crowded along a separate section of curb. He imagined how hectic the weekend traffic must be as he glanced at an arriving limousine.

The canoe drifted near the shore and the road that topped the sluice. They heard the cars before they reached the bridge and watched with anticipation for them to break free of the pitch pines.

"I hear a Packard," Andy said. "And what sounds like an Auburn."

Will listened carefully. Peepers filled the air behind them with high, bell-like ringing.

"There's another one," he said. "Sounds like a Ford."

His brother agreed just as the cars came into view. The first was a Packard, but the next two were Fords.

"Not too bad," he said, complimenting himself. Andy leaned back and let his hand fall complacently into the buoyant water. "When I'm finished school, I'm going to travel around the world and drive race cars."

"That would be swell."

"And dangerous. But that's okay because I'll be ready for it. When I get older, maybe I'll come back here and live."

"Let's hit the bathroom and do a couple of lines," Lou said as they entered the lobby.

Will followed him, seeing that he was familiar with the building's floor plan. People crammed every inch of the space, and Lou weaved his way through them. The clanging of slot machines permeated everything.

"A lot of folks with money to burn."

"There's always someone with money, my man, and there's always somebody who will take it."

"Some of these people don't look like they can afford it. And what about those kids?" Will commented after noticing a man and child who looked destitute.

"If they didn't have money they wouldn't be allowed in the building. Look at you. You fit in just fine."

"What about welfare checks?"

"The casino finds a way to cash them if the customer has an account."

They entered the men's room. Will was paranoid, thinking that someone might know what they were doing. He considered the headline and found the idea amusing in the circuslike atmosphere that surrounded him. Lou gave him a small vial.

"Go into the stall and snort this motherfucker."

"What about you?"

"Don't worry about Daddy," Lou said, holding another container close to his chest. "I've got three times as much as you." He smiled. "We're going to kill them out there man, absolutely murder them. You know?" He sniffled. "Slammin'."

When they emerged, Will was higher than he had ever been. He didn't have the spins like he would with liquor and found within his condition firm ground. He recognized the sensations and imagined he knew what to expect. He felt like singing, and as he traced Lou's footsteps he bumped into several gamblers, but it didn't matter. Music pushed above the garbled noise of the building.

"We going to Albert Hall?"

"What?"

"The music?"

"That's the lounge band," he said as they crossed an open hallway bordering the room.

"Do they play any country?"

"I don't think so, my man." Lou turned to face him but continued to walk. "You're high, dude." He laughed. "We have things to do. Have you ever played the wheel?"

"Roulette?"

"Yeah."

"At the fire hall. We have a charity night once a year."

"Far fucking out." Lou straightened his glasses. "So you're ready?"

"Damn right."

The casino was directly before them. Its floor was constructed six feet lower than where they walked. The walls and carpet were red except for the mirrors that appeared at regular intervals on the ceiling. A thousand overhead lights cast a tarnished gleam in cylindrical shafts on the players and tables. A layer of foglike smoke hung above their heads and reflected some of the light.

"Jesus," Will said as they stepped down to the casino floor.

"They have skeeter smoke in this place? Outside, martins are just as good."

"What in the hell are you saying now?"

"Pine chips and charcoal. You can burn it inside to keep the mosquitoes out."

"There ain't no mosquitoes in here, man. You're really zapped, dude. Toasted."

"What about the smoke?"

They passed the slot machines and their constant ringing made Will's head ache. A woman wearing a low-cut dress strided by. He could see most of her breasts as they bobbed freely above and under the sheer fabric.

"Jesus," he mumbled again.

The Wainwright girls entered the lake last. Both of the Jenkins' boys called to them, claiming that the water was warm. It was growing dark, and the two pleading heads in the water began to lose their definition. Finally, the two girls removed their clothing and rushed in. He and his brother watched from the protection of the woods, twenty-five feet from the water.

"It's about time, ladies," one of the heads said from the water.

"I thought you two liked to swim."

The girls splashed the boys and giggled, trying to make them avert their eyes.

"We do but not at this time of the evening and without our bathing suits," one of the girls answered.

"And not with naked men," her sister added.

"Is there any other way?"

"There's lots of ways," one of the girls said coyly.

"Andy..."

"Be quiet," his brother whispered.

The four started to swim toward the center of the lake. When they stopped, their features were beyond the boys' perception. Will thought their heads looked like ducks in the distance. A whippoorwill called in the empty space and was quickly followed by the whonk of a tree frog.

"Next time, I'm leaving you home."

"Why?"

"When we're spying on people, you have to keep your friggin' mouth shut. If they heard you, we'd be in trouble by now."

"What are they doing out there?"

"What do you think?"

"I don't know."

"You sure can be dumb sometimes," Andy said as he strained to see the swimmers.

"Let's get some chips," Lou said over his shoulder. "Do you want to play the twenty-five dollar tables?"

"Lead the way," Will remarked, taking his eyes from a woman, but finding another immediately. "You decide."

They passed between two long rows of blackjack tables. People crowded around each table, their numbers determined by which tables were hot and how much was being won. Two or three gamblers passed between the lucky tables, chips in their hands, ready to place bets. Then Will and Lou reached the roulette tables, their playing surfaces creating lines of wood, felt, and brass boundaries that stretched to the rear wall of the casino. Surrounded by the whirl of spinning wheels, the anxious and the curious paced the carpeted aisle.

The cars arrived for nearly an hour. He counted thirty-two and lost interest. He had never seen so many beautifully dressed people. The women's gowns created a radiant aura around their bodies. He thought that it would take a year's wages to buy one of their dresses then realized that the women wearing them didn't worry about money. Their escorts wore bible-black tuxedos as they whisked the women through the side gate and into the receiving line.

The mansion had been specially decorated for the birthday celebration which would be Olivia Jenkins' last. She was the final link in the line of resident owners, even though she was only a part-time occupant of the mansion. After her death, the house would be ignominiously carved into apartments then destroyed by fire.

"Place your bets," the croupier said as the men approached two empty seats at the roulette table.

The wheelroller held the ball on the back track as the chips were placed on the table. The pit boss stalked behind the rectangular group of tables. The ball was flipped clockwise around the track.

"Place your bets," the croupier repeated.

Lou quickly put fifty dollars in chips on the first column, then scattered more chips on a variety of numbers. Will hurriedly put twenty-five dollars on number twenty-six.

"No more bets please." The croupier placed an open hand above the table.

The ball fell from the back track and bounced erratically on the canoes for a moment, then stopped.

"Twenty-six, black," the man said.

The marker was placed on Will's chips and the remaining bets, if not winners, were swept away. His winnings were counted.

"What luck," Lou said, placing another hundred dollars in chips on the table. "I'll bet you can't do it again." He put an extra fifty dollars on number six. "Why don't you bet a column or square, or odd/even. You won't hit a straight bet back-to-back."

"I have a feeling about number eight," Will said, placing fifty dollars on it. "Number eight," he repeated to himself. He watched the other players frantically drop chips on the felt, covering most of the table.

"I guess you should go with it then, dude."

The ball spun wildly around the track again and landed on Will's number.

"All right," Lou said. "That's another one. Seventeen hundred and fifty dollars, my man."

Will watched the chips being stacked. His head still hurt. He blinked, trying to focus on his winnings. The green table seemed to be alive and breathing.

"I'll bet you fifty that you can't do that again."

"I think I'm hot, Lou."

"You're hot? Here's fifty bucks that says, no way."

"You're on, dude," Will said enthusiastically, knowing it was nearly impossible, but reason was beyond his grasp. He searched the table for the winning number.

161

"Place your bets."

Lou dropped chips around the table, looking for his first win.

"You're what they call a high-roller," Will said lightly, but the other man didn't smile. "I'm going to play twenty-six again." He put fifty dollars on the square.

"Man, you're not going to hit again. Give it up."

"I've got this feeling—it's Piney Power, my man."

"No more bets please."

The ball jumped around the wheel when it fell from the back track.

"Twenty-five, red."

"Yes," Will said, springing from his seat, his eyes filled with a kaleidoscope of colors.

"You blew it, dude," Lou said. "Chill out." He slapped him on the small of his back.

"Yes!" Will said again. His brain was moving faster than the roulette wheel had. "Goddamned son of a bitch!" he shouted. "I'm..." He stopped. As his eyes refocused he realized that people at the surrounding tables were looking at him. The pit boss approached the table as Will returned to his seat.

"You missed it, man. You know? He said twenty-five, not twenty-six."

Will glanced at the table and saw his bet was gone. Nothing was being stacked before him in his favor. The pit boss glared at him.

"Damn," he muttered under his breath.

"Where's my fifty?" Lou asked. You're one unlucky dude," he said as Will placed the chips next to him. "And my luck is about to change."

They continued to play and accepted several drinks from the scantily clad waitress who circulated between the tables. Lou was losing heavily, and Will was startled to see the amount of money he pulled from his pockets. He mentioned a credit line at one point and left his seat. A minute later he returned with a thousand dollars in chips. Will's luck turned mediocre for the next hour and his winnings began to slip from him. The thrill of the earlier hours had vanished. For each win, he had to lose ten or eleven times. He suspected his dream of a new truck would slowly evaporate until it was nothing more than a bittersweet memory.

"I'm going to play that black eight again."

"Do it, man. One of us has to walk with something."

Will placed fifty dollars on the number and held his breath as the ball hummed on the track. He knew that he wasn't a natural at the table and didn't believe in wasting money, but the fever of the moment combined with the drugs and alcohol overwhelmed any sensible inclination to stop. I am, he thought, playing with their money. When the ball rested, it was on number eight.

"Fuckin' A, man." Lou pounded on the railing with both hands.

Will looked at the chips being counted. He couldn't believe it but refrained from leaping from his chair.

"It's about time," he said, pulling the chips together. "It's about time."

Two women sat in vacant chairs flanking the men. Lou observed the woman next to him as she placed a meager stack of chips on the table. He elbowed Will.

"Look at this babe."

"What about this one?" Will said, cocking his head toward the woman next to him.

Lou glanced over the top of his sunglasses.

"Not bad."

"Let's see you do it again. I'll bet you one hundred bucks this time. You can't possibly do it. There's just no fucking way."

"You're on," Will said. "I'm getting a message, dude." He held two hundred dollars in chips against his forehead. "Lucky thirteen," he said. "It's lucky thirteen."

"You've lost it now, man. No way. Kiss it goodbye."

"Place your bets."

Will piled his chips on the number with authority.

The woman next to him put twenty-five dollars on a square that included thirteen and said, "I think you're a winner."

Will vaguely recalled a similar line from an old movie.

The ball seemed to hang on the back track for minutes

163

after the wheelroller let it loose. Will followed it until his eyes clouded. He gulped a mouthful of whiskey down before the ball halted.

"Thirteen, black."

Will sprang to his feet again. The room moved away from him for a second, and the lights dimmed. His knees felt as if they were going to break.

"Yes!" he screamed as seven thousand dollars in chips were counted. "I'm the King!" He raised his hands over his head and did a shuffle in front of his chair. "I'm the King, the King of the Pineys." He grabbed Lou's arm. "There's no doubt about it," he said jubilantly. "I'm the King of the damned Pineys. The King!"

TWENTY-ONE

1937

Agnes sat between her sons in the canoe as they paddled upstream. They stayed close to the shore, avoiding most of the river's current and the beaver lodge that interrupted the contour of the other bank. Trees grew in a tangled abundance around them and were occasionally punctuated by stands of white cedar. A turtle tumbled off a partially submerged log and broke the water with a sudden, brief plop. Along the bank a break in the cover revealed a savanna filled with tussocks and short red maples.

The air was calm but foreshadowed rain. She closed her eyes and listened to the paddles as they struck the stained water. On the opposite shore, which was less than ninety feet away, a pair of crows argued, but Agnes didn't open her eyes to look. Her mind was set on what might happen.

Since Elizabeth Worthing had reappeared in her home, Agnes tossed half-remembered facts around in her brain, trying to find a new connection, a clue that would unravel things for her, but nothing came. Samuel Worthing's son remained a victim of time, lost to her as well as his silent family. His fate was just as mysterious now as on the day of his disappearance. But the question remained. For years she had wondered what had happened to him, but her musings weren't intense or thorough. Nothing definite was known about his disappearance. Her sporadic interest had made absolutely no difference. There was a report in 1910 that he had been seen in Boston, but it was never substantiated. Beyond this not a word was heard, except for the persistent rumor that he had run off with a woman. With the discovery of the head, Agnes' imagination had been aroused. She pored over her collection of material, and when nothing new emerged she decided to take a look around the area where her son had found Elizabeth's head.

The dense snarl along the far bank thinned. A swampy patch of bottom filled with sedge and ferns appeared. The boys directed the canoe across the river and around a jog. They stopped in front of a dry spong that flooded with each hard rain. The canoe sat in a quiet pool where the water was dark under the ashen sky.

"This is it."

She glanced into the water and was discouraged by its color.

"Do you want us to go in?"

"No." Her eyes followed the bank. "Did you go over there?"

Andy shook his head as he paddled the canoe toward the unexplored bank. Agnes' hand slipped down to the handle of the shovel beside her. The canoe eased near the shore until a dull grinding sound rose from beneath them. Will leaped out and steadied the boat as Andy found the bottom with his paddle.

"Let's take a look," Agnes said.

Once on shore, they walked around for a few minutes. The boys kicked the ground, finding it pliant. Pieces of turf covered with green moss broke loose. Insects appeared.

"What are we looking for?"

"Oh, I don't know." Agnes rested one hand on her hip and bit her lip. "Anything that looks out of place, I guess. Anything unusual."

They moved closer to the spong. The area behind the junction with the river opened into a triangular savanna which wasn't totally visible from the river. An old, rotting corduroy road followed the periphery of the savanna until it reached the spong.

"Did you know that was here?" She pointed at the road.

"No," Andy said. "We probably could get the truck back here."

They crossed the spong, which gave out under their feet, and walked several yards on the road as it paralleled the depression.

"Looks like it went to the bank at one time," Agnes said without enthusiasm.

They returned to the river, and the ground became more waterlogged. A large mud-filled hole was on their left. One side of it had eaten its way into the river. Agnes poked the ground with her shovel.

"Let's try to find something." She edged around the hole. "Don't you boys get too close to this. I don't know how deep it is."

Will continued to kick soil away from the top of the ground. He walked to the river's edge. A badly rusted strip of metal protruded from the sand. He pried it loose and ran back to his mother with it.

"I've found something."

Andy crowded around them, then said, "It's only an old, rusty barrel hoop."

"Everything's important." Agnes patted Will's head and accepted it. "What do you think?" She looked at a disinterested Andy.

"Let's look a little more," he said, not wanting to disappoint her.

The boys moved back toward the river. Agnes followed the circumference of the hole until she stood on a thin strip of ground between the river, the spong, and the hole's edge. Rushes grew there in a segregated clump. She leaned on the shovel and batted the insects from her face. The sky had darkened and looked as if rain would fall from it without any more warning.

Agnes considered their chances of finding something of importance and decided that they would continue to look regardless of the approaching rain and the odds. She gazed into the hole, thinking that it could be thirty feet deep. The collapsed side had exposed a small section of wall that had been undermined by erosion. She studied the soil and pushed it around with the shovel blade. A small piece of shell or stone appeared. She positioned the shovel next to it, but it didn't move. She sank to her knees and reached for the greyish brown object. When it was free, she was startled to see that the piece of shell or stone was another piece of the statue—a partially destroyed hand.

"Andy! Will!"

The boys appeared at her side before the sound of her voice died.

"Is it a bone?" Will asked.

"No, sweetheart. It's from the statue."

"Here's another piece," Will said as he stooped to pull it from the mud. He handed it to his mother.

"This is a bone," Agnes remarked as she held it near her face.

"Probably from a goat. Crazy Bozarth must have a hundred of them on his place. They get lost back here sometimes," Andy said, looking closely at the fragment which his mother turned in her hand.

"I think you're right," Agnes responded. She examined the object for a moment. Her heart was pounding. "We should look around the rim of this hole. Get yourselves sticks so you can sink them into the muck." She turned the marble and bone in her hands, then placed them on the ground.

They worked for an hour but found nothing. Will was disappointed. His fear of a few days ago had turned into a delightful anticipation. Adventure was in the wind. He wanted to participate in a great discovery and when his mother said she was ready to leave, he objected, thinking that a minute more would allow them the time needed to uncover something important.

The trip back to town seemed longer than their journey into the woods, even though they floated downstream and the current pushed them toward their destination. Rain began to fall, creating thousands of sky-filled dimples on the river. Their shoulders grew dark with moisture. Agnes turned her collar up and slouched low between the gunwhales. At every bend and twist in the river, an opaque gauze of moisture hung before them. But this didn't prevent Agnes from considering the possible significance of their trip.

The boys were anxious to know if what they found had

any meaning. They foresaw bragging to their friends, especially the Wescoats, and thought that their names might appear in the newspaper. If the bone happened to be human and not from one of Bozarth's goats, they were certain that the person had been killed by New York gangsters. They started to ask their mother questions before they reached town. She purposely avoided answering them because she knew that any indication of foul play, especially related to the town in any way, would create a combination of fear and excitement in them which would be infectious. Before the day ended, the entire town would know about their trip that morning. She made them promise to be silent until they knew more. They agreed but she could see that it was given grudgingly and with disappointment.

The only certainty that existed was that they had found specific parts of the statue in the same location. Nothing pointed toward Worthing unless the location of the head was taken into account, and it had been suggested that the head had been moved. If coincidence didn't play a role in the location and the bone was not what remained of a long dead goat, other possibilities existed. A few of them terrified her.

When she telephoned Anse MacFarland, she avoided any contact with other county officials because she didn't trust most of them. He wasn't expected in his office until early afternoon. She left her name and telephone number with the secretary but no message except, "Call me. It's important." They were childhood friends and had attended high school together. In her opinion, he was the best sheriff the county had ever had. If something was amiss, he would devote his department to it until an answer was found.

The remainder of the morning passed slowly. The boys were playing down the street at the Wescoat house. She reminded them before they left to keep quiet about the morning's activities. Her husband was at work. The rain had ended only minutes after it began, and she was alone. The house needed cleaning, but she couldn't pull herself away from the kitchen table. She shuffled through her notes and ran her finger along the freshly cleaned marble. She had read each article and comment so many times that she found herself parroting the words before her eyes saw them.

Earlier, just after the boys had left, she decided to carry Elizabeth's head downstairs. She struggled with its weight and nearly dropped it on the stairs. She scraped her hand on the newel and blood swelled to the surface of her skin. Finally, she rolled the head onto the kitchen table. It gazed at her from the other side of the surface as she sorted through her papers one last time.

All of the available pieces were before her. If a crime had been committed, motivation was a problem. What did anyone have to gain by harming Worthing? His family owned the town. The estate battle had been fought and won. Mismanagement of company money, embezzlement, and blackmail were ruled out, although she couldn't say conclusively that they were beyond the realm of possibility. Revenge or jealousy could be elements worth considering, but he was the only son and his stepmother didn't have any close relatives. The town was essentially the same as when his father owned it except for its finances. A few of the employees had feared layoffs, but none had occurred. Robbery couldn't be ruled out, but what could be gained? The company paid well. An outsider could have been involved, someone who didn't stand to lose anything, but no one was seen in town on the day. His disappearance and her murder could have been connected, but how?

Agnes stopped and realized that she was letting her imagination get ahead of the known facts. She had to wait for MacFarland's call. With his help, she hoped that a solution would be found.

His call came early in the afternoon. Following an initial exchange of greetings—they hadn't seen each other for over a year—he asked about the importance of her earlier message. He was aware that she had been involved with the newspaper and had investigated the disappearance. For most of the county's residents, that was part of a forgotten past, but MacFarland knew that Agnes had never truly forgotten. He hadn't heard about Will's discovery, but the news didn't impress him. And finding another piece of the statue didn't alter his opinion. His interest warmed when she mentioned the bone, but he warned her not to rush to conclusions. He doubted the piece of bone was of any significance, especially in an area frequented by Bozarth's goats. And finding parts of the statue wasn't important because it was common knowledge that the destroyed statue was dumped into the river. The boys had merely stumbled onto the spot. His voice suggested calmly that the mystery, her mystery, wasn't one. Worthing had been seen with a woman, he said. The family didn't approve of her so he left them behind. But MacFarland would make a trip to the town to see everything. If anything proved to be more than he anticipated, he would want to see the place where all of the items were found. He promised to make it to Worthing Mills by seven o'clock that evening which would give them enough time before dark to look around. If they uncovered any evidence, he promised he'd be back at dawn with more men.

When Agnes hung up, her hopes were deflated. Anse MacFarland had always been a man who could defuse excitement. Speculation without a solid foundation of facts was worthless to him. She looked at the stone face and thought her enthusiasm had made a fool of her.

TWENTY-TWO

1889

Elizabeth noticed Zauber before he reached the house. From the open gate of the garden, she could see across the narrow lane and onto the main street. A telegram had arrived a week before stating he would be there on Sunday. He was a day late. By early Sunday evening, her husband was convinced that he had changed his mind and that an unforeseen problem had prevented his arrival. By late Sunday evening, Worthing was positive that they would never see him again, thinking that the advance sent to him was sufficient to move the man and whatever entourage he had to another city. He called him a charlatan, not because he was sure of it, but because a charlatan was easier to dismiss.

Again, Zauber was draped in a robe. He carried a bedroll and two rope-connected flour sacks filled with food and his belongings. He didn't appear to see the children who scurried in front of him or the houses lining both sides of the street. No questions were asked by him, although several women gathered in their yards to watch him. As he moved closer to the house, he saw Elizabeth standing in the garden. His eyes seemed to drop into the same hypnotic gaze used during his performances.

"Mrs. Worthing," he said when he reached her.

"Hello," she responded.

"This is marvelous."

"Yes, the garden is beautiful, isn't it?"

"Not only the garden, the whole village." He waved his hand around, gesturing theatrically in the air. "And you, if I may say so, the most beautiful."

"Thank you," she said, purposely using the tone she would with an employee. "We weren't expecting you since no word was received about your change in plans."

"My change in plans?"

"Sunday?"

"Oh, you know how things happen. Monday is just as good as Sunday." His face broadened, revealing his white teeth.

"Well..."

"Obviously, I haven't missed the person whom I most wanted to see because she's standing here in front of me." He bowed and gestured again with his hand.

"Unfortunately, my husband is not," Elizabeth added, implying with the tone of her voice that his friendliness was premature. "He has gone to look at a parcel of land and won't be back until this evening."

"So we must survive without his company, at least for a short while. What do you suggest?" Zauber gazed at the long grape arbor that covered the walkway leading to the rear of the house.

"Have you eaten? I could have something prepared. Or maybe you'd like to rest?"

"Rest?" His voice was distracted. He walked away from her toward a niche in the garden created by plantings and the brick wall. "I don't think I'm hungry at the moment," he said without turning to face her. "I would like to rest though. I am very tired."

He is an attractive although unkempt man, Elizabeth thought, but his manners are those of an eccentric. Every move he makes is unpredictable, as if he's working within a different sphere of order, she concluded, then said, "Mr. Zauber?"

He stopped in front of the niche and pronounced, "So this is the place." He looked at the ground and released a breath that deflated his appearance. He seemed to be several inches shorter. "It will stand here?"

Elizabeth was startled by the comment because it referred

to what her husband had discussed with her that morning. Her birthday was approaching, and he wanted to give her something extraordinary. Without her knowledge, he had managed to commission a prominent Italian sculptor, living in New York City, to create a life-sized statue of her. It would be placed in the garden niche. She was delighted. It was rare for such an artist to come to the Pines. What confounded Elizabeth was Zauber's knowledge of it. She thought that her husband was the only other person aware of the arrangements. She suspected that Zauber knew the man and had been to New York recently. Even with this doubtful connection, she didn't understand how he could know the exact spot in the garden where the statue would be placed. She respected his clairvoyant powers, but this revelation astounded her.

"Yes," she finally answered. "That is the place."

Zauber looked away from her and back to the area where he stood. His placid face became clouded and disoriented.

"Mrs...," he gasped once and his eyes rolled back. "Mrs. Worthing..." He bent over and wrapped his arms around his stomach. The color left his face, and by the time she reached him he had fallen. She knelt beside him, hoping to help him, but he was unconscious.

Zauber seemed to be lost. A physician was called, but he was unable to revive him. He feared the man was falling into a coma and said that there was nothing to do but pray. Modern medicine was at a loss.

When Worthing returned he was surprised that the spiritualist (this was what he had finally decided to call him) had arrived and was astonished to learn from his wife, as she led him upstairs, that he had collapsed. Zauber showed no signs of fever or unsteady pulse. It seemed to everyone that he was asleep and wouldn't wake until rested. The physician had even suggested narcolepsy, but couldn't be certain.

"Could his condition be due to drug use?" he asked after several perplexed grunts and a thought about Samuel Worthing's fondness for coca wine.

"I don't know," Elizabeth answered. "We've only known the man for a short time."

"Then anything is possible."

So they waited. There was nothing they could do, nothing that would improve his condition. For many hours, a noticeable pall hung over their conversations, reflecting a deadening of interest for the moment in each other's daily activities. Their guest had a disruptive influence on the household. The normally cheerful atmosphere turned sullen.

Even the land at which Worthing had looked received only a passing comment. The three thousand acre tract of mixed meadow, cedar swamp, bog, and pine forest would increase the size of Worthing Mills considerably and allow the company to mine more cedar for shingles—the West Indies' market was profitable and insatiable—as well as supply wood and charcoal for the town.

But the vigil which the Worthings were compelled to keep prevented the excitement usually attached to such important transactions. It was odd because Zauber was a virtual stranger to them. They knew little about his background and had hoped to find out more during his visit—a visit precipitated ironically by Elizabeth's desire to have him speak. The outcome was a guest in one of the bedrooms who wasn't even conscious. Elizabeth, unlike her husband, wasn't upset by the inconvenience.

The state in which she found herself during this period was unusual for her because she experienced a strong compulsion to care for the stricken man as if he were a family member. She felt what she thought was compassion for Zauber. It was true that he was an eccentric, although an ingratiating one, and persisted in presenting himself with an air of aloofness. Eventually, she decided that it was his beliefs and the intensity of his faith which fired her sympathy. She could have easily let one of the maids take care of him. But it was his very presence along with her interest in his welfare that brought her to his bedside.

On Wednesday morning his condition hadn't changed. Worthing decided that someone who knew him should be contacted. The logical starting point was the pier manager who had booked him to speak in Atlantic City. When Worthing set out that morning to make his rounds, he planned on sending word to the manager. He felt responsible for Zauber and didn't want him to die before an attempt was made to locate his family.

Once alone, Elizabeth mounted the stairs to the guest room. She could hear what she thought was his voice, but when she entered the room Mrs. O'Malley was standing next to his bed.

"Was he calling out?"

"No, missus. Not a word."

"I thought I heard him."

"No." Mrs. O'Malley stopped and rearranged the sheet so that it rested on his chest. "I wish there was something we could do for the poor soul."

"I know."

"Maybe this is the beginning of the end of his problems."

"Let's pray not, if you're saying he's going to die."

Mrs. O'Malley sat by his side and touched his hand. It was cold and there was no response. Both women remained silent for a moment, wondering if consciousness would return.

"I think he's going to leave us, missus."

"Don't say that Lucy."

"I can't think of anything else to do for him. I've even made loud noises, thinking he'd be able to hear them."

"Dr. Newbold said that we couldn't help him, only wait."

"I know, but I don't like feeling so helpless. I've heard of people hanging on for years like this."

"Lucy." She stepped closer to the bed. "Mr. Worthing is going to contact a man in Atlantic City. Maybe we can locate someone who knows if he has family in this country." She studied him for a second. "Granted he's unconscious, but he certainly looks like he's only sleeping."

"He's a handsome man, in a strange way."

"Yes."

"But I wouldn't want him seeing any of mine, if you know what I mean. There's something in his face that tells me he can be cruel. He's threatening—that's what he is—threatening."

Elizabeth could hear her but didn't search for the word to answer. She stared at his face, trying to find a sign that he would recover.

"The first day I saw him I said to myself he could be a mean one. I don't know if I could trust him, but he might be hard to deny. He looks like he could get you to believe anything."

Elizabeth continued to watch closely and saw nothing, although she imagined that there was a sound distinct from the other woman's rambling voice.

"Elizabeth."

She didn't answer because she doubted her own mind.

"Listen."

"And I think that he's addicted to a drug or cursed maybe. No one drops off like that. One minute he's wide awake..."

"It hurts. I feel the man...the statue..."

Elizabeth leaned forward. His eyes were closed as tightly as his mouth.

"Elizabeth."

"Lucy. Do you hear that?"

"Pardon, missus?"

"Can you hear his voice?" Elizabeth touched his lips with one finger.

"No, missus."

"I heard something," she said anxiously.

Lucy O'Malley looked carefully at the man who was as still as the floor beneath her feet. She shook her head.

"He's out cold."

Elizabeth regained her composure. "It must have been me. He hasn't moved?"

"No."

They focused on the prone body for a minute as the rumblings of a busy household came up the stairway and into the room.

"I'd better get about my business if I'm going to finish anything today." Lucy O'Malley crossed the room and paused at the door. "If you need me I'll be in the pantry."

"Fine."

She closed the door behind her leaving Elizabeth alone.

Elizabeth couldn't be certain that she had heard his voice.

With Mrs. O'Malley talking, the voice appeared to come out of her words like the sympathetic strings of a musical instrument. She sat quietly. Zauber was about thirty and was, as Lucy O'Malley suggested, handsome in a threatening way. She waited for twenty minutes, hoping to hear something and suspecting it would be inchoate at best. She considered what she thought he had said. It didn't make any sense to her. The statue was the subject, or was it? She noted the jugular pulsating on his neck. She was tempted to shake him but resisted.

After spending nearly an hour in silence, Elizabeth stood. She had several appointments that afternoon including one with an architect who was the designer of the opera house and another with two ladies who were interested in starting a weekly paper for the town and surrounding area. She straightened her dress and turned away from the bed.

"Elizabeth."

She froze, afraid that any sudden movement would end the sound.

"Elizabeth."

She moved carefully back to the bed, her dress rustling slightly. She wanted to speak but restrained herself.

"I..." The voice was hoarse but his mouth was rigid. "I can't..."

Silence. She grabbed his arm, pulling it free of the sheet, thinking that the motion would rekindle his ability to produce words.

"Mr. Zauber, Mr. Zauber!" Elizabeth finally exclaimed as she dropped to the edge of the bed. She needed more, some clue to understand what he had said before and what he was trying to tell her now. She recalled his seizures in the city and how nearly all of his words made little sense. A feeling of futility struck her as she waited and anxiously observed his face. But nothing came.

1909

He sat in the cab facing the rear of the garden. He put the truck into gear and it moved forward. The chains tightened. The vehicle paused, then inched ahead once more and the statue came off its pedestal. There was a pointed, short noise and then a thump. He didn't move because it didn't seem that he could; he merely sat with the engine running.

Suddenly, there was no garden or truck. Everything lost definition. Sound was muffled. He looked over the hood and thought he saw the distant outline of the Blackstair.

He walked along the Barrow with her. It was spring in Ireland. The rock-strewn river shimmered as it tumbled toward the sea. The sun was so brilliant that her hair was filled with strands of golden light. The irises were blooming yellow along the low marshy banks. They walked toward the town but had no intention of reaching it. They talked. He called to the cows that struggled to reach the spring grass through the pasture fence. Above them rose the Blackstair: dark, wrapped in flowing shadows, rocks, grass, and nothing more. Sheep moved lazily down one flank. He noticed a red figure gingerly following. The sound of the river brought him back to her.

"Mary," he said embracing her.

"I can't bear it."

"I don't know what else to do."

"There's no other way?"

"Quinn says not."

She broke from him, looked at the river and then at the stone steeple of the church that stood above the high crown of the hilly pasture.

"When things quiet down here and I make a bit of money I'll..."

"Don't say it because if you do I'll spend the rest of my days waiting. We should say goodbye, and if you decide to send for me I'll be pleased. But this way I won't be counting on you, and you won't feel that I'm waiting."

They started to walk again, not knowing what else to say. They reached a lockhouse. Carey wasn't there. His ducks waddled around the building and crossed their path. A cloud blocked the sun for a moment. The rich greens of the countryside grew somber.

"Why did you do it?"

"For Ireland."

"But why persist? The English don't seem to be budging."

"One day."

"We'll be dead and buried by then," Mary said sadly.

"That's possible."

"They think you killed those two officers."

"Let them think what they like."

"If they catch you..."

"But they won't. I've already sent a message to my sister and her husband. They'll be expecting me."

Mary knew that she would never see him again and tried to rid herself of the idea. This isn't anything unusual, she thought. Young men want to free the land of the English, and they only succeed in freeing themselves of the land—either by death or exile. The English match our stubbornness with their own adamant position. They refuse to leave. She didn't know the answer. She didn't want them in Ireland but would sacrifice that if he didn't have to go.

"It's impossible."

"What?"

"Everything, the whole damned situation."

He knew she loved him, and he told himself that he loved her and would send for her.

When they could see the bridge spanning the Barrow, they turned. Most of the town sat on one side of the river and was surrounded by sloping fields. They could hear the bleating of sheep. A fish broke the surface of the water. Its sound was quickly covered by the rushing current.

"I'll be going tonight. O'Farley will be taking me down to Cork."

"And from there?"

Straight to America, I think. That's if there's no trouble. O'Farley doesn't expect any."

"There's been enough."

He lifted his eyes and said, "You're right. Enough."

"So we have this afternoon?"

They started back on the same tow path. Their backs were to the mountains now. They became taciturn and each kept their own fearful thoughts to themselves. Mary saw the end: the finality of their relationship emerging from that very moment. The river, the trees, the occasional bird, flower, and cow meant the same terminable thing. She realized that he was leaving her but wouldn't totally accept it because the thought frightened her. It was a final loss of love, a defeat which wouldn't be easy to overcome.

He wondered what the next day would bring and tried to imagine what America would be like. He found that his thoughts of a new land and a new life obfuscated his concerns for the woman walking beside him. Absence, he suddenly thought, will make me forget not remember.

By the time they passed the lockhouse, a silent, unspoken agreement had been reached between them. There would be no promise beyond what had already been said. The future would find them together or not. Uncertainty would rule. They faced too many obstacles. Without this problem, they would have married and possibly drifted apart. Rather than waiting they would be apart in the beginning, and they thought that by way of a circle fate might bring them together again.

They made love that afternoon. It was their first time together in a bed. The fear of interruption was gone. Before they had employed the furtive practice of the young: meeting wherever privacy was available without regard for comfort or weather. Now, above their impassioned sighs and sweat, there hung a sadness—forlorn but without remorse. Their love-making was the last act of their relationship.

"Mary," he whispered. "Mary."

The engine was still running. He heard Worthing's voice and raised his hand. He turned the motor off, and the cessation of sound was followed immediately by the sound of a hammer breaking stone. He twisted in the seat and saw Worthing swinging the sledge. He got out of the truck and stepped toward him.

"You've decided to end your nap I see."

He watched Worthing as he finished the swing.

"Don't do that, sir," he said, noticing the severed head near the rear of the truck.

"You're ready to take over then?" Worthing stopped.

"No, sir."

"What do you mean?"

"I think we should end this."

"What?"

"She was...she was a good woman."

He raised the hammer again. Worthing wouldn't admit that he was right because principle had entered into the situation. He was an employee.

"Stand back man. If you won't do it I will," Worthing insisted.

"Don't." The other man grabbed the hammer's handle before it came down.

"I said stand back!"

"Don't, damn it!" He had both hands on the handle and tried to wrest it away from Worthing.

Worthing looked at the other man's hands, not knowing if he could resist his upper body strength. Each man held his ground for a moment. Then Worthing fell under the other's force. His elbow struck the truck bed, causing him to spin slightly as he fell. His head hit a piece of the statue with a crack. After that Worthing didn't move.

The other man watched him fall and strike the marble as if Worthing had choreographed the motion. The cracking sound startled him and the thought of an egg dropping to the floor entered his mind immediately. When Worthing didn't stir, he knelt next to him.

"Sir."

Nothing.

"Mr. Worthing." He slid his hand under the man's head. He was bleeding and a soft substance oozed from the wound. "Sir." He put his ear to his chest. Nothing could be heard. "My God." He looked up. Everything was quiet. No one was in the garden or directly behind the mansion. His eyes scanned the windows, and he didn't see anyone. With one instinctive movement, Worthing was in the truck and under the tarp. "God help me," he said in a low voice as he looked at the remains of the statue. Nichols will have to help me, he thought. Nichols owes me.

He worked quickly, lifting the smaller pieces onto the bed. He broke the larger sections, not thinking about his attempt to stop Worthing from doing the same only minutes before. If he stopped to consider what had happened, he knew that his self-control would disintegrate. So he methodically finished the job. When the statue was loaded and the tarp was fastened, he drove the truck through the rear gate. Once outside, he got out of the cab to gaze back into the garden. No one was there.

The truck moved along the river, heading toward the sinkhole. Occasionally, through the brush, he could see the water moving with a dead silence. Black gum created a mesh along the far bank. He didn't see the otter slip into the river as the vehicle passed or the egrets standing in a shallow brackish pool surrounded by curly fern. The sugar sand was deep, and he had to drive with two tires in the roadside underbrush to keep the truck free. The bumper flattened leatherleaf as it dragged against the undercarriage. Within twenty minutes, he reached the place that now seemed to be synonymous with his fractured life.

He dropped the pieces of the statue into the sinkhole.

When her head was in his hands, he paused and decided to throw it into the river. He carried it to the bank and pushed it away from his chest. The river sent a stream of water upward when the head disappeared beneath its surface. He wrapped the body with a few pieces of marble in the tarp and dumped it into the hole. Numbness overcame him as it sank from sight. His world and the life he lived had been shattered again. His fresh start in America hadn't helped him find the promised future but only the pit so often mentioned in his childhood catechism. He wished he had never left Ireland.

The first sign of the town was the swath cut into the forest. It formed a gigantic ring around Worthing Mills. Samuel Worthing had created the clear cut in the early 1890's in an attempt to protect his enterprise from the frequent fires. Just inside this ring, he had constructed a number of water towers which served the town as well as fires on both sides of the cut's perimeter. He felt his heart sink as he drove down the main street past the paper mill and mansion. He feared discovery and didn't relish the thought of revealing the accident to Nichols. He wanted to turn his back on the town and disappear. This was a comforting idea. The unknown was preferable. He thought about Mary and how she would have prevented all of this from happening, but Mary was gone.

1937

Zauber walked away from the institution the morning after Will Johnson made his discovery. Twenty-eight years had passed since he had been removed from the world. His appearance hadn't changed, except for the color of his hair and the deep lines that formed a web around his eyes and mouth. Until now he had accepted his unjust misfortune with stoicism, although not with total submission. Legally, he had had no recourse and remained confined, according to the laws of the state. But he had always combated the situation with his remaining spiritual strength. And this afforded him some comfort.

The night before he had a dream—what at one time he would have declared a vision. That was when he still spoke. Words, he had found, especially in his predicament, weren't necessary. Along with his decision not to speak came a complete halting of the powers which had flowed through him without control or prompting when he was young. During his years of confinement, he lost all hope that any of these powers would return.

But on the preceding night, this changed. Elizabeth came to him and said the identity of her murderer would be revealed to him. There was no indication that revenge was her motive, but Zauber felt it necessary. He was a bitter man. Any hope for a life beyond his confinement had vanished. His still copious physical energy was unharnessed until that moment. Now he would flee the institution and become her avenger.

The vision had startled him. He was tired and sat in his customary chair. An assortment of people ambled through the ward; all of them were ignored by him. He looked at an invisible point fixed in space just in front of the wall. The doctors had determined that he was a manic-depressive, but he found no use for labels. My loss, he thought, is more than most men could bear. He wanted to be alone with his misery. His interest in the outside world was gone. When she whispered to him, he recognized the voice. He had dropped into a light sleep, something that he did several times a day. It was a good way to temporarily escape his condition. For a millisecond, he thought it was a voice from the room finding its way to his dreamless brain. But within the same second, his mind opened and Elizabeth stood before him.

As she spoke, memories returned to him. It seemed to him that the past had faded from the reality of his existence. His mind dwelled there with less frequency each year. Now it returned with a definitive cohesion. He didn't have to struggle for the thread; it simply attached itself and enveloped him in its cocoon.

Long ago, when he first arrived in America, he was without employment. He wandered from city to city, worked occasionally, and earned enough money to feed and clothe himself, but nothing more. He was restless then, and this peripatetic lifestyle suited him. As a young boy, he had been a particularly devout Christian. He studied the Bible and planned on being a missionary. He lived with an uncle who decided to move to America. During the passage his uncle died, a victim of a ruptured appendix, leaving Zauber with a letter of introduction and a small amount of money. The promise of employment, guaranteed in the letter, didn't materialize. His search for work failed and he thought he was destined to live a vagabond's life.

Two years passed and his prospects were worse than when he had entered the country. He succeeded in finding a job as a laborer with a traveling circus. One of the sideshow performers was a self-proclaimed mystic called "The All-Seeing One." To amuse himself, Zauber would watch the man perform and try to guess the correct answers to questions posed by the audience for "The All-Seeing One." One evening he discovered that he could answer most of the questions—sometimes before they were asked. The personal lives of various audience members leaped into his consciousness. He informed "The All-Seeing One" and was invited to become his protégé, his apprentice in the divining arts. Within six months, his teacher succumbed to alcohol, and Zauber was his natural successor.

Fortunately, he had learned many tricks from the man, and these aided him in becoming his equal. After a year, he abandoned most of them because he found they weren't necessary. His power had increased, and chicanery wasn't required. Other performers in the side show said he was in possession of what was called the gift. He cultivated the look of a mystic or how he imagined one might appear. His cape came from "The All-Seeing One's" wardrobe. He allowed his beard and hair to grow until they reached his chest and shoulders. His eyes assumed an hypnotic quality. His touch had the ability to cure people of their ailments. Then Zauber saw that a connection existed between his newly found powers and his childhood studies. Like an evangelist, he started to formulate theories about the condition of the world and how people lived. His performances became laced with philosophy.

Not much time passed before he decided to leave the circus and establish himself as a main attraction, an attraction which was more attuned to religion, philosophy, and mysticism rather than entertainment. He concentrated his efforts on large cities and popular resort areas and promoted his ideas with fervor. His audiences were receptive, and he was recognized as a man with an important spiritual message. He toured the country and dreamt of accomplishing something worthwhile with the money he made. His income wasn't great, but he lived like an ascetic: very little to eat or drink, clothing only to cover his body, the use of transportation other than walking only when necessary. Many thought he was more than a man of faith. A few suggested that he was a new Apostle: someone sent to prepare the nation for the Second Coming. Others exclaimed madman when his name was mentioned. All of the comments made about Zauber proved that he was reaching the people, and he relished their sundry reactions to his preaching. He vowed to embrace all mankind whether receptive or not.

And then his life changed, but not for the last time. It was during his second set of appearances in Atlantic City. Elizabeth and Samuel Worthing sat in the audience. The moment he touched Elizabeth he knew that she would bring about a change in his life. When he arrived at Worthing Mills, he realized that his time there would last for more than a day or two. As his condition worsened, he found great comfort in her presence beside his bed and thought her role in his life might be larger than he had envisioned.

When he was well enough to leave, he headed west. He needed time to think and gave only a few lectures. When he reached Texas, his powers began to slip. His concentration weakened, and his focus became tenuous. Elizabeth Worthing filled his mind. He thought the end of his life as an evangelist and mystic was near. His imagined greatness became a joke, and his final appearance proved it. He couldn't find the words; his answers were unclear; his thoughts were muddy; he was booed from the stage. He began to drink and found that intoxication offered him a taste of euphoria—something he experienced after his sudden epiphanies. So he drank more and spent every cent he had earned. He found himself begging and stealing to get money for alcohol.

He drank until he hallucinated, but his aberrations offered only one, static image. He saw himself in the desert. Someone hunted him, or at least he thought someone hunted him. So he kept moving deeper into the wasteland. He began to feel that this wasn't an imagined scene and decided its repetition was not a coincidence. There was something waiting to be discovered in the desert. He hoped that he would find his lost powers there, but whatever the outcome he had to undertake the journey. He walked south into Mexico, carrying a blanket and a canteen. His body was impervious to the harshness of the land and the weather. Many times he looked over his shoulder to see a small dot in the distance. It moved relentlessly closer. This is the end, he thought, visualizing a tortured death. Sleep became secondary. He had no food. His appearance grew more frightening as his clothes became shredded. Children scattered when he entered a town. He had become a pariah, a madman lost in the desert. His detractors wouldn't have been surprised.

Over a year passed. He had no destination, so his wandering was often circuitous. Large geometric patterns were being scrawled by him on an invisible map, and he laughed at the thought of this madness. But his laughter ceased when he noticed the black speck still moving toward him. His self-amusement turned into fear, and an acute pain attacked his abdomen. The end never seemed nearer to him.

After a week during which he had nothing to eat, he accepted some mescal and bread. His desire to drink had stopped months before, but this was the only nourishment available at a time when he needed it. In the evening, he found a cave where he could sleep. He built a fire and sat behind it facing the mouth of the chamber. To his left was an outcropping of rocks which hid a man. The wood smoke filled the air, and the unseen man coughed. Zauber leaped to his feet, holding a heavy stick in one hand.

"Who's there?"

The man coughed again. Zauber moved closer, grasping the stick in front of him for protection, even though the man was prostrate.

"Who are you?" he repeated, straining to see the man through the fragrant smoke.

The man lifted his hand. The firelight lengthened his features. He looked more like an animal than a person stretched out on the ground.

"Don't you know?"

"Should I?"

"You've been looking at me for some time now."

He hesitated, trying to see him clearly, and said, "I've never seen you before, at least not that I remember."

"Not this close."

Zauber took a step back, holding the stick tightly. He thought he should strike him. The pain returned to his gut, and he was afraid.

"I've watched you stop many times and glance at me. You always had that same pathetic look on your face."

"You're the one?"

"Yes."

"Are you Death?"

The other man was entertained and said, "Not really. No."

"Then who?"

"Does it matter?"

"Why are you following me? How did you know that I would sleep here?"

"I haven't been following you. You've been walking ahead of me." He raised up on his forearm and chuckled. "Haven't you?"

"Riddles," Zauber said, brandishing his club. "I should kill you now before you get a chance to do the same to me."

"There's no need. I'm dying. You won't see me behind you anymore." His breathing was uneven.

"What's wrong with you? Are you ill?"

He shook his head and said, "Just old and tired."

"But if you're not sick?"

"No."

"Why are you dying? You don't look that old."

"Don't be deceived. Is there ever a satisfying answer when life faces death?"

Zauber didn't respond.

"That's a safe answer, although not very stimulating. We all grow old and sometimes sick as well. But death, we know about death. When it comes, nothing profound happens. We simply accept it because there isn't an alternative, and then we die."

"I'm..."

The man coughed again. Zauber continued to stand near the fire with the stick clenched in his hands, continued to watch the smoke-clouded form before him. He was nauseous and could feel the mescal burning his stomach and intestines. He vomited into the fire and it sizzled with each release; then he fell backwards. In his last waking thought, he said goodbye to life because he was convinced that death would take him before morning.

When Zauber opened his eyes, it was daybreak. He searched the cave and found the body of a man who had been dead for at least a month. His corpse had been picked apart by animals. He looked through what remained of his clothing and found nothing that identified him. Zauber left the only pieces of identification he owned in one of the dead man's torn pockets. When he left the cave, his direction wasn't a random one. He headed north.

By the time he reached the East, years had passed since his last visit. He arrived in Atlantic City and found a temporary job working for one of the amusement companies on the Boardwalk. His return to Atlantic City was due primarily to its location and Elizabeth Worthing. New York City, Philadelphia, Baltimore, and Washington were within easy reach. He attempted to renew old acquaintances, especially those who were contributors to his past crusade to found a school which would promote his philosophy. His devout adherence to his tenets returned. Unfortunately, his powers were still lost. There was an initial shock when he approached admirers from the past. His death had been reported after the body was discovered in Mexico. They were flabbergasted but glad that he was alive. His feigned death and supposed rebirth had a profound effect on some people, just as Zauber had anticipated. Several of them contributed to his school fund, although many suspected that the money would never be used for construction of any kind. It seemed tragic, some thought, that Zauber was still trying to find his place in the world.

Money accumulated, but his account wasn't large enough to construct and subsidize more than one classroom and its students. His dream included a school that would be free, and this added to his financial plight. He contacted Elizabeth Worthing, knowing that her husband had died. His affection for her and his belief that she would play an important role in his life at some point remained intact. His desire to see her wasn't based totally on his affection for her. She was a wealthy woman who could not be easily deceived, and he discussed his plans with her openly, using her as a sounding board. He thought after their first meeting that she was mildly critical. After several meetings, he found that his affection for her was genuine and discovered that she was sympathetic to his advances, if not his plans. Their relationship intensified and his desire to possess her grew. Her inheritance was threatened. She was concerned about appearances. Their love affair floundered and recovered and floundered again. He was forced to stay in the background. At one point, many months passed without any contact. His dream for a school never seemed so distant. Her money, he realized, would guarantee success. His slowly growing fund would permit him to open his school, but the size of it would be small—nothing as grand as he had envisioned. She visited him in Atlantic City less and less frequently. He became wildly suspicious of her social commitments and feared losing her.

Suddenly, one morning, he found himself accused of her murder and in jail. Jealousy was the motive, he was told, but he refused to acknowledge the charge. His silence was viewed as aberrant behavior and an admission of guilt. He was convicted, but not of capital murder. His unusual behavior and past were seen as indications of derangement. He was confined to a mental institution. Nothing could have been less anticipated by him at that time in his life. Madness was something he had escaped and left in Mexico. He continued his silence and refused to discuss Elizabeth's death with anyone. All of his hope for the future fled when Elizabeth died. It appeared that he had nothing to live for and therefore he had nothing to say. His one surviving illusion was that providence would bring him face to face with her murderer.

Zauber walked south, staying away from towns and open fields. He moved chiefly at night and was surrounded by stillness as he moved deeper into the Pines. Certain things had changed. Some of the roads were paved and power lines stretched in all directions. Except for agriculture and an incidental sawmill, industry had disappeared. One evening he crossed a burned plain. He walked for miles, groping in the night as the blackened ground crunched under his feet. The air was saturated with the scent of fire and charcoal. His thoughts were filled with Elizabeth as he traveled over the seared plain, and she guided him toward the person who had caused so much dissolution in his life.

1990

"**L**isten man, this bimbo has been coming on to me. She's been stroking my thigh man," Lou said beneath the chatter of the table.

"So?"

"What about the one next to you? I think they're girl-friends."

"She's said a couple of things."

"Does she want to do the nasty?"

"The what?"

"Does she want it?" Lou said, emphasizing the last word.

"I don't know about that."

"Well, find out, dude. I'd like to do this one, and it would be fine it you got fucked at the same time." Lou elbowed him. "Do it, man," he added, sniffling. "I'm not winning shit here, and you're starting to lose, too."

"What should I say? I don't even know her."

"Place your bets please."

"Ask her if her friend and her would like to get out of this place and go somewheres quiet. You know? Where we can get to know each other," Lou sneered.

Will glanced at the woman next to him.

Her eyes still observed the house where she had been carried. As he aged, her looks still fascinated him. She was a reflection of a different time, a time that appealed to him. He realized that people continually made the same errors, year after year, century after century, and those errors were caused by the same desires and vices, regardless of their place in time. So he wasn't surprised to see her face next to him. Why should

*he be? Everything must be duplicated at least once, he mused.
How many variations could there be until something or someone was a mirror image of the past or at least a small part of it?
She rested in the living room now, although that would change.
Before he left, she would be carried to the river and returned to
the torpid cedar water where he had discovered her. She didn't
belong at the gun club or traveling around the country packed
in a box. She belonged in the Pines where she was as much a
part of the river, where she would rest, as each individual drop-
let of water that comprised the stream itself.*

"What's your name?"

"Tara."

"That's pretty."

"Thanks," she said warmly.

"My friend wants to know if you and your girlfriend might
like to leave and find someplace quiet where we could talk?"

"No more bets please."

She looked at Will squarely for a moment and examined
his face and its rounded contours. Then she caught the attention of her girlfriend and motioned to her.

"I think we'd like to go to the ladies' room. Would you
save our seats?"

The women left and disappeared into the throng of gamblers who cruised the open aisle looking for luck.

"I told you, Will. There's action in A.C."

"Number fourteen, red."

Will watched the chips being cleared away and said, "You
did. I won't deny that. But don't they seem a little too friendly?"

"Hey man. You're winning, or at least you were. You
know women—money draws them like flies." Lou looked
behind Will in the direction of the restrooms. "You know this
is a fast city, dude. They probably figured that they'd hook a
pair of big fish for the night. But don't be surprised if they
don't stick around after they get it. They're like sponges.
Gimme. Gimme. That kind of stuff. After they get through with
us, they'll be back on the prowl." He raised his empty glass to
catch the attention of one of the waitresses. "What about you?"

Will nodded although he couldn't see across the room

clearly. The incessant din created by the crowd and the slot machines seemed to be absorbed by the atmosphere which magnified the noise into a visible curtain. Will leaned forward for a moment, then glanced at his companion.

"Place your bets."

"You lead the way, Lou. It just seems that those two are awfully friendly. They're probably going to want something."

"No shit," the other man said sarcastically. "I didn't think they were social workers. Of course they're going to want a couple of hundred. They're whores, man, but what the fuck?"

Will halfheartedly dropped chips on the odd box as he listened.

"You've heard the story of the old Greek cook, haven't you?"

"No."

"He never married and saved most of his bread. When he got the urge to get laid—I mean a strong urge—he took a few dollars and went to the city for a weekend. He found the most beautiful whore he could and bought her."

"Place you're bets."

"On Monday when he went back to work, someone asked him about his weekend in the city. He said that he bought a woman and had spent a lot of money. The other man told him that he should get married. That way, the man said, you get your ass for free. The cook laughed and asked the man how much money his wife spent all week, knowing that it was as much as the man made. You know? When the man thought about it, he realized that his wife was twice as expensive as the whore and three times uglier."

"No more bets please."

"The cook had the pick of the litter without the responsibility. You know? When he retired, he went back to Greece with a wad of cash. The other man was still working and ten years older than the cook, but he couldn't retire because he had to support his wife."

"You're saying that we should spend the money and forget about tomorrow?"

"Fuckin' A. Let's have a good time, man."

"Number twenty-four, black." The croupier marked the winner, and the table was cleared. Someone across the casino shouted after winning at craps, but the voice quickly subsided into the blanket of sound created by the ringing slots.

The women returned just as the drinks arrived. They were beautiful and attracted the attention of the other players.

"So you're in?" Lou asked as the women sat.

"What the hell," Will said.

"Awesome man. Totally fucking awesome." Lou directed his gaze at the woman next to him. "Did you ladies reach any agreement?"

"We have two rooms a few blocks from here," she whispered.

"You're kidding," Lou said, glancing at Will. "And?"

"We'd like to entertain you two, but it will cost two hundred apiece."

"That's pretty steep for horse flesh."

"Take it or leave it," the woman said toughly.

"I don't..."

"You won't get what we've got any cheaper."

"Well...you're probably right." Lou moved closer. "What's your name?" he asked, sliding his hand under the table and onto her lap.

"Faith."

"Glad to meet you," Lou said, "fucking glad to meet you."

"Place your bets."

Will could hear the tones of the younger man's voice as he talked to the woman next to him but couldn't understand what he was saying. Tara was sitting close to him, her leg pressed against his. His attention was drawn away from Lou when he felt her fingers touch the inside of his thigh.

"How old are you?" he said, thinking as soon as the words left his mouth that they were foolish and inappropriate.

"Any age you'd like," Tara replied quickly. "What's your name?"

"Will," he said as he placed chips on the even box.

"Are you going to have a good time with us tonight?"

"That's what Lou tells me."

197

"No more bets please."

Will looked at Lou's back as he faced the other woman. He had stopped betting.

"Are you ready, Lou?"

"Yeah," he said without turning.

"I guess we're leaving," Will said to Tara.

"Number twenty-one, red."

Will finished his drink and stood, but his legs wouldn't support him.

"Are you okay?" the woman asked as Will dropped into his chair.

"No problem," he said, putting his chips in his pocket. "I have to cash in." He shook his legs under the table trying to increase their circulation. He glanced at the croupier, hesitated, then put fifty dollars beside him on the table.

"Have a nice evening," the croupier said, taking his eyes from the play of the table for a second.

Will casually saluted him as he stood a second time and walked away.

"Indian Ann, Indian Ann," he sang in a low voice, "the last Indian in the land." His voice trailed off. It's the other woman, he thought. Her skin was dark, on the ruddy side. "I don't think she's an Indian," he said aloud. "Not here, not in Atlantic City." But why not? he reconsidered. His mother had taught him the song about Indian Ann, and he tried to remember the other lines but could only find the words baskets and Shamong in his riddled mind.

Will could feel his mother's disapproving eyes on his face and thought it absurd at his age. He had always felt that he had disappointed her though, not only at that moment. The day he had left for college was an important event in her life, and the day he received his degree was marked by her confession. She wanted him to leave the Pines and make his way in the larger world. The Pines had little to offer an educated man, she had said. You must get outside. The Pines will always be here, she added. Ironically, the little that the Pines had to offer was exactly what Will wanted. She disapproved of his decision to stay, but as she grew older and saw the land being transformed, her son's decision to remain didn't appear to be as wrong. The Pines wouldn't always be there as she had once believed. Each year, another piece of forest vanished. If he had left, its passing would have gone unnoticed by him except on brief visits, probably once or twice a year. Will knew that he had destroyed his marriage and any hope of a successful career outside the forest, but he had to weigh these losses against what he had gained by staying and living a life in the Pines, the integrity of which now had been nearly destroyed. With this knowledge, he thought his daughter hadn't been as lucky, even though she had left early and lived in California. And his grandchildren, whenever they heard their mother or grandfather tell stories about the Pines, thought the place mythical and an invention of overactive adult minds.

When Will reached the cashier's window, he removed seven thousand dollars in chips from his pockets. With the additional chips he carried in his hands, his winnings totaled almost eight thousand dollars, minus the one hundred and eighty he started with. On his way out, he stopped in the bathroom and stuffed a check for seventy-three hundred dollars inside one of his boots, enough he imagined to buy another truck.

"Everything chill?" Lou said when Will rejoined them at the entrance.

"Fine." He glanced at the women. "Should we get the car?" He could hear the breaking waves coming from beyond the shine of the electric lights. The widow maker, he thought.

"I don't think we need it. The place is only down the street. Let's walk," Faith said.

The road ran perpendicular to the Boardwalk and bordered the casino on one side. The first block was bathed in a yellow incandescent glow. Traffic obstructed the street, and people moved freely and happily around the casino. Behind them the Boardwalk formed a high barrier between the road and the beach. The women talked guardedly, as if they didn't want to reveal any details about themselves. Lou filled the silence with boasts of fabulously successful nights at the roulette table. Will walked stride for stride with him as Tara clutched his arm. He wasn't sure of exactly what should be said to the woman even though he would be making love to her within minutes.

The next block wasn't as congested and well-lighted as the first. Fewer people were on the sidewalks. Two men argued at the entrance of an abandoned storefront, one pushing the other. The buildings were black, their eyes blind. The back walls of parking garages appeared at random intervals. Screeching tires could be heard as parking attendants raced through the dimly illuminated tunnels.

By the time they reached the street that divided the second block from the third, the city returned to its natural state. The surreal qualities of the casino were behind them and their magical charms had disappeared. A different magic was at work in this section of the city. The smell of urine and rotting garbage tainted the salt air. The women turned left toward a motel that stood midway along the block. A flashing sign beat the message, 'STAY AT THE CASBAH AND SAVE $$$.' Green neon palm trees framed the entrance of the U-shaped building.

"Is that it?" Lou said.

The street narrowed and an alleyway opened to their left. Will looked down it and saw a cat scurry behind a trash can. As he tried to relocate the cat, Faith broke away from Lou and took a long step forward. She reached into her purse. Will felt Tara's arm stiffen then release.

"Hey baby," Lou protested as the woman turned to face them.

"All right, assholes," Faith said, holding a pistol close to her side. "Down the alley." She gestured with the short barrel.

"What the fuck's going on?" Lou asked.

Tara backed away from Will and joined her friend.

"What's it look like, hand job?" Tara said.

Faith raised the revolver and put her thumb on the hammer. "Into it, now!"

The men took several steps into the dingy passageway. The one streetlamp was broken and its fallen particles snapped beneath their soles. Will noticed a car parked at the far end of the alley. Garbage was heaped behind a loading dock. The cat reappeared. When they turned, the women were facing them.

"Okay. Money on the ground in front of you."

They didn't respond.

"Do it!" Faith snapped firmly.

Will dug into his pockets and dropped over five hundred dollars, but Lou remained still. Will didn't doubt Faith's willingness to shoot. Evidently, Lou did.

"I said now, idiot!"

Lou didn't move.

Faith stepped in front of him and jammed the end of the barrel squarely into his crotch.

"I'll give you ten seconds, asshole, or you'll lose what little you have between those scrawny legs."

Lou's hand went into his pocket.

"Just stay cool," he said.

"Now!" the woman replied as she pushed the barrel another inch deeper.

Lou let the money fall from his hand, and Tara scrambled to collect it.

It was late in the evening and Tommy's had been crowded all night. Dunphy was tending bar and exchanging small talk with the customers. Tommy sat on the last barstool of the counter, next to the kitchen door. He let the bourbon in his glass touch his lips. He wouldn't drink more than an ounce or two the entire night. Some of the customers thought it was amusing because Tommy owned the bar and could drink as much bourbon as he liked. Others thought he stayed sober so that he could watch Dunphy and count the receipts at the end of the evening. The truth was that he liked the taste of the bourbon but didn't care for the way it felt when the liquid reached his stomach.

Just as a song ended on the jukebox a man entered, wearing a stocking over his head. He approached the bar with a rifle extended from his hip. Customers moved away from him. Someone screamed. He placed a bag on the counter in front of Dunphy.

"Put the money in it," he ordered.

201

Dunphy took the bag from the bar, backed away, and then dropped to the floor. A shotgun blasted from the end of the bar. The intruder rose from the floor and was thrown back to the wall. When a customer checked the man's pulse, it was gone. Tommy had killed him. Two men carried the body outside, and Dunphy called the State Police. Another coin was put into the jukebox, and the patrons returned to their business.

"Get your faces against the wall," Faith ordered.

Lou was nervous now. Will's face paled as he wondered what was going to happen next. He considered the options and hoped that Lou would act with him when he made his move.

"Drop your pants," Faith demanded.

"Don't shoot me. Please don't shoot me," Lou pleaded suddenly.

"Shut the fuck up and take those stupid fucking sunglasses off."

"I'm sorry. I didn't mean anything I said earlier," Lou cried as he removed his glasses. "Please..."

"The pants!"

Will undid his buckle, and his stomach soured as his pants fell.

"Please, please," Lou continued tearfully.

"Your pants, cocksucker," Faith commanded.

Lou unfastened his belt.

"Get on your knees."

"I don't want to die," Lou said as he sank to the paving.

Will followed her instructions, praying that the worst wouldn't happen. He saw that Lou would be useless if he went for her. Faith wasn't a large woman and he was confident that he could overpower her, but he was worried about Tara. Did she have a pistol? He hadn't seen one, but if she did he wouldn't have time to prevent her from using it.

"Where's the rest of it, old man?" Tara said after calculating the amount of money in her hands.

"Back at the casino," Will said, hoping that his response would satisfy her. "I had markers out."

The women exchanged glances.

"Don't fuck with us," Faith replied.

"Not with that pistol," Will countered.

"Maybe you should go back with Tara so she can check on that while I hold a gun to your idiot friend's head."

"Faith," Tara said. "I don't think...I mean there's over twelve hundred..."

"Okay," her companion snapped. "Okay."

Nothing was said for a moment. Will could hear Lou's labored breathing.

"All right then. Don't move," Faith finally said as she backed down the alley with her friend. "Don't move or..."

The women broke into a run. One of them let out a relieved yell as they reached the parked car at the opposite end of the passageway.

"Assholes," one woman yelled as they both disappeared inside the car.

The engine started and the headlights whitened the intersecting street. The taillights cast a crimson shadow behind the car onto the men's bewildered faces.

"Fucking bitches! Cunts!" Lou shouted as he pulled up his pants and chased the car.

Will raised his pants and walked behind him. He could feel the flattened check pressing against the arch of his right foot. For a moment he thought he was sober, but the alleyway moved sideways as he rejoined the other man.

"At least they didn't shoot us."

"They got my fucking money, man."

"The casino got more of it," Will reasoned.

"Whores."

"Hey, better your money than your ass. She could've killed us."

"They took my bread." Lou sniffled and took a small vial from his jacket pocket. "This is all I have with me. I'll give you some when we get back to the car, dude." He lifted the container to his nostril, released the cap and the white powder disappeared. His eyes rolled for a second.

"Now what?" Will said, wondering if the man wanted to return to the casino.

"I've had enough of this fucking dump. I've lost all my cash. Now I can't get laid. Shit, man. No pussy."

"You don't want to try your luck again? Maybe we could play craps instead," Will said, noting Lou's change in attitude.

"What fucking luck? Those bitches put an end to that. They put in the last nail. Let's get out of this hole, man. You know? We'll buy some beer, smoke some crack. I have some special weed with dust on it. You'll like that. If I fly, I can hit the bars in the burbs and get some action. I have a lot of favors out. People owe me, dude. You know?" Lou brushed his clothing off and straightened his sunglasses. "Let's bag it."

1909

Nichols arrived in Worthing Mills the morning after he received Kelly's message. When he first read it, his day was almost over; it was late afternoon and he felt no inclination to rush to Worthing Mills to speak with a man whom he controlled and disliked because of it. When the morning brought the report of Worthing's disappearance, Nichols left immediately. After speaking with Sooy, he found Kelly working behind the mansion.

"Have you heard?"

"About Worthing?"

"Any leads? Is there a witness?"

"What are you talking about?" Nichols asked.

"The missing man," Kelly said, continuing his work.

Nichols studied him and saw that something was wrong. Kelly seemed nervous although Nichols had always thought Kelly uneasy.

"Okay. Out with it."

"I know where he is." Kelly stopped and looked at the other man.

"Where?"

"With the girl."

"Girl?"

"The one from the club."

Nichols stepped toward him. He started to shake and felt a flash of heat touch his neck.

"What have you done?"

"Nothing, really."

"Kelly!"

He saw that Nichols was angry and might strike him. He considered what had happened and started to cry, not convulsively but with single tears that streaked individual paths from his eyes across his cheeks.

"Listen. Before I tell you what happened, I want you to help me. If you don't there'll be hell to pay, and you will be doing it with me," Kelly said emotionally.

In the past, Nichols had deliberated about the possibility of Kelly implicating him but felt that he could use him in the future. As long as I can manipulate him, he had thought, the man will not be a threat to me. He had already used Kelly for a variety of services, and if another difficult occasion arose he thought he would use him again. Once Kelly's usefulness ended so would his life if Nichols still felt threatened by him.

"All right," he said, finally consenting but without any conviction about his willingness to do so. "But calm down."

Kelly took a deep breath and glanced along the garden wall; then he said, "Give me a few minutes." His voice was thick and broken.

Nichols started to talk about general topics: sports, local gossip, automobiles. Ten minutes passed. The other man seemed to have checked his emotions.

"Now," Nichols said after a short pause.

"I was tearing down the statue of Mrs. Worthing, and we had a disagreement. Nothing great. I mean I didn't want it to continue and told him that it wasn't right. The thought of doing it a second time frightened me and brought back what happened. He fell and cracked his head on a section of the statue. That was the end of him. It happened so fast." Kelly coughed, forcing the phlegm in his throat to move. "I loaded the body onto the truck bed along with the rest of the statue and dumped everything into the hole." There was a cold distance in his voice.

"Christ!" Nichols said, throwing his arms in the air wildly. "You can't be serious." He turned to one side as if he would walk away. "This is too damn much. You have an argument, and the man falls and he splits his head open." He spat and tried to contain his anger. "I guess this is what they call the luck of the Irish?" he said vehemently.

Kelly didn't respond. His eyes flickered back and forth like a small, frightened animal.

"And what do you think I can do?"

"Just what I said." Kelly's voice quivered. "Unless you prefer facing the executioner and for some reason I don't think you do."

Nichols reconsidered his position. Suddenly, he questioned his ability to manage Kelly. Normally, controlling him wouldn't be a problem, but he heard the man suggest that he was willing to be a martyr as long as they both paid the price. If arrested Kelly would confess because there was nothing to lose. Kelly didn't have anything, or at least he seemed to think this in his present state of mind. The fear of being sent to prison or back to the English was outweighed by his fear for his sanity and maybe his soul. With a confession, Nichols' life would be ruined; his career would come to a inglorious end, and his name would be disgraced. He looked closely at Kelly's eyes and saw endless possibilities there, including a nervous breakdown.

"I agree," Nichols finally replied. "But you have to follow my instructions. Don't speak to anyone about this. If you do, don't say anything beyond what Sooy already knows. I spoke with him and he told me that you saw Worthing last, that you finished with the statue and left him alone in the garden. So keep it at that. Don't speculate and don't let that running Irish mouth of yours get going. I'll take care of the rest. No one will suspect you. There are no witnesses as far as I know." Nichols touched his damp face.

"I won't say a thing."

"Don't. One slip and we'll be buried under all of this."

"You don't need to worry."

"I'm going to do the normal things here. When something like this happens, especially with someone important like Worthing, procedure has to be followed. If you notice me around town asking questions don't get nervous. We need to present what looks like a normal investigation."

"All right."

Nichols noted that the other man was calmer and more self-assured. He wiped his forehead with his handkerchief.

"Have you heard anything from the foreman?"

"No."

"No questions about the girl from her people?"

"I suggested to her padrone that she ran off with a customer. He looked relieved. I know he couldn't handle her. She wasn't related to anyone there, so no one asked questions."

Nichols stuffed the handkerchief into his pocket and said, "They bought it completely. And nothing from the club?"

"No."

"Good." He started to walk away. "Remember Saturday night," he said.

The other man started to object, but Detective Nichols didn't look back.

Nichols drove slowly toward the county seat. He decided that Kelly's future was bleak. With another shift toward instability, Kelly's life would have to end. He would let Worthing's disappearance blow over and keep up the investigation for the appropriate time, then close the case. It would remain unsolved. This went against his instincts. He had arrested Zauber on a false charge, but to contrive another false solution might be dangerous, especially on the heels of the previous one.

He thought about Agnes Lippincott and how she had confronted him. He wasn't fond of reporters because of their persistent nosing around the business of the law. For a woman of her age, she was impertinent. Her determination to impress Crawford might be of use to Nichols, however. Her eagerness for information, which he could present to her as specific and truthful, might allow him to influence the reports in the county newspaper in a beneficial way. Spurious information would help him, if used properly, and hurt Agnes Lippincott as well as the newspaper's credibility. Nichols' investigations would remain his business, if he had anything to do with it.

He entered the county seat from the east. He drove out of the orchards and fields planted with peaches, corn, and tomatoes and into one of the residential sections of town. Substantial homes and large shade trees graced each side of the street. Young children played on lawns, and prams were pushed by mothers. He waved to a passing car and glanced at the ice wagon stopped at an intersection. Gradually the large homes gave way to smaller houses and churches. Corner stores started to appear. He noticed how at certain points the brick sidewalks bulged above the roots of the gigantic buttonwood trees that lined the street. A black iron fence started on his left, delineating the boundary of a graveyard whose grass and mossy headstones looked cool and tranquil. The spiked fence ran to the cemetery gate and a Quaker meetinghouse, which was perched on its unwieldy stone foundation, causing it to rise above the small corner lot and crown the top end of the business district.

Nichols turned at the intersection and parked in front of his office. He could see the monstrous, grey county jail, constructed nearly a century ago, from where his car sat. It reminded him of a dungeon inside, complete with iron rings pinned to the floor and walls. There had been discussions concerning the modernization of the structure, and he was against the very idea. That jail, he had said, is a deterrent. Change it, make it comfortable, and criminals will be standing in line to get a bed just like a hotel.

Later that day in his office he heard the church bells ring six o'clock. He stopped working and walked to the hotel restaurant diagonally opposite the meeting house. He sat at his customary table. As he ate alone he reconsidered what Sooy had told him once more, trying to uncover any clue that would lead someone to Kelly.

"I don't know what has happened to him."

"You've contacted Beatrice Worthing?"

"Yes."

"Has he done this before?"

"Never or... not that I know of."

"Have you asked around town to see if Kelly was really the last person to see him?" Nichols twisted his hat in his hands.

"He was the last as far as I can tell."

"What does that leave us with?"

"Pardon me?"

"Have there been any problems here with labor—disputes of any kind?"

"Just the everyday things."

"What about the layoffs?"

Sooy hesitated for a second then said, "Layoffs?"

"At the paper mill. A lot of men work there. I understand it's losing money."

"Nothing has been decided regarding that," Sooy said, wondering where Nichols had obtained his information.

"No ruffled feathers yet?"

"Not that I know of. Mr. and Mrs. Worthing always managed to keep things going. I think the employees at the paper mill expect his son to do the same."

"So," he mumbled vaguely. "What would I do in his place?"

"Good question."

"I'm betting that he went to Philadelphia or Atlantic City and forgot to leave word. Let's not panic for now. There's no sense in sounding alarms yet."

"It seems irregular not to do something."

"Leave that to us. We'll issue a report, and I'll see you in a few days."

"And if I hear anything, I'll let you know," Sooy said.

"Contact me directly," Nichols suggested. "And where is Kelly?"

"The mansion."

When he left the office, Nichols knew that Kelly was involved. His day-old message was folded in his pocket and as he walked his fingers crumbled it. The spectacular frame house rose above him as he rounded the first corner of the main street. He passed the company store, and an acquaintance on the porch saw him.

"Detective."

Nichols turned his pink face toward the porch.

"Hello."

"Come down to find Worthing?"

"He'll turn up."

"Probably running around with a woman." The man snickered.

"Maybe." Nichols wondered why the man had snickered. Was there a woman? he asked himself. He continued to walk, hoping that there was.

"Good luck to you," the man called when he realized Nichols wasn't interested in continuing the conversation.

The detective didn't like to discuss police business with anyone, even his own colleagues. The more mysterious his movements stayed, the more miraculous his solving of crimes remained. Keep them guessing was his credo. Without all of the facts, no one could disprove the solution. He had found this to be the best procedure, and it helped him cultivate a larger-than-life image. His quest for prominence in the county and state could only be complimented by such a persona, so he strived to maintain it.

1990

A tlantic City and its promise of one big night sank into a purple vapor as Lou and Will left the causeway and stopped at a traffic light. Darkness waited a few miles ahead. Lou passed a joint to the man next to him.

"What a fucking day!" He held his sunglasses, checking them for damage.

Will inhaled deeply.

"Taken by two whores," Lou remarked as he accepted the smoldering joint. "And to top it off, I lost at the tables. Can you believe it?" He pushed the glasses onto his birdlike nose.

"There's always the next time."

"Not for me." He held the joint between his lips.

"You're finished with the city by the sea?"

Lou waved his small hand emphatically as he attempted to hold his breath.

"No more roulette? No more babes?"

Lou exhaled and said, "No more bitches, no more casinos, only business. I collect my cash and fuck the rest. You know? I can get plenty of action without driving through the sticks for it. The only business that's going to bring me here is with Eddy T."

"Sticks?" Will questioned, looking at the over-developed strip of gas stations, motels and hamburger stands. "Where?"

"In a few miles, man. You should fucking know. Who in the hell owns it all anyway?" He coughed.

The sign read, 'Heavenly Hills Estates, For further information contact H. Jones Inc., N.Y., N.Y.' He watched from the pickup with his brother as two men tamped around its base. Behind the sign, the Plains with its five-foot-tall pygmy pines rolled for thousands of acres.

"Who would live out here, Andy?"

"I don't know. The wind whips around here like a hurricane sometimes. There's no water or shade either."

"You think somebody will be interested?"

"Probably. People from the city who have never seen the place will go for it. The guy who owns it won't ask much for an acre. City folks will think it's a steal until they come down here and take a look."

"I'd be mad."

"They will be too, but that Jones guy will be gone by then. More than likely he doesn't own the land to begin with. I'll bet it's a scam."

"Everyone has a piece. That's how it looks to me. The feds, the state and the farmers and a few corporations control most of it."

"Who in the fuck would want it?"

"A lot of people. Some want to make the Pines their mistress; others want to make it all their whore."

Lou didn't reply.

"Even a damn fool would rather be a mistress than a whore, right?"

"Yeah. Whatever."

"Ever heard of the National Reserve?"

"No."

"The Wharton Tract?"

"Don't think so."

"Wharton was a Quaker who bought over a hundred thousand acres of it. He wanted to supply Philly with water. He wanted to establish a series of reservoirs and pumping stations."

"No shit."

"There's seventeen trillion gallons of potable water in the Cohansey Aquifer, no more than thirty or forty feet below the surface."

"No shit."

"Nothing like it left in the East." Will took the last hit and burnt his fingers. "The state finally put a stop to it."

"Let me tell you something, my man. I don't mean to change the subject, but I'm not taking any more shortcuts tonight. You know? I want to get back early enough to make the bars. If we get stuck in the woods I'll be fucked for the night, and we've been fucked more than once already." Lou reached for the radio.

"Could we hold on that for now?" Will asked.

"No problem. You okay?"

"Yeah. I'm fine. My head is on backwards, but I'm fine."

"Pass me another can of beer," Lou said as he lowered his window and threw his empty outside. "We should have bought a case rather than two sixes. But I guess that will have to do."

"I don't think I can hold much more."

"You're getting old, dude. When you stop consuming, you stop living."

Will handed him a beer.

"Now take me. It's early. The night is young as they used to say. I'll drive back to my crib and check my answering machine for messages. Then I'll head out to the bars where all the good looking bitches hang out. If I see one I know, maybe I'll hit on her again. If I see somebody who owes me, I'll ask them about who's hot. Last week I was introduced to the sweetest piece of meat—big tits, nice ass—by some dude who owed me. Her name was Alisha and she could do it man, let me tell you. If I bump into her look out. She's really into coke, and she knows I'm the man who has as much as she wants. You know? If she isn't around, I'll try another piece—just like eating candy. When you find a piece you like, eat it. But if you don't like the looks or taste of it, spit it out. Variety is...what's that old saying?"

"The spice of life."

"Fuckin' A. Anyway, if Alisha ain't around I'll find another bimbo. No doubt about it. Just about every bitch in the burbs knows about me." He raised the beer can to his mouth. "Do you want to know my real secret?"

"Real?"

"Yeah. You know? Not that I have coke or weed. The real reason why I'm so well known."

"Why?"

"My cock is twelve inches long." Lou laughed. "And when a bitch hears that, she has to find out for herself."

"Bullshit."

"Hey man. I'm not lying. They call me Big Boy all over the burbs. Word travels. You know?"

"Hmm."

"So tonight I keep looking for a piece that is hot. Within a hour or two, I'll have a prime cut. And by tomorrow morning, I'll have another notch on my..."

"Why don't you have these connections in A.C.?"

"A few reasons. A lot of people down there are from out of state. If I do one, she goes back to Iowa or Ohio or someplace like that and it puts a kink in building a following and I go to A.C. to relax, do a little business maybe, but to relax and gamble or to see a fight or show. If I see something good I'll buy it, if it's for sale. That whore tonight would have paid me after I gave her a taste of Big Boy. You know? I don't want to be mobbed when I hit the town. It's better that I don't have the rep there. I wouldn't be able to blow off any steam."

"From your work?"

"Fuckin' A." He sniffled.

"But you're not going to A.C. anymore, except for business?"

"I may have spoken too quick," Lou said. "The casinos are a release. A.C. is a change of scene for me once a week. And I can tell you that I win big usually. Last month I won fifty grand."

"What did you do with it?"

"I lost it the next time I was there, but on the third trip I won most of it back. This past weekend I walked with an extra ten grand in my pocket."

"Did you invest that?"

"Fuckin' A."

"Drugs?" Will asked, knowing the answer.

"I can trust you, right?"

"Yep."

"I mean I have..."

"Nothing you tell me will leave this car."

"Yeah. But nothing that will hurt people. Weed and coke. That's it. I do quite a bit myself."

"Ever get arrested?"

"For drugs? Hell no. I'm like those rum runners. I just bring it to the man. I don't sell the shit on the streets."

"Like a smuggler. Used to do a lot of that along this coast."

"They still do, don't they?"

"Everyone has to make a living," Will remarked, finding his dislike for the man next to him growing with each passing mile.

"Fuckin' A. Do you want to know my philosophy, dude?"

"Uhh..."

"The world is our hell. If there's a God, he's making us pay for shit everyday. We live in this hell, and then we die. No one knows what happens after that. I think the reason for living in this hell is so we can get ready to stay dead forever. What else could it be? Now you have people who accept that. You know? And you have people who fight against the hell. The people who take it are the humble ones. They work their shift—nine to five—or whatever, make peanuts, have a nagging, fat wife, and pain-in-the-ass kids who grow up and spit on them. These people go through life and never fight, never try to turn the tables. They're victims but never see it. You know? And then there are the ones who refuse to accept life as it's been dealt to them. They use life and take everything they can because they hate to be pathetic victims. The idea turns their stomachs. Look at me. I have a small business, with flexible hours, and I make a ton of money—more in a few months than most fuckers make in a year. And that's what's important. Right? Bread, man. You know? Without it you're shit, but with it you can be king. I'm not saying that life doesn't kick me in the ass occasionally, but I kick it back twice as hard. I'll take everything that I can get my hands on, dude, everything that I can squeeze out of life."

"So those two tonight were only taking what they could get?" Will interjected.

Lou ignored his comment with a frown and added, "Isn't that what this country is about? Making it? That's the American dream, right?"

"The meek shall inherit the earth."

"No fucking way. The meek will get fucked, and that's the truth."

"A lot of people get screwed in this world without reason. I'll grant that," Will said.

"Being meek is reason enough. You don't need an explanation or reason besides that. You could say they deserve it. They had it coming. As long as I beat it, that's all that matters to me. I could care less about those other bastards."

Will asked himself how Lou had managed to lure him to Atlantic City. He admitted that his interest was heightened by the alcohol and other drugs. His ability to stifle his curiosity was weakened to the point of tacit consent. He had never touched an illegal drug in his life. The disappointments of the morning had obviously pushed him into the situation. He needed companionship, someone to take his mind away from his depressing predicament. To his amazement, the wish to flee his personal reality had led him to the very thing he truly wanted to avoid—the larger reality which had created his own.

"Whatever you say," Will finally offered, accepting the conclusion that an argument would be fruitless. Is this the future? he wondered and decided that it was. Lou was a new subspecies, part of a new breed. He tried to see beyond the passing veil of darkness. The gaudy strip of buildings and lights had given way to forest and cool autumn air. He saw a face dangling from a tree, then another, dangling like Christmas ornaments. He blinked and realized when they disappeared that he was hallucinating. Deer larger than draft horses crashed through the woods. Entire houses lifted from the ground as their roofs flexed at their peaks and flapped above the walls like wings. "Shit," he mumbled.

"Something wrong?"

"I'm seeing things."

Lou laughed and said, "You're fucked up. Too much stuff. The dust will do it every time."

Will sipped his beer.

"Yep, fucked up." He rested his head on the back of the seat. "What about you, Lou? Are you fucked up?"

"I'm always fucked, man. I do a pretty good job of hiding it though. Can you tell?"

"Definitely."

"It's the glasses. My eyes are redder than fire. The sunglasses hide it."

"True."

"Some people—the users that is—know what's happening. They see the glasses and say that dude knows what's chill. I'll bet he's wasted on coke or something." He sniffled. "Wired."

"I imagine they do," Will said.

Will was tired. His body was filled with substances that prodded his organs in contrary directions. His eyes burned. The other man's voice hurt his eardrums. He was anxious to reach home, but the thought of soon having to leave the town where he was born tempered his yearning. He moved his stiff legs, trying not to crush the loaf of bread that had slipped from his grocery bag next to his feet.

The car vibrated as it crossed a ribbed patch of gravel. He held his legs together and glanced at his mother as she drove. His friend's birthday party was over, and his mother had come for him. To his chagrin, she had to drive to the county seat and he was going for the ride whether he wanted to or not. Unfortunately, the five sodas he had gulped at the party had worked their way into his bladder. He didn't mention his need to relieve himself and was in pain by the time his mother finished her errand and started for home. Embarrassment grabbed at his throat, and he didn't know why. He sensed his bladder was altering its shape with each new bump. Trees stood in solitary clumps and were surrounded by open farmland. Blueberry fields began to appear. Some of them were small and occupied less than an acre; others stretched for thousands of feet along and away from the road, head high rows of dense green leaves that seemed to be more a part of the landscape than the wild scrub and cedars. One more bump, he thought and it'll come out. Then the inevitable happened. A tremendous mound threw the tires up and the car reacted with a crash. The jarring reaction banged his insides, and he felt a trickle of warm fluid run down his thigh and back into his crotch.

"Mom, could you pull over?"

"Why?"

"I have to go."

She stopped the car and watched him get out. An oval-shaped dark spot covered part of his pants.

"Will."

He hesitated and looked sheepishly at her.

"Why didn't you say something?"

"I thought I could hold it but..."

"Well, go on," she said, raising her voice. "We don't want another accident."

They drove for half an hour, and the sensation Will tried to suppress only increased its hold on him.

"I have to take a piss," Will finally said.

"Now? We're almost there."

"It'll only take a minute."

Lou whipped the car from the road and onto the shoulder. Will opened the door and stepped out.

"Thanks," he said, undoing his fly. Steam rose from the ground as the hot liquid reacted to the night air. The smell of urine mingled with the scent of dead leaves and pine needles. He noticed an unpaved road that sliced away from the asphalt only a few feet from where he stood. When he finished he turned toward the car. His door was still open and he could see that Lou was adjusting the radio. Music blasted from the speakers. Before Will reached the door, the other man hit the accelerator. Gravel flew wildly through the air as the car shot forward. Will covered his face with his hands and reeled. Cinders stung him. The tires screeched when they grabbed the paving. When he dropped his hands, Lou's taillights had started to disintegrate in the distance.

"Son of a bitch!" Will kicked the shoulder and lost his balance, hitting the damp ground with a jarring thump. "Son of a bitch," he repeated as his back reacted to the fall. Taking a deep breath, he tried to sit. His body was numb, but after two failed attempts he managed to reach an upright position. The night was cloudy and moonless. From the edge of the shoulder, he stared at the narrow sand trail that parted the trees and vanished in the darkness. He remembered that the overgrown road would lead him to the back of Worthing Mills. "It's that way or the long way," he mumbled. "Four miles, four damned miles." He had thought Lou would take him to his house because Will didn't think he could walk, didn't have any confidence in his legs' ability to carry him, but that hadn't been in Lou's plans. Eventually, Will stood and tried to find his way off the hole-filled shoulder, pushing an empty beer can away from his path with one foot, as he entered the trees.

1937

Nichols stood in the doorway of Kelly's ramshackle cabin, which was half-covered with drooping, black tarpaper and was surrounded by an assortment of garbage. In the center of the cabin's only room, Kelly sat behind a table piled with dirty dishes and open food containers. The two hadn't seen each other for nearly fifteen years. They had lived their lives, each somewhat secure with the knowledge that he held the upper hand.

"I decided to make the trip," Nichols said, glancing around the newspaper-covered walls.

"It's been a long time." Kelly stood as if he were going to offer the man his hand, but he reached for a chair. "Close the door," he said as Nichols studied the room. "Sit down." Kelly pushed the straight-backed chair toward him.

Nichols looked at Kelly as he returned to the table. He had aged, and Nichols thought Kelly would be unrecognizable to him on the street. He remembered the last time he saw him. It was in town—his town—not Worthing Mills. They didn't speak or offer any form of greeting except for a silent instant when their eyes met and said, I still know so keep your mouth shut and I'll see you in hell. Nichols wondered why he had come to the cabin but dismissed it as curiosity and an interest in protecting a fragment of his past history.

"I stopped by my office. I was down in Cape May." Nichols removed his hat. "The girl said you dropped by to chat. I had a little something to take care of in the neighborhood so here I am."

The other man had no desire to know what Nichols had

been doing in the vicinity of Worthing Mills. He had learned years ago that the detective extracted a price for any information he passed on.

"So what is it?" He looked around the room with displeasure. "Kind of rough, isn't it?"

"I make out." Kelly fell silent, knowing what he had to say would upset the other man. He had survived for years without contact with Nichols. Somehow this lack of closeness seemed to relate to his personal freedom, and he wasn't willing to risk its security now.

Nichols continued to look around the cabin.

"Well, I suppose it's okay for a Piney. You people like it this way," he added.

"They found it," Kelly blurted out as if a switch had been tripped inside him and a current had raced from his brain to his mouth. "In the river."

"What?"

"Some boys," he said, rubbing his hands together. "The Johnson boy—Will—and his friends. They found her head after all of these years." Kelly saw that he had the other man's attention. "Who knows what will happen next? This morning Agnes Johnson went up there with her sons. She was carrying a shovel when they left, and I didn't see them come back. They must have landed at a different spot."

"And the statue is in the same..."

"As the girl and Worthing. You do remember the girl?" Kelly stood, moving nervously around the table toward him.

"Shut up," Nichols said. "And sit down."

Kelly dropped into his chair behind the table.

Nichols played with the brim of his hat, seeing that Kelly feared the worst and didn't realize the impossibility of connecting him to any of the crimes.

"Nothing is going to happen. It's been too many years."

"But..."

"Shut up and give me a fucking minute to think."

"But..."

"Shut up, I said."

Retirement was the first word that entered Nichols' mind,

not what Kelly had said. The threat of an atrocious end to a brilliant career horrified him. He wanted to allay the other man's fears and even considered killing him for a second. Kelly was the only man alive who could connect him to a large segment of his marred past, but he had always taken pride in the fact that he had let him live for so many years. He had his thumb on the man, and his knowledge of Kelly's sins was his leverage. But, as he looked at him across the room, he saw that Kelly was old and desperate. Kelly's needs were few, and it appeared that he would die naturally and silently in the stench of his own obscurity. Nichols decided to placate him.

"You promised that you'd help me years ago. Don't forget I know..."

"Shut up." Nichols stretched his legs in front of him, noticing the mud caked on one of his shoes. "I think you're in the clear. Limitations come into play and time handles the rest."

"But I'm afraid she found something."

"Do you recall the exact spot?"

He replied, "I can't forget it."

"We could take a ride over there and see if everything is in order."

Kelly nodded.

"We can get back there with your truck?"

"I think so. It's probably overgrown but..."

"Good."

"I don't have to worry?"

"No. Even if Agnes Lippincott, I mean Johnson, found something, how in the hell could it matter? She's been snooping around the county for years. She's just a stupid bitch looking for a thrill."

"But what about the statue?"

"Coincidence. Do you know how many people get lost back there? Plenty. We find bodies all the time. The mob uses the place for its private morgue. They dump them; then we find them and ship the remains back to Philadelphia and New York. This will blow over. If she did find something just remember who Patrick Nichols is," he said forcefully, thinking his words would soothe the man's anxious mind and prevent him from doing anything rash, just as they had done in the past.

"You'll go with me and take a look?"

"Yes," Nichols responded, knowing that it wasn't necessary. "I'm willing. We'll go in a few hours—after the town has
quieted down. Anything for an old friend to eat?" he said dryly,
glancing at his watch. "It's almost suppertime. Do you have
any grub in this dump?' He hooked his hat on the back of the
chair. "What about a beer?"

Kelly cooked their meal, and Nichols listened to him talk.
He was amazed how much Kelly had changed. His altered
physical appearance was normal considering the years, but his
outlook on life—his philosophy about the world and his existence in it—was different. He wasn't the same man with
whom he had associated twenty or twenty-five years ago.
Kelly's memory of that time was shadowed by an intense remorse. It was as if his middle age had been lived as a testament. He had sacrificed his life, living in his isolated, decrepit
cabin and working around a dying town, for what Nichols
imagined was a higher ideal. Kelly was doing penance and
had become what Nichols could only describe as a righteous,
rather meek man. This disgusted Nichols. Kelly won't be
missed when he dies, he thought. The man is faceless at this
point.

The word reappeared in his mind—retirement. His
thoughts were of Florida and he closed his eyes. He wouldn't
let Kelly take it away from him. There would be no room for
accusations. His career must end without any problems and
preferably with a flourish. If he was threatened by the other
man, Kelly would be the first to fall.

Another possibility existed as well. If a way to solve the
one great mystery in the county could be arranged before he
retired without casting any suspicion in his direction, Nichols
would grab it. This would complete the cycle and satisfy his
dream of ending his service with another successful trip
through the labyrinth. He promised himself that this intrigu-
ing idea would remain a viable option.

After eating Kelly spent an hour listening to Nichols recite
the history of his career, beginning with the early days before

they began their association in 1909. Kelly was astonished that a man like Nichols had managed to achieve so much, some of it by illegal means, without ever having to pay for it. He thought that his own sins had been paid for, at least in part, with his suffering. His dealings with Nichols and what he represented had ended long ago. But Nichols had continued in exactly the same manner for years without sorrow or pain. He was the quintessential villain, masquerading as the epitome of justice. Nichols moved in respectable circles, circles which Kelly could only stand outside of, waiting for an order. He would retire a wealthy man. Kelly knew that extortion and bribery must have contributed heavily to his nest egg because a county detective's salary wasn't large. Regardless of his questionable activities, which even included ties to the Klan, Nichols had created a model image: tough, aggressive, and dedicated. He charmed all of those who counted and damned the rest, including Kelly.

Kelly's one chance to destroy Nichols' career and put him in jail or send him to his death was delayed by his own sudden moral paralysis, and when he recovered Nichols had him cornered. Many times he wondered why Nichols hadn't killed him, but he finally decided that Nichols had never purposely killed someone in cold blood with his own hands. There was the girl, but Kelly reasoned that Nichols had been drinking and had misjudged his strength. He knew that Nichols had shot several people, including two women, in self-defense. His way of harming people, Kelly surmised, came by way of other people—proxies who had been drawn into his trap. His distaste for blood was evident on that night twenty-eight years before. Behind his cold boasting, Kelly detected not only his suppressed horror but a dissatisfaction with his own reaction to the girl's death. As he listened to Nichols' autobiography, he couldn't help feeling that the man's personal life was sterile and unfulfilling. His friends were no more than professional allies. He had never married or fallen in love and probably found little to discuss with his sexual partners. He marveled at the man's ability to keep so much hidden and escape any castigation.

Kelly feared the retribution that Nichols seemed to evade or ignore without effort. He feared his final years being spent in jail and the hood being drawn over his head. He feared his past deeds being made public. He possessed enough fear for both of them and wondered if Nichols would ever be made to suffer while still alive.

It was early evening when they left the cabin. Nichols had had several bottles of beer, and he continued to brag about his courageous life in the face of criminals' hostilities. He seemed to be in a good mood, although Kelly couldn't trust his own senses when it came to the man. They drove in a wide arc, bypassing Worthing Mills and anyone's observation. They traveled on sand roads—two-track fire lanes and old logging roads. The truck bounced violently because of Kelly's constant zigzagging to avoid deep pools of water that had collected at low points in the road. He usually enjoyed being in the forest during the evening. The hot sun was low in the sky. The sand started to cool after absorbing heat all day. Swallows filled the air. The light was fleeting and created pockets of deep color between the trees. All of the sharp edges were muted. At dusk, the world appeared to be more accommodating. Generally, Kelly found solace alone, in his truck, riding at a lethargic pace through the woods. But tonight his mind was filled with apprehension.

1909

For most of the morning, he waited just off the road, hidden behind a tangle of laurel and huckleberry bushes. It was hot. Gnats were swarming in the spring air. He didn't want to be there and decided to leave but stopped himself. His only alternative would be to flee the state just as he had done in Ireland, but he decided against that. Nichols would find me, he thought. Kelly knew that Nichols would do everything he promised if he didn't do this. The truth was clear however. He wasn't a murderer. It wasn't in his heart. He had been involved with the Fenians in Ireland, but somehow that was different. Nichols always seemed to be watching him, and he was afraid of the man. Why didn't I spurn him? he asked himself. But Nichols had had the upper hand even when they first met.

Over a year had passed since Nichols had discovered the source of Kelly's supplementary income. At that time, Kelly didn't feel his sideline was wrong. The women and girls he used would make a little money—certainly more than they would working in the fields. They would have a chance to spend time at a prestigious club—probably their first and only chance. They were usually alone or orphans or had a family to support and frequently didn't speak more than a few words of English. The following day they were paid and happy. No one was harmed. The men who bought their services were satisfied and normally returned to him to repeat the arrangements. There was no coercion, at least not in Kelly's mind. He had managed to save money and felt that his small business could provide him with a comfortable retirement. This was before Nichols appeared.

His plans began to fall apart the day after a girl got hurt and was found by Nichols along a seldom used road. Kelly was flabbergasted by the coincidence, but the detective seemed to be everywhere. He had a nose for the abnormal. Kelly considered the chances of him finding the girl, and they were astronomical. The size of the county wasn't relevant. The wildness of the area around the Chatsworth Club was of little hindrance. Nichols was there. He took her to the nearest physician who stitched together her lacerations. Then he returned her to the place where she was staying. Between the time of her discovery and the moment she left his car for good, Nichols knew everything. Within an hour, he was in Worthing Mills. Kelly tried to remember his exact words and how they forced him to this place along a deserted sand road but could only find confusion about what had happened.

"I've found one of your girls."

"What do you mean?"

"Don't bullshit me."

"I don't know what you're talking about."

Nichols grabbed his shirt and said, "I'm talking about the Chatsworth Club."

"I've never been there."

"In that case, I guess the best thing to do is take you in. I'll bet we can find something on you."

Kelly tried to look into Nichols' eyes but found them grey and cold.

"The girl," Nichols reasserted.

"I brought her to the club for a gentleman. I had nothing to do with it beyond that."

"Stop fucking around. You've been pimping for certain gentlemen, as you call them, for quite a while. You're a well-known man. Anyone over there who wants a girl sends word to you. Now isn't that right?"

Kelly tried to fabricate a lie, anything that would lead the man away from him, but he saw Nichols knew too much.

"I'm waiting."

"I never forced any of those girls."

"You're still a pimp."

"What are you going to do with me?"

Nichols put his hands in his pockets.

"You are going to help me in the future. And if you ever mention any of this, you'll be on a boat back to Ireland. I suspect that you don't want that to happen."

"No."

"You know who I am and what I can do?"

"Yes, but what can I do for you?"

"Don't worry about that. I'll let you know." Nichols started to walk away but paused. "Not a word. Do you hear me?"

A month passed before he heard from Nichols again. He continued to run his operation, but more cautiously. His inside man at the club had to be more selective. Definite arrangements for transportation were made. He realized that one loose end could lead him back to Nichols. But Nichols hadn't forgotten him.

"I've done some checking. You're quite a fellow back home. The English seem to have a few complaints about you and your friends," Nichols said one evening.

"I don't know much about the English."

"Nothing about the I.R.B.?"

"It seems that you have the advantage."

At that moment, Kelly's world began to fall apart in a resounding way. He had never liked to be controlled by anyone and had shown that in Ireland. But Nichols wasn't an ordinary man. He was as conniving as any thief. After their first meeting, Kelly was certain that Nichols would want a woman. This proved to be true. He wanted a woman—a young girl actually—free of charge. Kelly consented because he had no other choice. This was the beginning of a regular habit. Nichols wanted someone every weekend—usually on Saturday evenings. He told the other man not to reveal anything about him when he left the girls at his hunting cabin. Not only did Nichols expect him to deliver the girl but to pick her up as well. Kelly did this without complaint although as the weeks passed Nichols' demands became more unusual. Younger girls—children actually—as well as boys were needed to satisfy him. He objected but Nichols threatened him, and Kelly knew that his own position was weak.

This arrangement continued for several months. Kelly was still in business, still supplying women for his clients. He did his best to obtain what Nichols wanted. Nothing changed except for an occasional shift in desire on the detective's part. Often Kelly daydreamed about escaping. He had a premonition about Nichols and his sexual appetites. He remembered the bloodied girl and how Nichols had helped her. There seemed to be a trace of humanity in Nichols' heart, but when Kelly returned the young back to their tents and shacks in the fields he noticed the terror in their eyes and the bruises on their bodies. He was convinced that something horrible was waiting to happen.

One evening a costume ball was held at the Chatsworth Club. The event was attended by important people from around the state as well as many of national prominence. Vice President Sherman was there. Tickets for the affair were scarce, but Nichols managed to secure one. He demanded that a room be reserved for him and Kelly's inside man arranged it. There was only one request for a girl that evening, and it came from Detective Nichols. She was to be placed in his room and was not allowed to leave. She must be younger than thirteen.

Kelly wasn't completely aware of what had happened that evening, but it had involved Elizabeth Worthing. When he left the girl in Nichols' room, Nichols wasn't there. Evidently, he arrived at the club late; the party was already in progress. Nichols had been drinking, and his mask, an odd combination of two faces, had been damaged by a fall. Several guests attempted to discover his identity but failed. He continued to drink as the guests left or went to their rooms. It was after one o'clock when Nichols stumbled upstairs. The girl was asleep when he entered his room.

Elizabeth Worthing was staying in the room next to him. An hour passed before noise disturbed her sleep. When she opened her eyes, the sound stopped. Thinking it was a dream she closed her eyes, but a girl's muffled cries came through the wall. She wasn't anxious to interrupt another couple's pleasures, but the cries persisted and Elizabeth decided that something was wrong. She got out of bed and opened her door. The hallway was deserted. After knocking several times on the door at the end of the hallway, it opened. Two eyes stared through the crack.

"I heard someone..."

"She's better now."

"What was wrong?"

"Too much to drink." The man's hand reached up to adjust his mask. Blood covered the backs of his fingers.

"Are you sure that everything is fine?" She noticed the blood and at the same instant could see a bare leg hanging from the bed.

"Yes. Everything's fine."

A moan rose from the bed. The man cleared his throat at the same instant.

"Signor Patrick," the voice said weakly.

The mask glanced quickly into the room then back to Elizabeth. She was uneasy and thought it strange that the man would still be wearing his disguise.

"Goodnight, Mrs. Worthing," the man said as the door closed abruptly.

Elizabeth went back to her room and listened for ten minutes but heard nothing, except an occasional sigh. The man's voice was vaguely familiar, but she couldn't connect it to a face. Being recognized by strangers wasn't unusual for her, so she didn't think it peculiar that the man knew her. She assumed, just before falling asleep, that nothing was wrong although the voice from the bed sounded younger than it should have. Elizabeth had been drinking and concluded that her own impressions weren't reliable so early in the morning.

Nichols came to Kelly's cabin about four a.m. He said there had been an accident. His voice was strained. The girl was injured and possibly dead. Nichols told Kelly to return to the club and bring the girl back to the cabin. He didn't want any witnesses, so he warned the other man to be careful. This wasn't difficult because Kelly had a key for one of the service entrances and a pass key for all of the rooms. By sunrise he was home. The girl was under a blanket in the trunk, dead.

Kelly was distraught. He didn't want to be involved, but it was too late. Nichols' earlier nervousness was gone, and he calmly informed him that he was part of it as well; he was a pimp and an accomplice to murder. Nichols ordered him to take the body into the woods and dispose of it. When Kelly returned Nichols was eating breakfast as if nothing had happened.

"You took care of it?"

"Yes."

"What about the family?"

"She was an orphan," Kelly lamented.

"No one was looking after her?"

"She was with a group of migrants."

"Any trouble with her not returning?" Nichols chewed his food.

"I'll tell them she got a better job, or that she ran off with someone."

"Positive?" Nichols mumbled.

"They knew she was a whore."

"You're sure?"

"Yes."

"How old was she?"

"I'm not sure." Kelly looked away from the man.

"She was sixteen if she was a day."

"So?"

"You know what I like."

"She said she could pass for twelve or thirteen. She was small."

"Bullshit."

"I'm sorry."

"It's a little late for that," Nichols said wearily.

"Not for you. I'm sorry for her."

"Wonderful. She was just another wop and a whore to boot. They're like vermin. Every damn one of them. Immigrants. All of them. Worthless." Nichols sipped his coffee. "We have another problem."

"What," Kelly asked as he moved nervously around the room.

"Someone saw me with her."

"Jesus."

"We'll have to get rid of her." Nichols' voice was cold.

"What do you mean?"

"An accident or something."

"Who?"

"Elizabeth Worthing."

"Are you crazy?"

"Listen, we're in this together. If I go down, you're coming with me. If I have to die, so will you. You're in this thing and there's only one way out."

"You can't be..." Kelly felt his stomach turn sour.

"She has to go. She's the only person who can tie me to that girl. You didn't tell what's his name about the girl?"

"No, I handled it."

"Good."

Kelly waited for the car. He held the rifle. A tree limb blocked the road which ran a long thousand yard loop around a cedar swamp. He didn't know if he could do it. His hands sweated. Nichols' threats tormented him, and if he failed today he would probably be in jail tomorrow. He heard the car round the top of the loop and start down his side. Nichols had told him what to do and where to wait, suggesting he might have to stay there the entire morning and possibly the afternoon. Elizabeth Worthing used this road—a shortcut never used by regular traffic—when she returned from her weekend trips to Atlantic City. The sun struck the curved surface of the hood and it gleamed, blocking the image of the driver from Kelly until the car was closer. When she reached the limb, the car halted. The woman looked at the obstacle for a few seconds then removed a rope from the backseat of the car.

Kelly watched her. She was going to pull the limb from the sand road with her automobile. If he didn't fire now it would be too late. His hands shook. He aimed, closed his eyes, and a shot sounded as she stooped over the limb. Her head jerked up with a grotesque motion and turned toward the bushes; then she fell to the ground.

It had happened quickly. Kelly didn't check to see if she was dead but hastily assumed the bullet had struck her in the head. He found himself running and couldn't remember squeezing the trigger. He dragged the rifle behind him as he ran into the swamp, not caring about his direction. Eventually, he found himself standing next to the riverside sinkhole that had been created by the decaying roots of an enormous, fallen oak tree and an underground stream. The girl's body rested there. His breathing was sharp and a pain gripped his left side. He threw the rifle into the water and mud-filled hole and fell to his knees. He cursed Nichols and couldn't believe that he had shot her. If I did pull the trigger, he thought, how could I have possibly hit her?

When his mind cleared, he saw the slender tips of the cedars etched against a starkly blue sky. Gnats gathered around his head again. The ground was green. He heard a woodpecker but didn't follow its tap. A slight wind made the trees bend. He listened closely, thinking that someone might have heard the shot and followed him. The metallic tap-tap of her still-running automobile edged its way through the trees. It was more than a mile back through the dense swamp bottom, but he could hear it. He covered his ears, trying to deaden the sound, but it only grew louder.

Kelly left the sinkhole and moved steadily through the brush, snapping everything that stood in his path. The ground gave way several times, and his boots sank into the muck of the damp forest floor. He fought through bright green briers and didn't feel their sharp thorns as they creased his flesh. He was exhausted but didn't stop as he tried to put as much distance as possible between himself and her body. When he reached the town and his cabin, the ping of the engine still reverberated in his ears, even though it was far away.

T H I R T Y

1937

After a day of rain and clouds, the evening air had a slight chill to it. Kate Harris walked slowly toward the Johnson house. Her mother had just revealed everything to her without knowing what Kate's reaction would be. The long wait, her mother said, had been agonizing for her. She feared rejection and losing her maternal place in Kate's life. For years, she had thought little harm would come from her reticence. With the discovery of Elizabeth Worthing's statue and a few casual remarks made by the Johnson family as well as Kate, she felt the time had arrived.

"Kate," she said. "I have something to tell you, something that I should have told you years ago. Your father doesn't have to know about what I'm going to say unless you want him to."

This offering came immediately after Kate had mentioned Andy Johnson's innocent comment about Elizabeth Worthing's statue. Kate found it amusing and had passed it on to her mother with the same innocent tone. What happened afterwards shocked her and propelled Kate out of her mother's sight. She had never suspected her mother or father of being anything else but her parents. The thought was alien to her. At times, she had wondered why her parents didn't have a larger family. They had been good parents. But she never pressed her question beyond her mother's remark that another child wasn't part of God's will. Nothing other than that was needed by Kate. As she grew older, Kate decided that her mother wasn't physically able to have another baby.

Now she knew that her conclusion had been correct, but

with one minor alteration. Her mother had always been barren. Kate wasn't the daughter of the woman who had always been a mother to her. Biologically, they weren't linked. Different blood flowed through their veins. When Kate heard the words, it seemed as if her blood was suddenly heavier than her mother's and her heart was straining to pump it. A forcible pressure exerted itself against the undersurface of her skin. She felt dislodged from the secure world of her everyday existence. Her mother tried to touch her hand, but she intentionally drew it away. This woman is a stranger to me, Kate's mind said. But reason swarmed around that thought and said her rejection wasn't truly intentional. Their eyes met: her mother's were filled with uncertainty and fear and anguish; Kate's revealed her confusion and anger. Kate opened her mouth and a thousand words rushed toward her lips, but somewhere they stopped except for one.

"Who?"

Her mother tried to explain why it had taken so long, why they had pretended to be her natural parents. Kate was only one month old when she was placed in their care. She had been born in another state where her real mother had spent some of her pregnancy with strangers. No one in Worthing Mills was to know that she had been born, which wasn't difficult because the Harrises lived several counties away at the time. They were to care for her until specific legal problems were resolved. Everyone was told that Kate was a niece and her mother was ill. The person who arranged for Kate's protection and care was her mother's aunt, Lucy O'Malley. Then, her real mother died suddenly and her father was unaware of his daughter's existence. Her mother had wanted it that way. It seemed natural to raise her as their own. In time, they moved to Worthing Mills where her father found work in the machine shop. And they had done a good job, her mother added. No one asked questions and everything fell into place. Before Kate had been born, her mother had prayed to God for a child because she couldn't have her own. Kate was her miracle.

With this Kate sprang from her chair and started to cry.

Her mind was clogged with conflicting thoughts and emotions. She tried to breathe deeply but found the air in the room unyielding. She paced across the floor once as her mother pleaded and apologized, asking to be forgiven. There was money as well, she said, money left for her. But none of it mattered to Kate at that moment. She had to absorb the initial impact of the revelation. Her heart felt as if it would burst. She looked at her mother again, and in three long strides she was outside. The door slammed behind her.

When Kate started to walk down the street, away from the house, her intent wasn't clear. After a moment she found, to her surprise, that her legs carried her toward Agnes Johnson's house. She saw that the machine shop was still open. Cars lined the small lot. Aromas from cooking food filled her nostrils, mixing together into one solid odor that reminded her of baking bread. She passed a row of houses without looking up. People spoke to her, but she didn't answer because their words were distorted in the reverberation of her own thoughts.

Her desire to reach the Johnson's house was overwhelming. Then the reason came to her as suddenly as the acknowledgment of her intention. She must look at the face of Elizabeth Worthing again but with different eyes. She must search that face for the answer to the one obstinate question inundating her every conscious impulse.

"Who am I?" she heard herself ask. "Who am I?"

She attempted to leave this and think about her mother's words which had been spoken only minutes before, but found that she couldn't react rationally to them. Suddenly, at twenty-nine years old, she felt like an orphan. Her home, her parents, her life were all fragmented. Her possession of them was merely partial now. She didn't have a husband or children of her own. She thought she would end up a spinster librarian but wasn't disturbed by the prospect. There had been interested men, but beyond common civility she had spurned them. She had created in her mind the image of a perfect man, as most women do, but unlike most women, she refused to abandon the ideal and reach a compromise. Now she wished she had. Even if her marriage was an unhappy one, her husband and children would be part of her. Her foolish dream of the ideal mate had left her stranded. Her parents never complained about her lack of interest or tolerance when an eligible man was attracted to her. They said she would always have a home with them. Regardless of their feelings, her security seemed at risk. A place would always exist beside them, she told herself, but belonging next to them was an entirely different question now. For a moment she considered marrying the first bachelor who approached her, but she wasn't positive that an eligible man could be tempted to do so soon. As Kate aged, the pool of available men had dwindled. And her enthusiasm for learning to live with another person wasn't great. Her life had been altered from a stable, peaceful acceptance of what the world offered to one which suggested an existence plagued by unnerving fears and doubts.

When she reached the Johnson's house, her mind wasn't any clearer than it had been when she left her mother. She pulled her hair back and wiped the teary corners of her eyes, then knocked.

"Miss Harris," a boy's voice said from inside.

"Is that you Will?"

"Yep."

"Is your mother home?"

"Nope."

"Your father?"

"He'll be here soon. They're working overtime again. But Andy's here."

"Could I come in?"

Kate entered the living room and tried to stay calm. She looked at the boy and folded her hands together.

"Could I look at the head, Will?"

"If you want...but you saw it twice already."

"I know, but I'd like to take one more look."

"Sure. It's in the other room. Andy's in there, too. He's mad because the sheriff left him here with me."

She followed him into the kitchen. Andy sat at the table with his head and arms resting on the tabletop.

"Here it is," Will said, bounding around the table until he stood behind the stone face.

She stopped and saw it as if there had never been a first time. Her heart raced. It was true. She studied the curve of her nose and chin. She noted the shape of her eyes.

"Mother," she said softly without thinking. "Mother." Tears reappeared.

"Are you okay?" Andy asked as he stood.

She couldn't answer.

"Do you want a glass of water?"

"Yes," she said awkwardly, sitting at the table. "When will your mom be home?" she asked, staring at her face.

"She went with the sheriff," Andy said, handing her the water.

"Why?"

"We found another part of the statue."

"And an old goat bone," the younger boy added.

"Where?"

"Same spot we found this." Andy's hand rested on the head. "Sheriff said he didn't have room for us in the canoe. He didn't think they'd find anything, but he wanted to make Mom happy so he said he'd take a look. They left about fifteen minutes ago."

"Mom sort of thinks it's where that man's son is. The one that the town's named after," Will said, trying to contribute to the exchange.

"He disappeared the same year that she was murdered and her statue was thrown into the river," Kate commented absentmindedly.

The boys agreed, realizing that the town's history was already known by her.

"But the sheriff doesn't think she's right?"

"He said they should take a look," Andy speculated. "But I don't think so. I sure wanted to go with them, but Dad isn't home yet and Will..."

"We couldn't both fit."

"And Mom didn't want to leave you here alone."

"That's not true," Will said defensively. "Anyway, it's not

my fault that Dad's late."

Impulsively, Kate felt she had to go to the place. She looked at the face and felt an irrepressible connection to Elizabeth and the town and everything that had happened there. She wanted to be part of it because she was tied to each event and person and building. Kate needed answers to all of the questions teeming inside her and became lightheaded when she considered the possible answers. The room seemed to be tilting and forcing her to move through the door and down the street toward the river like she was a rolling ball. She wanted to see the spot where parts of her mother's effigy had been found, and if there was something more to discover, she must be part of it because it was part of her.

"I can get a canoe," she said.

The boys were stunned. They had never suspected that she would elect to go. They hadn't even considered it.

"Well?"

They looked at each other and smiled.

"You'd better leave a note for your father," Kate added.

"Miss Harris," Andy said as they left the house, "why do you want to go up there?"

"Just to see for myself."

"But you've been on the creek before. I'm sure you've been past the place a dozen times easy, and it's going to be dark soon."

"You're right, Andy. But everything is different now."

They didn't speak again until they reached the river. She hadn't offered the boys any further explanation about her sudden urge to go upriver, so they formed their own theories. Will didn't consider any beyond the one which he had—adventure. The thrill of finding more bones or another piece of the statue was enough to excite him and make him want to go upstream. But Andy knew that Kate Harris wasn't seeking adventure. He had heard her whisper mother when she looked at Elizabeth Worthing's face. Was it true? he asked himself, thinking it might be. His attraction to her was greater than he had imagined and he decided that whatever the reason, he would do everything in his power to help her. As they paddled, he traced the outline of Kate's head as the light faded and the background shifted with each new twist in the serpentine river. He felt himself drifting away. It was night and he was in bed. He imagined the sheets brushing against his naked body, and then he was asleep, floating on the impenetrable river of his dreams.

When they cleared the last bend and entered the dead pool before the spong, voices reached the canoe through the white mist, overcoming the banging of the carpenter frogs and scratching tremble of insects. For a second the voices weren't distinct, only a mixture of undefined sound. Then the sounds became clear to them as if they had been asleep and had just opened their eyes. Andy steered the canoe from the stern, directing it toward the sand and gravel shore.

"Nichols," someone insisted in a tone that verged on hysteria. "Nichols...he..."

More talk. Several voices sounded without separation. They could distinguish Agnes' voice from the sheriff's, but the others were unfamiliar to them.

"There's no question," another voice said. After a moment of garbled objection, the same voice responded. "He led me here after he confessed. He's been right here under our damn noses for years."

The river existed and flowed beneath them, but the deepening blanket of fog denied it. The canoe moved silently, floating on air as well as water, still undetected by the others only a few yards from the bank. As they struck bottom Kate stood with perfect balance, emerging from the mist like a spirit from another world. Her sudden appearance was met by a deafening scream that rattled across the savanna.

Zauber darted from the cover along the edge of the clearing. His hair and beard were the color of smoke. He howled again as he surged toward the group gathered near the river. Nichols stepped foward and reached for his revolver.

"Elizabeth!" Zauber shrieked as his eyes caught sight of Kate rising from the mist. "Elizabeth!" he screamed, thinking this was the sign he had anticipated.

Before Nichols could draw his pistol from his shoulder

harness, Zauber was on him. The men fell to the ground, disappearing into the low fog. An explosion flashed. The air responded with a fluttering surge; another shot followed, grafting itself to the remaining sound of the first and piercing Nichols' face and skull. The others recoiled. In the canoe, they watched as the sheriff pushed Agnes to the ground. Kelly tried to bury himself in the muck of the sinkhole, wanting to escape what he thought would be his fate. Kate collapsed back into the canoe, knocking Will down as he strained to see the two men enmeshed in the fog. The sheriff had drawn his revolver and was moving toward the men, but before MacFarland reached them, Zauber reared up, his eyes electric in the black night, and bolted into the forest.

"Stop or I'll shoot," MacFarland yelled, leveling his pistol. "Stop," he repeated, firing once. He started to pursue the man, sprinting in the direction he thought the assailant had taken, trying to follow his trail into an impenetrable thicket, but Zauber had vanished.

1990

The woods were dark. Will tried to find the sky, but it was blackened by the dense canopy of trees. He heard what he thought was a bear, then laughed for considering the idea. A lone whippoorwill sang plaintively. An animal moved delicately along a parallel road to his left. His lungs burned with the night air, and each breath left a frozen white shroud on his face.

He wondered why Lou had left him and concluded that he had tired of him; he had used Will for his personal entertainment and abandoned him. It seemed to Will that they had reached the same conclusion simultaneously. Will had had enough, yet he didn't regret spending the day with the younger man. It allowed Will to see part of the new and improved world which was and would be dominated by Lous. There will be no place for anyone different, Will predicted. Lou is the new Everyman, part of the great, fast everything society—consumable, replaceable, disposable, fuckable. Oh yes, he thought. That has to be. Fuckable is more important than anything. Suddenly, Will was glad that he wasn't young, glad that his youth was spent in the Pines. His one short evening with Lou had voided any lingering fantasies about a different life, a life with fewer sacrifices and more luxuries. Give me age and memories of the past, he thought. Lou is what happens when there is no past to believe in. Without a center, there's nothing to clutch, nothing to hold. Nothing. He stumbled over something large and solid but didn't stop.

"Lou. Lou. Lou," he said loudly, hearing his words reverberate between the colonnaded pines. "The wave of the future. Forever...and ever," he added, comforted by the presence of his voice. "Lou!"

Twenty minutes passed, but it felt like three hours to him. The uneven road slowed his progress, and the cold air started to find its way under his clothing. He paused to zip his jacket. White vapor fell to his chest, then rose around his cheeks and into his hair before it dissipated. A fingerboard stretched before him. The road that paralleled his entered the junction from the left and separated into three roads when it continued to the right. Directly ahead, his road split and the right fork divided again within a few feet. The sand was deeper in the center of the intersection, and he knew that his loosely laced boots would be filled with it before he reached Worthing Mills. He considered the fork opposite him and remembered where each branch would lead. Every blink of his eyelids created additional choices. One road became three, then vanished and returned as two lanes. His legs had left him long ago. He was still numb from his waist down, and he wasn't certain what was transporting him.

"The right fork, straight ahead, then to the right at the split," he said, still standing before the fingerboard. He hadn't used this entrance to Worthing Mills for ten years. Or was it fifteen? Some of the road was impassable; sugar sand was piled in high, undulating ridges. To his left, a small bridge that crossed a cripple had collapsed. Brush closed in so tight at several points that an entire vehicle would be encased in a tunnel of grinding undergrowth if it tried to pass. "Thirty minutes and I'll be home," he said as he entered the fingerboard and selected his route.

As the fork arched sharply to the right, Will became aware of his mistake. This will run down to the river, he remembered. If it was still there, he'd have to use the old savanna road that ran along the stand of white cedar. He considered turning around but calculated, in his disordered mind, that the distance would be the same after he recovered the mile he had traveled already.

"Forward," he promptly commanded with a slur, and his legs mysteriously obeyed.

The forest was alive for a fall night. He tried to ignore the sounds which seemed menacing. His brain fought his attempt to harness it. Objects appeared again. Bats flapped near his face. He stumbled and reached for an invisible weapon to ward them away. For a second he worried that he was lost, that he had somehow succeeded in missing the river, but reassured himself that the road would end at the river and somewhere along the bank another would ricochet off toward Worthing Mills. He glanced at the sky, but it was still inseparable from the upper reaches of the forest.

His father had told him not to go far from camp without his brother, but he hadn't listened. He stood on a dead stump and looked as far into the forest as possible. There was no break in the monotony. Each direction presented the same picture. As daylight faded, he decided to make large looping circles, first clockwise, then counterclockwise, hoping to rediscover his trail. He worried about wild animals searching for food and recalled a story of a boy who was raised by wolves, but wolves hadn't roamed the Pines for decades. He considered being raised by bears, but they were gone as well. His eyes searched the forest. He paused and tried to hear a voice or movement. Finally, his patience was rewarded. The faint sound of an axe came to him, and he followed it. He caught a glimpse of his brother's flannel shirt, appearing like a flag through the shadows. His father was reading a newspaper and smoking his pipe when he entered camp. Andy asked him where he had been. But Will didn't admit to his brother or his father what had happened because he was ashamed.

He neared the river. The inconspicuous rush became his focal point. A break in the trees opened to his left, and the sky created a gaping void above it. There wasn't any variation in light tone, but Will imagined it had grown darker. He stopped on the dissolved edge of the forest as it broke down into scrub then completely gave way to the yawning bottom. Something moved twenty yards ahead of him. A branch snapped, and the noise was followed by what sounded like footsteps to him. He dropped to the ground and tried to quiet his breathing. Pine needles punctured the palm of one hand.

He wanted to see the person first, finding it odd that someone would be wandering through the woods at that hour unless he was poaching. Will touched his chest and could feel his skin rippling. More movement, this time to his left. He crouched lower, fixing his eyes on the spot where the noise had originated, and waited.

Several minutes slipped by. When he raised his head above the scrub, he realized that he was much closer to the river than he had thought. He glanced quickly to his right and could see the dim outline of its banks as the water filtered past like honey being poured. The identical place, he thought, startled that he had failed to perceive it earlier and hadn't recognized exactly where the road was leading him. The triangular savanna fanned out to his left. Cedars bordered its periphery. The river elbowed to touch the narrow edge of the clearing. With this recognition came better sight. The sky's color seemed to lighten, and the mist that rose from the river absorbed the additional illumination, turning gossamerlike. The movement had stopped, and he immediately thought he had made a mistake. No one trudged around this part of the woods at night. It was a deer, browsing in the thicket and looking for food, he decided. But he still wasn't sure. Another dry snap came from his right. Fear overwhelmed him. Heat formed beneath the skin of his neck and he panicked. He closed his eyes. Then, without warning, he felt his knees buckle.

Will opened his eyes as the sky turned toward morning. The air was cold and he was stiff. His head throbbed as he stood. A towhee called along the river. He rubbed his eyes and looked toward the empty clearing which was overgrown and deserted. The road vanished before it reached the water. His eyes followed the line of clustered cedars, trying to discover the other road, the one which would lead him to Worthing Mills. A trace appeared but nothing more. The corduroy road that divided the savanna and cedar stand had virtually disappeared.

He walked to the river and dipped his forearms into the water, bringing his cupped hands to his face, then to his mouth. The bank was different than he remembered. The sinkhole had dissolved into the river and swamp. Only a shallow depression remained. The spong which had separated them was dry and filled with trees. The towhee called again. He sat on the bank and rubbed his wet hands on his pants.

The river was low. Autumn had been dry, and the few deciduous trees that bordered it had a brittle look. Their still clinging dead leaves contrasted vividly with the luxuriant color of the evergreens. He followed a patch of iron-oxide as it brushed the bank, leaving a bubbling foam in its invisible wake. Behind him, the sun hit the lip of the savanna and began to warm his back. The water became streaked with deep, black shadows. Between the shadows, it turned brown and red, then copper. In spots, especially close to the shore, the water was clear and colored by the light grey sand beneath it. Green eelgrass grew a few feet from the bank and its long, slender blades waved flat on the river's surface like a woman's hair being caressed by the wind.

He glanced downstream to the point where the river hooked away from his sight and toward the lake at Worthing Mills and listened as if he had never been alone in the Pines before. The current of the river remained constant, but was filled with a dying languor. The towhee called again, and this time he tried to find it along the opposite bank, but it wasn't there. He tossed a stone over the water and watched it arch gracefully before it struck the surface. The impact caused concentric rings to open until they became too minuscule for his eyes to see.

When the sun was fully above the savanna and filled the sky with yellow-pink light, he was ready to walk. He found what remained of the old logging road. As he weaved along it and tried to avoid the leatherleaf, he could see into the stand of cedar.

"I'm going home," he murmured, knowing the place he called home, the place of his nativity, no longer endured. The same earth that gave him breath and nurtured him would not cradle him in death. But sometime during the night, he had decided to hold fast and not to grieve. "I'm going home," he repeated calmly.

PINELANDS

The wall of black gum, briers, and laurel that snarled the edges of the vanished road subsided. Beams of sunlight angled into the cedar swamp's vaulted heart where surviving insects gathered in irregular swarms around hassocks and tried to capture the evanescent warmth of autumn. Moss-covered mounds of fallen trees and silent pools of stagnant water hugged the swamp's floor. The towhee sounded once more, and Will tried for a second time to pinpoint its location, but that was impossible.